George. A saint's name, the name of kings and now the name of Feversham's new owner.

But oh, when did Fan begin thinking of him like that, as George instead of his string of titles? She was his housekeeper, his servant, not his friend and certainly not his lover. To address him with such familiarity would be one more slippery step downward to her own ruin, with no way ever to climb back.

That kiss on her hand had been another. Why, why hadn't she pulled away? Could she only protest when there were others watching? Or was she so weak that she'd cared more for that shiver of heady pleasure that came from his touch?

* * *

The Silver Lord
Harlequin Historical #648—March 2003

The SILVER LORD

Miranda Jarrett

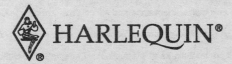

HARLEQUIN®

TORONTO • NEW YORK • LONDON
AMSTERDAM • PARIS • SYDNEY • HAMBURG
STOCKHOLM • ATHENS • TOKYO • MILAN • MADRID
PRAGUE • WARSAW • BUDAPEST • AUCKLAND

ISBN 0-373-29248-1

THE SILVER LORD

This edition published by arrangement with Harlequin Books S.A.

® and TM are trademarks of the publisher. Trademarks indicated with ® are registered in the United States Patent and Trademark Office, the Canadian Trade Marks Office and in other countries.

Visit us at www.eHarlequin.com

Printed in U.S.A.

Please address questions and book requests to:
Harlequin Reader Service
U.S.: 3010 Walden Ave., P.O. Box 1325, Buffalo, NY 14269
Canadian: P.O. Box 609, Fort Erie, Ont. L2A 5X3

For TFR,
For believing there are second acts!
With Affection & Regards

Chapter One

Feversham Downs, Kent
March, 1802

The fog clung close to the coast, so gray and heavy and icy-wet that it seemed like an extension of the sea itself, risen up into the night sky solely to increase the misery of any shivering creatures it might touch. This fog had stolen away the moon and stars along with all earthly landmarks, and even the great rush and crash of the waves seemed muffled and muted. It was a night fit for neither Christian man nor beast, and certainly not for a lady.

But for Fan Winslow, it was the most perfect night imaginable.

"Keep the light covered, Bob," she said briskly to the man on the horse beside her. "Even in this murk, I won't have the risk of a glimmer to betray us."

Dutifully the man tugged at the hinged window on the tin lantern swinging from the stake in the sand, the awkward bulges in his coat betraying the pistols in his belt. Though there was seldom any trouble, they were always armed; in this trade, it would be foolish to take the risk of doing otherwise. Now only the tiniest pinpricks of light showed through the punched holes on the back of the lantern, and Fan nodded her approval, drawing her black cloak more closely around her huddled shoulders.

Faith, as if that could keep out more of this wretched cold! The fog would always have its way, icy fingers that could creep through the woolen layers of petticoats and stockings and mittens and shawls under her cloak. The only real warmth came from the sturdy little horse beneath her, for Pie's shaggy rough coat had been bred for weather like this. Fan wasn't as fortunate, and she pulled the scarf higher over her face, trying to preserve some semblance of a ladylike complexion, even as the salty wet chill made her cheeks ache and her eyes tear, and plastered the few loose curls of her hair like clammy seaweed against her forehead and neck.

Yet still she and Bob Forbert waited on the beach, steadfastly staring out into the fog to where the little boat must be, squinting so hard to see what Fan prayed would be there that her exhausted eyes teared from the effort. Except for those careful few who knew the truth, no one would guess her place by day at Feversham Hall, or understand the risk she took by coming here on this night, and on scores of others like it.

Furtively she puffed her breath against the rough wool of the scarf pulled over her mouth, hoping to warm herself however she could, and twisted the reins in her cold-numbed fingers. It was a perfect night for their trade, exactly the weather she always prayed for.

A fog like this kept secrets as surely as the grave itself.

But how long had she been standing here by the sea, the spray that blew towards them like tumbled flakes of snow? Had it been one hour, two, even three? She could reach for the heavy watch she wore at her waist, but to do so would make her look weak and unsure of herself, as if she hadn't planned and anticipated every last detail of this night. She couldn't let Bob sense her uncertainty. She couldn't let him, or any of the others, ever see her be less than absolutely confident.

But hadn't Father taught her that, never to show doubt to those who depended upon her? These folk are our people, Father would say, his black brows bristling with seriousness, these are the Winslow Company. They're our responsibility, and you must be ready to put them first. That's how it's always been for us Winslows, daughter. We must be brave, be sure, be true. We must, my girl, else we'll never hold their respect and their loyalty, nor shall we deserve it.

But then Father would never have imagined her in his place here on the beach, waiting with the lantern and pistols and praying that she'd said the right things to make the men follow....

"Leastways they'll be no red coats after us tonight, mistress," said Bob, spitting in the sand as an extra measure of contempt. "Nor blue Navy ones, neither. None of them bastards'd take their fat rumps from the hearth in this cold."

"They're all fair-weather rogues, true enough," said Fan. "Let them stay by their hearths, I say, and leave us honest folk to ourselves."

It had been a warm, clear night early last summer,

the air full of the sweet scent of hay and new clover, when Father had let a bellyful of unwatered French brandy at the Tarry Man in Tunford rob him of his common sense. Off he'd stumbled towards the marshes and the beach with his old friend Tom Hawkins, the pair of them bellowing wicked songs about the king beneath the bright crescent moon, certain that there'd be a boat coming in from Boulougne.

And to her sorrow, it was the last she or anyone else had seen of either her father or Tom. Some said they'd drowned and been washed out to sea. Others were sure they'd been murdered, shot dead and their bodies hidden away by some rival company. There was even one version, still popular at the Tarry Man, that they'd simply hopped aboard some vessel for France on a whim, and were there now, drinking their fill of brandy and chasing the ladies and blithely turning their backs on their old lives.

Yet the stories were no more than guesses, without any proof one way or the other. All that Fan knew for certain was that her father had never come back, and that she missed him dreadfully, and that ever since that night, she'd been standing here in his place, waiting and hoping and praying for his return.

"There, mistress, there be the boat!" exclaimed Bob, pointing out through the fog. "Just like you said it would be, mistress! Just like you said!"

Fan nodded again, hiding her relief. She hadn't been nearly as certain that Ned Markham would risk bringing the *Sally* in on such a night, but now she could see the bobbing yellow light on the sloop's prow for herself. The pattern of the signal was the same they'd always used: one quick flash, two slow.

Fan leaned forward to uncover the face of her own

lantern, and answered the signal in reverse with two slow flashes, one quick. Then, at last, Fan uncovered her flame and let the beam shine bright and steady, a kind of makeshift lighthouse here on the beach. The *Sally*'s pilot would need such a signal, for without the lantern's light, he'd have the devil of a time guessing exactly where lay the mouth of the narrow channel called the Tunford Stream.

On the far side of the dunes the others were waiting, the trusted Company men with the horses, as well as the porters and carriers hired for the night. They all would work together with the *Sally*'s crew in well-practiced efficiency, bringing seven hundred pounds of China tea ashore without paying a single penny to the Customs House or the Crown.

She watched the boat drawing close, the sail just visible through the mist and fog. The tedium of waiting here on the beach was nearly done, and the next few hours would fly by, a race against the dawn. If everything went as planned, she would see the last pony, laden with tea, off over the hills before the night began to fade on the eastern horizon, and be back at Feversham with the cock's crow, and so weary she'd barely be able to climb the back stairs to her bed.

"Who be takin' our tea this time, mistress?" asked Bob, hopping up and down beside her with excitement, or maybe the cold. "The innkeeper in Lydd, same as last week, or that new bloke clear from London?"

"Hush yourself, Bob," ordered Fan sharply, appalled he'd speak so freely. "Haven't I told you before to keep your peace about our affairs here?"

"But mistress, I—"

"No chatter, Bob, not even to me," she answered, cutting him off. "Or is that the path you're wishing to take, Bob Forbert? Betraying us all with your idle guesses and follies?"

"Nay, mistress," said Bob, anxiously wringing his hands in their fingerless gloves. "Nay, mistress, not by half."

"Not by halves nor wholes nor quarters, either," said Fan. "If you wish to share the Company's profits, then you must abide by our rules."

"'Course I shall, mistress!" cried Bob defensively. "I've my family to feed, mistress! I'm not like you with only yourself to look after!"

That hurt; that *hurt,* but since it was the truth, what could Fan say? "Off with you, Bob," she said, hiding her bitterness, "and tell the others the *Sally*'s nigh. I'll follow on my own, as soon as I'm sure they've followed the lantern."

At once the man turned his pony and trotted away across the sand, while Pie whinnied and shifted restlessly, eager to be off as well. Swiftly Fan drew the pony in, wondering unhappily if Bob's haste was because he was trying to prove his loyalty, or if he simply wished to be away from her criticism.

She'd heard what some of the men in the Company said behind her back, how since her father had disappeared, she'd become sharp-tongued and hard, the worst kind of shrill spinster. It didn't matter that the Company had continued to prosper under her leadership, or that the runs were planned with greater efficiency now, or even that their profits had grown while the government's patrols had increased along the coast with the end of the war. All they had to grumble over was the trial of taking orders from a leader in petticoats, even if she was Joss Winslow's daughter. She didn't want to consider how much longer they would listen to her, or what she would do if they stopped altogether.

But because Father would wish it, she'd done her best to hold the Winslow Company together, taking each day and night as it came. Whether with the Company or in her place at Feversham, she'd always taken pride in being a hard worker, in doing things the proper way.

Yet now nothing seemed right or proper in her life. Ever since last summer, she'd exactly the same feeling as she had standing on this beach tonight: empty and cold and joyless, and absolutely, completely alone.

Chapter Two

Always prepare for the worst, and you'll never be disappointed.

This was hardly the sort of cheerful altruism that guided the lives of most English peers. Blue blood and privilege didn't generally go hand-in-hand with such sturdy pessimism. But although Captain Lord George Claremont had in fact been born the legitimate second son of the Duke of Strachen, he'd learned from hard experience that the worst could be lurking around the next corner, and all too often was.

No wonder, then, that as George leaned back against the musty leather squabs of the hired carriage, he concentrated on how best to attack the rest of this gray Kent morning.

No, not *attack*. He was in the civilian world now, and civilians did not take kindly to attacking of any sort. He must remember that, even if it broke a habit of eighteen years' standing. Impatiently he brushed away a speck of lint from the gold-laced sleeve of his good dress coat, refusing to believe it had been quite so long that he'd worn a uniform of the same dark blue.

Sweet damnation, it *had* been eighteen years, hadn't it? He hadn't paused to do the figuring for a while, but the facts were still the same. He'd been only eleven when he'd been unceremoniously sent to sea, as wretched and homesick an excuse for a midshipman in His Majesty's Navy as was ever created. But the Navy had given him a structure and values that his own family had never had, and against all his wishes he'd survived, even prospered. Now, at twenty-nine, he had risen to be a full captain of one of the fastest frigates in the service with a crack crew of seamen to match, and as thoroughly content with his lot as any man had a right to be in this life.

Or rather he *had* been content, before the politicians had signed that infernal peace and he'd been deposited on the beach like every other good sailor. At least he was better off than most of his fellow-officers, and with a grumbled oath he remembered the fantastic good fortune that had, finally, brought him here to Kent.

He glanced once more at the printed sheet that the property agent had given him in London.

FEVERSHAM HALL
A Most Handsome & Agreeable Seat of the
First Order in the County of Kent
Discreetly Situated & Elegantly Appointed
Highly Suitable for a Gentleman's Family
Available for Immediate
Consideration & Possession

The crude drawing beneath this proclamation showed an old-fashioned, rambling house from the stately days of Queen Bess, with dark timbers crisscrossing white plaster walls and diamond-patterned windows. Roses bloomed on either side of the front door and handsome old trees shaded the curving drive, and in the distance was a picturesque glimpse of shining water and an improbable winged goddess with a trumpet hovering over the waves.

Ever skeptical, George frowned at the illustration. "Elegantly Appointed", hah: most likely there were bats in the chimneys and mice in the walls, and the slates on a roof that old were sure to let in the rain in torrents. He'd no more real use for a grand house in the country like this one than he did for a three-legged cockerel.

He didn't hunt and he didn't give grand entertainments that lasted for weeks, the two usual reasons for country living. He didn't feel the imperative to have a home tagged onto his name, of always being referred to as "Lord George Claremont of Pretentious Hall." Besides, he'd no intention of lingering on land any longer than he had to, and as for the family that required the suitable arranging that the advertisement had promised—he certainly didn't have so much as a wife, nor, given his career, was he ever likely to acquire one.

Yet for the first time in his life he had the means to support the title he'd been born to. He hadn't inherited the dukedom or their father's debts with it, thank God, the way his older brother Brant had, but he was still a Claremont, and there were certain obligations to the family that should—and now could—be maintained. He was an officer of the king, too. He couldn't spend the rest of his life ashore living in the same ragtag lodgings over a tavern in Portsmouth.

The carriage slowed to turn off the main road, and

with new interest George studied the landscape. There was a wildness to this part of Kent that he'd always liked, so different from the plump, sunny contentedness of his native Sussex. It had the additional advantages of being far enough from Portsmouth to excuse him from calling on admirals' wives, yet almost exactly equidistant between Claremont Hall, where Brant lived, and Chowringhee, the oddly named house that his younger brother Revell had built for his new wife Sara.

On this overcast day, the flat gray of the sky seemed to merge with the silvery sweep of the Romney Marshes, a place that fell somewhere between land and the restless waters of the Channel. This coast was known to have an unhappy history, replete with shipwrecks and smuggling, and it looked it. The few scattered trees had been bent and gnarled by the wind, and as far as the horizon stretched George could see no friendly curls of smoke to mark a cottage chimney. He'd not be troubled by inquisitive neighbors, that was certain. A desultory handful of gulls riding the wind and a herd of shaggy brown sheep, huddled along a stone wall for shelter as they grazed at the stubbled grass, were the only living things in the entire bleak picture.

The driver turned again and swore as he struggled to control the weary horses. The new road was narrower and even more rutted, and George braced himself to keep from being bounced from his seat to the floor. One more way to hold unwanted visitors at bay, he thought wryly, and craned his neck for his first glimpse of the house that surely must be near.

And once again, he'd been wise to expect the worst.

Clearly the London artist who'd been called upon to draw the house had never seen it for himself, but had made his illustration based on another's description. Like the blind men and the elephant in the old fable, the stark results were based far more on imagination than reality. The ancient timbers and the white plaster and the diamond-paned windows were there, true, but there was no sign of the gracious old oaks or the rosebushes, and the drive was neither curving nor welcoming, but scarcely more than another rutted path to the door.

"Here we be, M'Lord Cap'n," said the driver as he opened the carriage door for George. His face was ruddy from the cold, his breath coming in white puffs, as he kept a suspicious eye on the scruffy boy who'd appeared to hold the horses. "Feversham Hall, M'Lord Cap'n."

George nodded, too intent on studying the house itself to venture more. The old timbers were splitting and silvered, the plaster needed patching, last summer's weeds still dangled from the eaves, and nothing seemed to be parallel to anything else. Even that wretched boy with the horses would have to be taught to comb his hair and stand properly. If he took the house, he'd have plenty of work ahead to make it shipshape and Bristol-fashion. He'd have to bring in his own people up from the *Nimble* to see that things were done right, beginning with filling in the ditches in that hideous excuse for a road.

He nodded again, allowing himself a wry smile of determined anticipation with it. A right challenge this would be, wouldn't it? If Addington and his blasted treaty had put the French out of his reach, at least for now, why not direct his energies and those of his idle crewmen towards replacing rotting timbers and split shingles? Perhaps "attack" had been the right word after all.

Purposefully he climbed the stone steps to thump his knuckles on the front door. The agent in London was supposed to have sent word about George's arrival to the caretaker who lived in the house—a caretaker who was not only negligent in his duties, but dawdled at answering the door, decided George impatiently as he counted off the seconds he waited. *If* he took the house, one of his first tasks would be to send this worthless fellow packing.

George knocked again, harder. Where in blazes was the rascal, anyway?

He heard a scurry of footsteps inside, the clank and scrape of the lock being unbolted, and at last the heavy old door swung open on groaning iron hinges that needed as much attention as everything else. That much George had expected.

But he'd never anticipated the woman now standing before him.

She was tall, nearly as tall as George was himself, and even the simply cut dark gown that she wore with the white kerchief around her throat couldn't hide that she was a handsomely made woman, one that would draw his eye anywhere. Just enough thick, dark hair showed beneath her cap to emphasise the whiteness of her skin, and her mouth had the kind of rich fullness that lonely sailors dream of. She seemed as if she'd been fashioned with the same contradictions as the landscape around her, dramatic and unyielding, beautiful yet severe, with thick-lashed eyes the mysterious smokey-gray of the mist that rose from Romney Marsh.

Yet though she wasn't some giddy maidservant ripe for dalliance—she was too self-possessed for that—she wasn't a lady, either, not answering her own door. The housekeeper, then, to stand with such authority. She was most definitely a different kind of beauty from the dithering, highborn London ladies he'd spend the last fortnight with, women so overbred and insubstantial in their white muslin gowns that a good west wind would have blown them away. But not this one, not at all, and George caught himself studying her with considerably more interest than he should.

"Good day, sir," she said. The clipped words sounded more like a warning than a greeting, nor did she step to one side to invite him to enter. "We have been expecting you, Captain Claremont."

"Captain *Lord* Claremont," he corrected, his smile intended not to soften his words, but to show he meant them. "If you have been expecting my arrival, then you should know how to address me properly. 'Good day, Captain My Lord', not 'sir.'"

Her eyes might have narrowed—he couldn't be certain from the way the shadows fell across her face—but she most definitely did not smile.

"As you wish," she said, pointedly omitting any title at all as she finally stepped aside and held back the door.

He walked past her, tucking his hat beneath his arm. As his eyes adjusted from the gray light outside, he could see that the interior of the house was in much the same state as the outside. Everything was well-ordered, scrubbed and swept, clean and in its place, but the cushions on the chairs were threadbare and the walls needed paint, the sorts of shabbiness that came from a lack of money, not inclination.

"Mr. Winslow is to show me the house," he said as he ran his hand lightly along the carved oak leaves on the newel post. "Please summon him directly."

"Mr. Winslow isn't here," she answered, so quickly that he was sure she'd been anticipating the question. "He is—he is away at present."

"Is he indeed?" George was surprised; he knew the agent had been quite specific about his visit since there'd been so few inquiries about the house.

"Indeed, he is." She flushed as she noticed his gaze shift to her clasped hands, looking for a wedding ring. "Mr. Winslow is my father, not my husband. I can show you the house every bit as well as he."

He held his hat before him and bowed, just from the waist, and smiled. She deserved that from him. It wasn't any of his business whether she had a husband or not. Still, for some reason he was glad she wasn't married to the ne'er-do-well caretaker, but instead merely burdened with the rascal as her father. "Then show away, Miss Winslow. Show away!"

She didn't smile in return the way he'd hoped, though the flush remained in her cheeks. "You will not like the house."

He frowned. "Why are you so certain?"

"Because none of you fine London-folk do."

"Then it is a good thing I am neither from London, nor what you would deem 'fine', being a sailor," he said, wondering why the devil she seemed so determined to warn him away. "You are not quite as knowledgeable as you believe yourself to be, Miss Winslow."

"Nor am I quite so ignorant as it pleases you to

think," she said. "Even here in Kent, we have heard
of the 'Silver Lord'. Rich as the king himself, they
say you are now, and all from plundering that Spanish
treasure ship."

"'They' do not always tell the truth, Miss Winslow." He should have realized his new fame would
have preceded him, even to this remote place, and he
doubted he'd ever grow accustomed to that hideous
soubriquet that his own brother Brant had concocted.
But unlike the greedy admiration and interest his good
fortune had brought him in London, this woman
seemed disdainful, her gaze patently unimpressed as
it swept over his uniform.

"Now shall you show me this house, Miss Winslow," he asked, "or will you leave me to find my
own way?"

He couldn't tell if she sighed with resignation, or
irritation, or simply took a deep breath as she turned
towards the first room to the left of the hall.

"The oldest part of Feversham Hall was built in
1445 by Sir William Everhart," she began, lecturing
like a governess with her hands folded before her at
her waist. "It was supposed to be called Rose Hall,
but the Feversham stuck instead because of the fevers
and miasmas that rose each summer from the
marshes. They say from fear of fevers, Sir William
wouldn't come down from London until he'd been
assured of a killing frost."

"I can understand the old gentleman's reluctance,"
said George as he followed. "I saw what yellow-jack
could do to an entire fleet in Jamaica. I wonder that
you don't worry for your own health, Miss Winslow,
living so near to the marshes."

She paused, staring at him as if he'd asked the most

foolish question in the world. "I have always lived near the marshes, and I cannot imagine living anywhere else. Besides, it's only the outsiders that are stricken with the fevers. We folk that live here always are never touched."

"So if I were to make this my home," he asked, "then I should never be touched either?"

"Shifting your home to here would make no difference at all," she answered firmly. "Not even you can have whatever you wish to buy. At Feversham, you would always—always—be an outsider. Now here, this is the front parlor."

He frowned, tapping his thumbs along the brim of the hat in his hands. He was accustomed to being obeyed by his crewmen and most everyone else he encountered in his life, and he certainly hadn't been corrected with such directness by a woman since he'd left the nursery.

The same woman who'd just turned her back to him—to *him!*—and was now walking briskly away as if he were nothing more than that lowly stable-boy.

"Miss Winslow," he said, his voice automatically marshalling the authority of the *Nimble's* quarterdeck. "Miss Winslow. Have you forgotten that I have come here solely to inspect this house for the purpose of making it my own?"

Slowly she turned, her hands still clasped before her, and gazed at him over her shoulder with unsettling evenness, almost as if they were equals.

"I have forgotten neither your purpose nor mine, no," she said, her head tipped to one side so the pale light slipped across the curve of her cheek. "You are here to see Feversham, just as I am here to show it."

He let out his breath slowly, unaware until that moment that he'd been holding it. "I am glad you have recalled your duty, Miss Winslow."

"Yes, Captain My Lord." She turned her head another fraction to the left as she dipped a quick curtsey of unconvincing contrition. "I recall everything. My duty, and my miserable low station before my betters. I shall not forget either again, Captain My Lord."

Before he could reply she'd swept into the next room, tugging aside the heavy curtains at the windows. Weak sunlight, swirling with motes, filtered through the tiny, diamond-shaped panes and drifted over furniture shrouded in white cloths like so many ghosts. Miss Winslow didn't glide through the parlor like London ladies, but went striding across the patterned floor so purposefully that her black skirts flurried and fluttered around her ankles in white-thread stockings.

But the skirts and the ankles were the least of it. Why in blazes did he have the distinct impression that by agreeing with him as she had, she'd still somehow bested him?

"There are sixteen chairs made of the same Weald oak to match the panelling," she announced, twitching aside a dropcloth to display the tall-backed armchair beneath it. "It is considered most rare to have the complete set like this."

Most rare the chairs might be, but George was in no humor to appreciate it. "That chair is a right ugly piece of work, Miss Winslow," he said testily, "whether it has fifteen brothers or a hundred, and I'd wager it's barbarously uncomfortable in the bargain."

"That is your judgment, My Lord." A fresh spark of challenge lit Miss Winslow's gray eyes as she flipped the cover back over the offending chair. "The last master, Mr. Trelawney, appreciated the old ways in his home.''

"Or perhaps," said George, "Mr. Trelawney was simply too tightfisted to make the necessary renovations to bring the old ways up to snuff with the new."

"And what if he was, Captain My Lord, or what if he wasn't?" she demanded tartly. "It's been four years since Mr. Trelawney died, and nothing has been changed in that time. I told you the house wouldn't suit you."

George raised a single brow. "I haven't said that it didn't, have I?"

"You've as much as said it, saying everything's gone fusty and shabby," she said, her voice warming. "The other Trelawneys up north aren't about to keep up with London fashions and improvements when what's here will serve well enough. Times are hard, what with the wars and all, and the Trelawneys aren't the sort to go tossing good coins after bad for no reason."

"But what a wonderfully fine thing their carelessness is for me, Miss Winslow," countered George, "especially if the shabbiness of the 'old ways' lowers Feversham's asking price."

She dipped her chin, letting the words simmer and stew between them. Too late she'd realized he'd been teasing her, and clearly the knowledge hadn't made her happy with him, or herself, either.

"Through these doors lies the dining room," she said curtly, turning with an abrupt squeak of her heel to lead the way.

George followed, keeping his little smile to himself. He'd won this particular skirmish handily, and he suspected there'd be more to come before they were done. Clearly Miss Winslow hated losing just as much as he did—which was making this tour a great deal more interesting than the old-fashioned furniture and creaking steps.

Their truce lasted through the tour of the dining room, the drawing room, and another dark little parlor pretending to be a library, though the shelves appeared to hold not books, but a mouldering collection of badly preserved stuffed gamebirds. The same uneasy peace held between them as they went downstairs and through the empty servants' hall, past the laundry and the dairy and the echoing catacombs of the pantry, scullery, and kitchen, where George decided there was nothing more desultory than a kitchen bereft of the bullying chatter of a cook and the savory fragrances of roasting and baking, or sadder to see than a cold, clean-swept hearth with a row of empty spits above it.

How in blazes did Miss Winslow live in the middle of this? Surely she couldn't be spending night and day alone among these shrouded chairs and mouldering walls, not and keep that straight defiance in her back and the sharp spark in her eyes. Surely there must be some other small, snug cottage on the land where she and her old father lived, some other place that was home.

But if that were so, then why did she still have so much pride in the old hall, shabby as it was? And why, when he had the power to restore it, did she seem so resentful of such a possibility? Why was she so intent on chasing him away?

And why, really, did he care?

"This is the mistress's bedchamber," she was saying as she threw open the shutters of the next-to-last room upstairs. "It has not been used in a long time, Mr. Trelawney being a bachelor-gentleman."

"But doubtless at least one visiting queen or another has slept here," said George, gazing at the enormous canopy bed, the heavily carved posts and the faded white and gold brocade hangings still maintaining a rare, regal grandeur. "Isn't that always the case with the grand beds in these old houses?"

"No," she said quickly. "Not here, not at Feversham. No lady's ever slept in that bed that hadn't a wedded right to it."

Unable to resist such an opening, he patted the bed's faded coverlet. "You've not been tempted to try it yourself, Miss Winslow? Not once, for a lark, to see how the mistress slumbered?"

Fiercely she shook her head, even as she blushed. Ah, he thought, so she *had* tried the bed, no matter how severe and proper she aspired to be. What woman wouldn't, really, when tempted with a bedstead fit for a queen?

Or fit for a smoke-eyed woman with a queen's own bearing....

"You have not asked of the roof, My Lord," she said hurriedly, wishing so clearly to move from the topic of the bed that he almost—almost—regretted twitting her about it. "Most of you Londoners ask after that."

He glanced up towards the ceiling, where the white plaster was stained yellow from obvious water damage. "I assume that there is one?"

"Of course," she said. "It is made of tiles, to replace the old thatch."

"And does it leak, Miss Winslow, this tiled roof?"

She looked upward, too, following his gaze. "Rain

is a part of our life here, Captain My Lord. Raindrops and sea-spray—why, we scarce notice them, nor the marks that they leave.''

He smiled, knowing inevitably what would come next. ''But the Londoners notice?''

''Oh, yes,'' she said with undeniable triumph in her voice, and for the first time she smiled in return, quick and determined, in a way that seemed to link them together for that instant. ''They do. Here is the last room for you to see, My Lord, the master's chamber. You shall understand for yourself why it is the most perfect room in the entire house.''

His own smile lingered as he followed her, thinking of how that grin of hers was already as close to perfection as anything he'd see today. He'd tolerate a good winter's worth of water-marked plaster to be able to see her look at him like that again.

But as soon as she pulled back the heavy velvet curtains, he forgot everything else but the view that rolled away before him. Here the old-fashioned diamond panes had been replaced with newer casements, freeing the landscape. The overgrown remnants of a garden huddled close to the house, then a band of wind-stunted oaks and evergreens that ran to a ragged edge of sandy land, and then—then lay the restless, shimmering silver of the sea, the horizon softened on a gray day like this so the waves and sky blended into one. What he would see from these windows would never be the same twice, just like the sea itself, and just like the sea, he'd always be drawn irresistibly back to it.

''Mark what I say, Captain My Lord,'' said Miss Winslow swiftly, realizing too late the cost of sharing perfection. ''There is so much wrong with Feversham that you cannot see for yourself, not in so short a time! Every chimney needs repointing, and every fireplace smokes. I cannot count the panes missing from the windows, the lead in the mullions having gone so brittle. The last cook left over how the bake-ovens are crumbling to dust from the inside, and there's so many bats living in the attic that they'd come down into the servants' quarters, too, making the maidservants all give notice from fright.''

He was only half listening, because none of it mattered. He would make whatever was wrong into right, wouldn't he? There'd be no better way to spend his Spanish silver than this. He would have the curtains taken down from these windows, and he would never replace them. He would want to wake to this, his own private square of sea, and he would want to fall asleep to it each night as well.

''Shall I call your carriage, Captain My Lord?'' the gray-eyed woman beside him was asking. ''You should begin your journey now, before it grows later. Your driver will not wish to take his horses on our roads after dark.''

''Thank you, Miss Winslow,'' he said gently. He could hardly fault her if she wished to keep such a magical place as this to herself, could he? But if he hadn't come, then someone else would, and at least he would be sure to give her and her worthless old father a handsome parting settlement when he let them go. ''Tell the driver I shall be ready in half an hour's time.''

''You will leave, then, Captain My Lord?'' she asked, the relief in her eyes strangely sad. ''You will be gone from Feversham?''

He nodded, wishing for her sake that the truth

didn't feel like deceit. He would leave, but he meant to return, and then he wouldn't leave again until he'd new orders from his admiral. He would always come back to Feversham because, like every wandering sailor, at last he'd found his home. He'd prepared for the worst, and been granted better than he'd ever dreamed.

He'd found perfection.

Chapter Three

Fan stood on the bench and gazed out over the score of expectant faces turned up towards her, her hands clasped before her to hide any trembling. The candle-light from the lanterns flickered with the drafts that found their way in through the barn's timbers, and the men of the Company were waiting so quietly that she could hear the horses at their hay, rustling and nickering in their stalls behind her.

"I know there's talk at the tavern in town," she began, "and I'm not the kind to pretend otherwise. The hard truth is this—that a Londoner came to look at Feversham with an eye towards buying it."

She let the muttered oaths and exclamations settle before she continued. "But this *fine* gentleman found the house old and inconvenient, with much lacking," she said, adding a bit of purposeful scorn to her voice for extra emphasis, "and I do not expect him to bother with us again."

"You didn't show him this barn, did you, mistress?" called one man to the raucous delight of his friends. "He wouldn't've found much lacking there if'n you had."

"Nay, Tom, not the barn, nor the privies, either," she answered dryly. "I kept our secrets to ourselves, where they belong. But I did take care not to show him the house in the best of lights, just to be sure. The sight of old Master Trelawney's moldy stuffed pigeons seemed enough to send him racing back to London, his driver whipping those hired horses for all he was worth."

They laughed again, as much from relief as from amusement, and pushed and shoved at each other, as if to prove that way that they hadn't been worried, not at all. But Fan knew she wasn't entirely free of the questions, not as long as Bob Forbert stood in the front of the crowd, chewing on the inside of his mouth and shifting nervously from one scrawny leg to the other.

"The boy that watered the coachman's horses, mistress," he said, his voice squeaking as he strived to make himself heard. "The boy said the man weren't no regular Londoner, but a fancy lord and a king's officer, a Navy man in a coat all glittering with gold lace. Do that be true, mistress? That some bleeding gold-lace officer was here poking his long nose around our affairs?"

Instantly the laughter and raillery stopped, and all the faces swung back towards Fan for an answer.

"Yes," she said slowly, carefully. "He was Captain Lord George Claremont of His Majesty's Navy, but all that interested him was the house."

Smuggling took money from the king's pockets, and in turn the king took catching smugglers most seriously. Officers like Captain Lord Claremont were sworn to capture smugglers as enemies of the crown, especially now with the country at peace with France.

Such an officer could destroy her life as well, if he learned of her role in the Company, and there wasn't a man in the barn who wasn't thinking the same.

How simple it sounded that way, how clean and uncomplicated, when in fact the captain's visit was still twisting away at her, as sharp as a new-honed knife. When she'd received the letter from the Trelawneys' agent in London, she'd imagined the captain to be the model of Navy cruelty, with a twisted, squinting face as weather-beaten as a cliff to reflect the wickedness of his personality.

But an aristocratic captain: what could possibly make for a worse combination? To be sure, she'd next to no experience with arrogant noblemen, though she'd heard enough tales of how they were all riddled with the pox and fat from too much drink and wickedness. And considering this one's reputation as a famously daredevil frigate captain—the agent had made quite a point of that—he'd likely also have lost an arm or leg in battle, or be hideously seamed with scars. She had pictured the visitor like this in alarming detail, steeling herself for the unpleasant task of showing him the house.

But what she had never imagined was the reality of Captain Lord Claremont who had presented himself on Feversham's doorstep.

She had, quite simply, never in her life met such a gentleman, let alone found one standing on the doorstep before her. He was appallingly handsome, tall and broad-shouldered and lean, and the dark blue coat and white breeches of his uniform were so closely fitted that she'd no more need at all for her imagination.

It wasn't just that he had all his limbs, unlike the

Captain Claremont she'd been picturing in her mind. This Captain Claremont stood before her with an assurance that was new to Fan, a kind of unquestionable confidence that came from inside the man, not from any tailor's needle. She could see it in his eyes, his smile, even the way his dark hair waved back from his forehead. She'd known her share of brave men, but their bravery had come from muscle and force, while this one—this one would have the same muscle and force, true enough, but it would be his intelligence and his conviction that he *would* win that would always give him the advantage.

And God help her, he already had it over her. He had begun by treating her like the lowliest parlor maid, and she had responded as was fitting for the housekeeper of Feversham: dignified and aloof, and justly proud of her position and the old house. He'd respected that, or so she'd thought at first.

But somehow things had shifted between them while she'd shown him the house. He'd challenged her, dared her, badgered her, until she'd done it all back to him, and not only in defense, either. She'd enjoyed testing herself against such a clever man: that was the horrible truth of it. She'd enjoyed the banter, and she'd enjoyed being with him. By the time they'd reached the bedchambers, he'd been out-and-out flirting with her, and, wretched creature that she was, she could only smile and blush like some simpleminded maid.

Her only solace came from knowing Captain Claremont had left Feversham the same day he'd come, and wouldn't return. He'd made that clear enough, hadn't he? She'd made a shameful fool of herself once, but at least she'd be spared doing it again. And if she let his handsome, smiling face haunt her dreams, then that would be her penance.

That, and the questions and doubts of the men before her.

"But why Feversham, mistress?" called Will Hood from the back, and others rumbled along with him in a chorus of uncertainty. "There's scores o' other grand houses for the likes o' him. Why'd he come here if he'd no reason?"

"He wished a house by the sea," answered Fan, raising her voice, praying she sounded more sure of herself than she felt. "That is what the Trelawneys' agent in London wrote to me. He saw a drawing of Feversham, and was much taken with it. But he found the real house much lacking and inconvenient, and left disappointed, determined to find another."

She was unwisely repeating herself, and she saw the uneasy glances passing back and forth.

"Captain Lord Claremont saw nothing to make him wish to return," she continued, "nor anything of our affairs here. None of this barn, or your ponies, or the boats near the stream."

"This Captain Lord Claremont, was he the same captain what made all the fuss last year?" asked Hood. "The one what stole all that silver from that dago treasure-ship? Was he your gentleman here?"

"He's not *my* gentleman," said Fan quickly, but no one else noticed the distinction, or cared.

"Likely this Claremont's friends with the old bloody Duke o' Richmond, too, may his bones rot in the blackest corner of Hell," said Forbert darkly. "All them nobles are kin, aren't they? I say this one's come to see us broke and strung up for the gulls to pick apart, like they did to those poor blokes on Rook's Hill near Chichester.''

"And I say you're daft, Forbert, making no more sense than a braying jackass," said Hood, wiping his nose with a red-spotted handkerchief. He was a sensible man, an old friend of her father's, one she trusted and one the others listened to as well. It was also whispered in awe that Hood was strong enough to row single-handedly across the Channel to France, which doubtless added extra weight to his opinions. "Those black days o' Richmond were your grandfather's time, not ours."

"But who's to say they won't come back?" demanded Forbert peevishly. "Who's to say they're not here now?"

"Because they're *not*." Impatiently Fan shoved a loose strand of her hair back under her cap. "Do you think I'd purposefully lead you astray, Bob Forbert, just for the sport of it? Do you think I'd put my own neck into the noose first? You know I've ways to tell Ned Markham to keep back his tea for another week if the customs men are here. Why would that be changing now?"

Hood nodded. "And mind, we're a small company, and always have been. No high-and-mighty lord-captain's going to bother with us, not when he can go fill his pockets as deep as he pleases catching dagos and frogs. Mistress here will tell you the same. We're not worth the bother."

Forbert gulped, his Adam's apple moving frantically up and down. "But there's a peace now," he persisted, "and if this captain is idle, then—"

"The peace won't last, not with the French," said Fan quickly. "The London agent said so in his letter.

He said Captain Claremont wanted to find a house at once, since he expected to be sent back to sea soon. Ned Markham's said that, too, that the word of a Frenchman's not worth a fig.''

"Well, then, there you are," said Hood. "And if mistress says this lordly bloke's not coming back, then he's not, and that's an end to it."

"Yes," said Fan, her old confidence beginning to return. Captain Claremont was no more than a single day's inconvenience in her ordered life. Why, in another week, she'd scarce remember the color of his hair, let alone the way he'd grinned to soften his teasing about the mistress's bed. "That *is* an end to it, Bob Forbert, and to Captain Lord Folderol, too. Let him take his Spanish dollars and settle in China for what I care, and a pox on anyone who says different."

Hood nodded, the lines around his mouth creasing through the graying stubble of his beard as he smiled. "True words, mistress, true words," he said, clapping his hands. "How could it be otherwise with you, considering what the Navy would do to the likes of us if they could? Ha, that old bastard of a captain-mi'lordy's lucky you didn't shoot him dead there in his fancy carriage, just because you could!"

The others laughed, pleased by the vengeance Hood was imagining. But while Fan laughed, too, her conscience was far from merry.

Shoot the bastard dead, that's what they wanted, dead on the step of his fancy carriage.

And forget forever the way he'd smiled, just for her, just for her....

George sat in the small office, ignoring the dish of tepid tea that the bustling clerk had brought, and considering instead the murky fog in the street outside. Though landsmen failed to mark the difference, London fog was nothing like the clean, salty fog at sea. The stuff that clogged the London air was gray and heavy as a shroud, so weighted with coal smoke and grime that he wondered the people who lived in the city could breathe it without perishing.

Not that any of them seemed to notice it, let alone complain. That in itself would set him apart from the true fashionable Londoners like his older brother Brant, His Grace the Duke of Strachen, as much at elegant ease in the chair across from him as George himself was not. If it weren't for his uniform, George wouldn't have the slightest notion how to dress himself, while Brant not only knew the fashions, he set them, from the precise width of this season's waistcoat lapel to the cunning new way to wear a peridot stickpin in the center of one's cravat.

Once again George smiled to recall how blithely Miss Winslow had lumped him in with the other Londoners, and smiled, too, to remember how she'd lifted her chin with such charming defiance when she'd done so. Yet he'd felt more instantly at home in that windswept corner of Kent than he'd ever felt in his family's vast formal house on Hanover Square—a contradiction he intended to correct as soon as possible.

"Ah, ah, Your Grace, Captain My Lord!" exclaimed Mr. Potipher as he scurried into the office, bowing in nervous little jerks like some anxious little waterfowl in old-fashioned knee-breeches and steel spectacles. "I am so honored to have you here, so very honored!"

George didn't even give him time to circle around

to his desk. "I have come about Feversham," he declared. "I have decided to take it."

"You have?" exclaimed Potipher, so shocked that he briefly forgot his manners. "That is, Captain My Lord, you have found the property pleases you?"

"I have," George answered without hesitation. "And I wish to buy it outright, not merely let it. The house requires so many improvements—which, of course, I intend to make at my expense—that it would be imprudent not to."

"You would buy Feversham outright, Captain My Lord?" asked Potipher, shocked again. "You would make an offer this day?"

"Indeed, I will make it," said George, "just as I expect it to be accepted. I understand the family that owns the property has had little interest in it for years, and should not be overly particular."

"No, no, no, they shall not," agreed the flustered agent, taking down a wooden box from the shelf behind him and rustling through the sheaf of papers it contained. "Yes, here we are. You are quite right about the Trelawneys, you know. Times being what they are, I am sure they shall be delighted to accept whatever you offer."

George nodded, and smiled with satisfaction across the room at his brother. Brant had always been the one among the three brothers with a head for business and investments, and Society had long ago dubbed Brant the "Golden Lord", after his ability to draw guineas seemingly from the air, while their brother Revell had been called the "Sapphire Lord" for his success in India.

It had, of course, followed that George would be labeled the "Silver Lord" on account of that single stupendous capture, a title that George himself found wretchedly embarrassing. But after today, he'd have more than that ridiculous nickname. When he left his office, he'd no longer be just a rootless, roaming sailor, but a Gentleman of Property.

But Potipher was scowling through his spectacles at a paper from the box. "You should know that there is one small consideration attached to this property, Captain My Lord."

"My brother's credit is sufficient for a score of country houses in Kent," drawled Brant. "That should be no 'consideration' at all."

"Oh, no, no, there was never a question of that!" Potipher smiled anxiously, the plump pads of his cheeks lifting his spectacles. "It is the housekeeper, Miss Winslow. I believe you must have met her at your, ah, inspection of the house, Captain My Lord?"

George nodded, striving to remain noncommittal. The last thing he wished was to confess to this man, and worse, to his brother, that he'd been thinking of that self-same housekeeper day and night since he'd returned, with no end to his misery in sight.

"Then I am certain you shall be willing to oblige this request from the current owners, Captain My Lord," said the agent, his lips pursed as he scanned the letter in his hands. "Miss Winslow's father was the house's former caretaker, and most kind and useful to old Mr. Trelawney before his death. But it appears that recently Mr. Winslow himself has met with some manner of fatal misfortune."

At once George thought of the young woman's somber dress, how she'd said her father was only away, and how long it took for her to smile.

"I am sorry, on Miss Winslow's account," he said softly. "She is young to bear such a loss."

"Then you will honor the Trelawneys' request that she be assured her position as long as she wishes to retain it?" asked Potipher hopefully. "They have made it a condition, you see, Captain My Lord, having great respect for the father's services as well as regard for Miss Winslow's own abilities. She would certainly ease your entry into the neighborhood, recommending the best butchers and bakers and such."

George sat, suddenly silent. To keep a lone young woman in the house once he'd settled it with his own men from the *Nimble,* his steward and other sailors who knew his ways and would readily adapt them to land—it would not do, it would not do in the least. He was certainly fond enough of pretty women, but he hadn't lived in the same quarters with a female presence since he'd been a child, and to do so now could bring nothing but absolute, appalling trouble.

And then he remembered the wistfulness in Miss Winslow's face when they'd stood together in the last bedchamber, when the view from the windows had convinced him to make the house his own. He'd realized then that she'd saved the best for last, at once hoping and dreading that he'd love it the same way that she did. Clearly she did love the weary old place as if it were her own, and he understood the depth of her sorrow at seeing it go to another. She'd already lost her father, and now she was faced with losing her home as well. He understood, and he sympathized, a good deal more of both than was likely proper.

And now there was this damned clause imposed by

those damned Trelawneys, tying his hands and hers too....

"I shall leave you to consider it, Captain My Lord," said Potipher as he rose behind his desk and began bowing his way towards the office's door. Feversham had sat empty for years, and clearly the agent meant to be as obliging as possible if it resulted in a sale. "Pray take as long as you need to reach your decision. But I fear I must remind you that there is not another property with Feversham's special charms in all my lists, and keeping the housekeeper is such an insignificant, small condition for such a fine estate!"

"'Special charms', hell," grumbled George as the door clicked shut. "The place is such a rambling, ramshackle old pile that they should be paying me to relieve them of it."

Not that Brant cared one way or the other. "The housekeeper, George?" he asked, pouncing with unabashed curiosity. "You've been keeping secrets from me again, brother."

George sighed mightily. "No secrets, Brant, for there's nothing to tell."

"Nothing?" repeated Brant archly. "I'd wager ten guineas that this Miss Winslow isn't the sort of black-clad old gorgon who ruled our youth with terror, else you would have already described her to me in the most shuddering terms. Instead you haven't even mentioned her existence, which tells me infinitely more than any words."

"You will make a wager of anything," grumbled George. This was precisely the kind of inquisition that he had wished to avoid. If there was one area where Brant delighted in displaying his superiority over his younger brother, it was his far greater experience with women—a markedly unfair advantage, really, considering that George had spent most of his adult life at sea and far from any females at all, while Brant, with his fallen-angel's face and a peer's title, had absolutely wallowed in them in London.

"Well?" asked Brant, undaunted. "Is she?"

George glared. "Miss Winslow is neither old, nor is she a gorgon, though she was dressed in black."

Brant waved his hand in airy dismissal. "Black can be an elegant affectation on the right woman."

"Not if it's mourning," said George sharply. "You heard Potiphar, Brant. The poor woman's just lost her father."

But Brant would not be discouraged. "Is she sweetly melancholy, then? A delicate beauty, shown off by that black like a diamond against midnight velvet?"

"You would not find her so," said George, his discomfort growing by the second. He'd never cared for Brant's manner with women. True, his brother's attitude was shared by fashionable gentlemen from the Prince of Wales downward, but the way Brant combined a connoisseur's fastidious consideration with a predator's single-mindedness seemed to George to include almost no regard or respect for the lady herself.

Which, of course, was not how he'd felt about Miss Winslow. "She is tall," he said, choosing his words with care, "and handsome rather than beautiful. Dark hair, fair skin, and eyes the color of smoke."

"Ah," said Brant with great satisfaction as he settled back in his chair, making a little tent over his chest by pressing his fingertips together. "You sound smitten, George."

"She is not that kind of woman, Brant," said George defensively. "Put a broadsword in her hand, and she'd become St. Joan and smite her villains left and right, but as for leaving a trail of swooning beaux in her wake, the way you're saying—no, not at all. She's prickly as a dish of nettles."

"But you *are* intrigued," insisted Brant. "I know you well enough to see the signs. You've had the sweetest cream of fair London wafting before you this last month, and not one of them has inspired this sort of paeans from you as does this housekeeper."

"Paeans?" repeated George incredulously. "To say she is prickly as a dish of nettles is a paean?"

Brant smiled. "From you it is, my unpoetic Neptune of a brother. I say you should take both the house and the housekeeper. Regardless of her housewifery skills, she shall, I think, offer you other amusements."

"Amusements, hell," said George crossly. "That's not why I'm taking the blasted house."

"Oh, why not?" said Brant with his usual breezy nonchalance. "Our dear brother Rev has gone and married a governess, and now you fancy a housekeeper. I'll have to look about me for a pretty little cook to become my duchess, and make our whole wedded staff complete."

"Just stow it, Brant," growled George. "Just stow it at once. Potipher!"

The agent reappeared so quickly that George suspected he'd been poised on the other side door, listening.

"You have reached a decision, Captain My Lord?" he asked, hovering with cheerful expectation.

"I have not," growled George. "What if Miss

Winslow wishes to leave my employment, eh? Is she a slave to the wishes of these blasted Trelawneys as well?''

Potipher blinked warily behind his spectacles. ''Oh, no, Captain My Lord, not at all. Miss Winslow will be under no obligation to remain whatsoever.''

George sighed with a grim fatalism, drumming his fingers impatiently on the arm of his chair. At least that was some small solace. He would not wish any lady, especially not one as fine as Miss Winslow, to be obligated to stay with him. Yet if he wanted Feversham—which, of course, he did, now more than ever—then he was trapped into keeping Miss Winslow with it. George did not like feeling trapped, but least Potipher was also offering him a way out: what respectable woman, young or old, would wish to remain long beneath the same roof with the crew of the *Nimble?*

But then George thought again of the way Miss Winslow had smiled at him, bright and determined, as if she'd enjoyed their skirmishing as much as he had himself. Although he'd nobly scorned Brant's suggestion that he ''amuse'' himself with the housekeeper, he couldn't keep from considering all the wicked possibilities and justifications the circumstances would offer, and he nearly groaned aloud at the willfulness of his wayward thoughts and willing body.

Blast, he didn't even know her given name….

Abruptly he rose to his feet. ''Then it is decided, Mr. Potipher,'' he said. ''I shall take Feversham, and Miss Winslow with it.''

And trust the rest to fate.

* * *

"Ooh, miss, those look most wonderful fine on you!" exclaimed the girl behind the counter of the little shop as she held the looking-glass for Fan. "They say all the noble ladies be wearin' such in London and Bath."

Fan turned her head before the glass, making the gold earrings with the garnet drops swing gently back and forth against her cheeks. While her Company specialized in bringing in tea, there were others along the coast that carried more jewels and lace from France than in most of the shops in the Palais Royale, and even here in the tiny harbor village of Tunford, not three miles from Feversham itself, Fan could let herself be tempted by earrings that likely were the same as the noble ladies in London were wearing.

"You'll fetch yourself a handsome sweetheart with those a-glittering in your ears, miss," promised the girl, nodding with mercantile wisdom. "Less'n you already have a good man, and you want me to set these aside for him to come buy for you."

Wistfully Fan touched one earring, catching the sunlight in the faceted stone like a tiny ruby prism in the golden filigree. She'd never had a sweetheart, old or new, let alone one to give her anything like these earrings. Father hadn't permitted it, claiming that all the Tunford boys were beneath her. Fleetingly, foolishly, she now let herself imagine what kind of roses and jewels Captain Claremont would lavish on his lady, just like the heroes in ballads.

For that matter, Fan couldn't recall the last time she'd bought something so frivolous for herself. Instead she'd always dutifully put her share of the company's profits into the double-locked strongbox inside the wall of her bedchamber against hard times, the way Father had instructed. She was always conscious of that, of how she wasn't like other women with a husband to look after her. She'd no one now but herself to rely upon for the future. She'd no one to blame, either, if she died in the poorhouse, or if some cowardly fool like Bob Forbert finally decided to turn evidence against her to the magistrates.

Yet the earrings *were* lovely things, and Fan let herself smile at her reflection as the red-tinged sparkles danced over her cheeks.

"Them garnets are as right as can be for you, miss," coaxed the girl. "You won't find any finer on this coast, not in Lydd nor Hythe, neither, and I vow—la, what be *that* ruckus?"

The girl hurried to the shop's doorway, the looking-glass still in her hands, and curiously Fan followed. Tunford was a small village with only a handful of narrow lanes, sleepy and quiet the way country villages always were.

But it wasn't quiet now. Two large wagons piled high with barrels, trunks, and boxes were coming to a noisy stop before the Tarry Man, Tunford's favorite public house, their four-horse dray teams snorting and pawing the rutted soil while their drivers bawled for the hostler. Dogs raced forward, barking and yelping with excitement, and children soon came running along, too.

Even before the wagons had stopped, the eight passengers who'd been riding precariously on top began to clamber down, laughing and jumping to the ground as nimbly as acrobats. They were strong, sinewy, exotic men, all burned dark as mahogany from the sun, with gold hoops in their ears and long braided queues down their backs: deep-water sailors, man-o'-war crewmen that were seldom seen in a group like this outside of the fleet's ports.

"What d'you make of all that, miss?" marveled the shopgirl. "Looks like half the Brighton circus, come here to Tunford!"

But it wasn't the Brighton circus, half or otherwise, thought Fan with sickening certainty as she watched over the other woman's shoulder. Over and over she had told herself this wouldn't happen, until she'd let herself believe it. What was arriving in Tunford, and soon after at Feversham, was going to outdo any mere circus, and cause a great many more problems.

Because there, riding on a prancing chestnut gelding as he joined the wagons carrying his belongings, was Captain Lord Claremont.

Chapter Four

It took considerable determination for Fan to make herself walk slowly across the lane towards Captain Claremont, as if she'd been planning all morning to do exactly that. What she really wished to do, of course, was to race back to Feversham, lock every door, and bury her head beneath her bed pillow upstairs like a terrified cony in her burrow. But Father had taught her that danger was best confronted face-to-face, and so she did, even managing a polite smile to mask the thumping of her heart.

"Good day, Captain My Lord," she called as he swung down from his horse. "I did not expect to see you again so soon."

Clearly surprised, he turned at her voice, ducking around the chestnut's neck to find her. He smiled warmly as she came closer, and swept his black cocked hat from his head to salute her, there in the middle of Tunford.

"Miss Winslow," he boomed, his voice so cheerfully loud that she was certain they must be hearing it clear in Portsmouth. "Good day to you. I did not expect to see you here, either."

She'd forgotten how very blue his eyes were, as if they'd stolen the brightest color from the sky above, so blue that she had to look away, towards the wagons and the grinning sailors watching them with undisguised curiosity.

"You are making a journey, Captain My Lord?" she asked, foolishly saying the obvious as she hoped and prayed he was going somewhere on the far side of the world.

"I am," he declared, the sunlight glinting off the gold buttons on his coat. "And likely you have guessed my destination as well. Feversham, Miss Winslow. Feversham, my new home port. You have received the letter from Potipher, I trust?"

"No," said Fan faintly, the awful certainty knotting tightly in her stomach. "I have had no letter from anyone."

"No?" The captain frowned, his blue eyes clouding. "Potipher was to have written to you. So you'd know, you see. So you'd be prepared."

"No letter," she said again, and swallowed hard as she tugged her shawl higher over her shoulders. She didn't want to know, and she didn't want to be prepared. "I've had nothing from—"

"Miss Winslow!" The shopgirl came puffing up beside them, her expression as stern as her round face could muster. "Miss Winslow, if you don't be wanting them garnet ear-bobs, then I must be taking them back to the shop."

"Oh, I am so sorry!" Fan flushed, her fingers flying guiltily to the earrings. "I forgot I even had them on. Here, take them back, if you please. I do not think they suit me after all."

"I think they suit you vastly well," said the captain gallantly. "A spot of color is just the thing for you."

The flush in her cheeks deepened, more scarlet than any miserable garnets, and hastily she pulled the earrings from her ears.

"Thank you," she said, pressing them into the girl's waiting palm. "Besides, they're too dear for me."

"How dear can they be?" asked the captain. "What's the price, missy?"

"Twenty-five shillings, M'Lord," answered the shopgirl, simpering up at him as she brazenly tripled the price that she'd asked of Fan earlier. "They be French garnets and filigree-work."

"And now they shall belong to Miss Winslow," he said, reaching into his waistcoat pocket for the coins, "for I cannot imagine them hanging from any other ears than hers."

"No!" gasped Fan. True, she'd been fancying them, but fancies didn't account for gossip, or whispers, or how accepting such a gift from him would rob her of all respect from the men in the Company. "You cannot! I will not take the earrings! That is— that is, it's not proper for me to accept such a gift from you!"

His face fell, and he rubbed the back of his neck, a rare, restless little gesture of indecision for a man like him.

"It is not intended as a gift such as that," he explained. "Not as a gentleman to a lady, that is. I meant it to make up for Potipher not sending that dam—that letter to you, as he ought to have."

"Why?" she demanded, though she was already guessing—no, she already *knew*—the truth. He would be the new master, for as long a lease as the Trelawneys would grant him.

"Because I haven't just let Feversham, as I'd first intended," he said, unable to keep the satisfied pride from his voice. "I've bought it outright."

She stared at him, dumbstruck. He'd *bought* Feversham? Had his captain's share of that Spanish treasure ship truly been so vast, or were even younger sons of dukes wealthy enough to make such a purchase with ease?

"That is where I'm bound now," he continued, "to take possession. There's nothing to be gained by wasting time, is there?"

Aware of her shock, his smile turned lopsided as he answered quickly to fill her silence. "No, no, there isn't, not at all. But this will be easier for us both if we—"

"No." Abruptly she turned away from him. Everything in her life would be changed by this impulsive purchase of his, from warning the men, to changing the place along the stream where their tea was landed, to making sure no further messages were delivered to her at Feversham.

Oh, yes, and more change as well: she must leave the house where she'd been born and find a new place for herself to live. No wonder she was walking so fast now she was nearly running.

"Hold now, Miss Winslow, don't flight off like this," he said, his long stride easily keeping pace with hers. "We've matters to discuss."

She kept her gaze straight ahead, quickening her step. "We do not."

"And I say we do." He wheeled around, blocking

her way. "Isn't there some place more private than the middle of the street where we can talk?"

"I told you," she said, trying to step around him, "there is nothing to be said!"

"But there is." He caught her arm to stop her, his grasp through the rough linsey-woolsey of her sleeve hard enough to make her gasp indignantly. "I don't give a tinker's dam if we talk here where the whole world can listen. But knowing these are your people, I'd think you'd want it otherwise."

Fan glared at him and jerked her arm free, rubbing furiously at the spot where he'd held her as if to wipe away his touch. What he said was true; there was never much privacy to be found in a village like this, where everyone knew everyone else's business. Even now she and the captain were drawing a sizeable audience, curious faces peering from open windows and over walls, and she didn't want to think what sort of tales the company men would be hearing.

"This way, then," she said curtly, heading across the lane and leaving him to follow her into the yard of the little church, stopping when they were surrounded only by overgrown headstones of long-dead villagers and the empty graves of sailors who'd perished at sea. "There's no one here who'll spread gossip."

"Very well," he said, glancing dubiously around at the old slanting headstones, the carved names and dates softened by the wind and patched with moss and lichen. The breeze from the marshes and the sea blew more insistently here in the open, tossing the heavy tassels on her shawl against her hip and ruffling his hair across his forehead. "Dead men tell no tales, eh?"

"Why should the dead trouble you?" she demanded bitterly. "Considering your trade's as much killing as sailing, I'd vow that you'd be more familiar with the dead than the living."

"You cannot have life without death," he said quietly. "One goes with the other, doesn't it?"

A chill shivered down her spine. No matter how often she'd pleaded with him to stop, her father had often spoken that way of death as well, as if he almost wished to court his own end. How was she any better, speaking like this while standing among so many graves?

"Life goes with death, yes," she countered, striving to put her darker thoughts aside, "but few can find as much profit in it as you have."

"Luck is as unpredictable as death, you know. I could as easily have been shot to pieces by French guns as be standing here with you now." He tried to smile, but his expression seemed clouded now, without the earlier happiness, and she wondered if he, too, felt the grim pull of the burying ground. "You are angry because I have bought the house you regard as your home."

"It is not my place to be angry," she said sadly, for of course he was right, "even if you are taking away the only home I have ever known."

He shook his head, frowning. "Hold now, I've not said that."

"You didn't need to say a word, not when your actions are so clear!" she cried forlornly. "You've no use for our old ways here, and you've even brought your own people as servants. What place can there be left for me at Feversham?"

"Have I asked you to leave?"

"Have you needed to?" She lifted her chin, determined to not let him see her cry. "I'll not trouble you overmuch, Captain My Lord. That's not my way. I shall gather my things and be gone by nightfall, and you'll need not give me another thought."

"The hell I won't," he said sharply, his frown deepening. "You're not to leave, not unless you wish it. I'll have need of your special knowledge of the house, the tradespeople in this county, the neighbors—a thousand things, I'm sure, if you'll but share them. I've no intention of sending you out of your home, especially not with your father gone."

"My father's not dead," she said quickly, shoving aside a piece of hair that had blown free of her cap and across her forehead. "I know it. He *will* come back."

"I'm sure he will," he said with gruff kindness. "And he should find you at Feversham when he does."

Her resolution wobbled, and tears stung behind her eyes. How long had it been since anyone had shown her any manner of kindness at all, gruff or not? To take her father's place leading the Company, she'd had to appear twice as competent, twice as emotionless as Father had ever been. Such leaders didn't expect sympathy or kindness, nor did they get it. To feel it now, standing in the windswept burying ground and from this man, was almost more than she could bear, and far more than she could wish.

"Father would never look for me anywhere else," she said softly. "I was born at Feversham, you see. My mother was the cook, when the old master still had guests to look after. Not that I can remember those times, or my mother, either."

The captain nodded, more understanding than she'd expected. "I can scarce recall my mother, either, she died so young."

"It fell to my father and my aunt to look after me," she said. She didn't know why she was telling him this, for surely these ordinary details of her life would be of no interest to anyone else. "My aunt was the housekeeper before me, and trained me well in the skills and arts of running Feversham. 'The mysteries', she called them, as if she were a very witch, and not the most pious woman in the parish."

He smiled, the lines crinkling around the corners of his eyes the way she'd remembered. The last time he'd smiled at her like this had been when she'd shown him the mistress's bedchamber, and he'd teased her about trying the bed. He'd made her heart thump and her thoughts race off in all kinds of wrongful ways.

"I expect you were the most attentive and adept of students," he was saying now, "whatever the day's mystery."

"Oh, hardly," she said, recalling how often her aunt had rapped her knuckles with the long handle of a wooden spoon. "Aunt called me Miss Fan Fidgets, on account of my never paying proper attention. I always longed to be out-of-doors when I was little, you see, and didn't always heed her explaining how to take the tea-stains from the Irish linen and mildew from the plaster, or how always to speak as much like the gentry as I could."

"That's what your aunt called you? Miss Fan Fidgets?" His smile widened with obvious relish. "I can't repeat any of the names my brothers called me, they were so foul. It's quite astounding how many mangled versions of a simple 'George' boys can concoct when they set their minds to it."

She smiled then, too, more amazed that he'd confide in her that his brothers had teased him with foul names when they'd been boys. She couldn't picture having such a conversation with any of the other men she knew, even the ones she'd known since they'd been children together. Perhaps this was another way titled gentlemen were different than ordinary men, or perhaps, more dangerous for her, this was simply the way this particular titled gentleman behaved with her.

"I was the only child of the household," she confessed wistfully, "which made me more at my ease around my elders than the lads and lasses my own age."

He glanced at her sideways, beneath the brim of his hat, as if to show how thoroughly he doubted her. "Though surely that is no longer the case."

She shrugged, twisting her hands into the ends of her shawl. She'd already told him more than enough; he didn't need to know how few her friends of any age were, or how lonely she often was, or, most revealing of all, how much pleasure she was finding in this conversation with him.

"How fortunate for you to have had brothers!" she said with the wistfulness of an only child. "To have them to count on, to know you are always bound together by blood and birth no matter how you stray apart—what a rare, wonderful thing that must be!"

"Oh, aye, the Duke of Strachen's three sons, as wild a little pack of ruffians as you can imagine," he said fondly. "We fair raised ourselves in the country, you know, without much guidance or interference, and turned out deuced fine in the end, too."

"Surely your father could claim his share of the credit," she said, only half in jest. His father had been a duke, after all, a peer, and only a step or so below the king himself.

But clearly he didn't agree. "My father had other occupations that kept him in London," he said, his expression abruptly losing all its merriment and closing against her. "His sons were not among his favorite interests."

"I am sorry," she said softly, realizing too late that she'd inadvertently misstepped. "The love of your parents—that's a precious fine thing for a child."

"I would not know," he said curtly, his face once again the stern officer's mask, impersonal and unemotional. "Shall you accompany me to Feversham now, Miss Winslow?"

"Have I a choice, Captain My Lord?" she asked, made wary by his sudden shift of moods.

"You are a servant, not a slave," he insisted impatiently, though that insistence was enough to make her believe otherwise. "This is England, not the Indies. But you will oblige me greatly by remaining as Feversham's housekeeper."

A servant, not a slave, and the formality of obligation: how quickly things had changed between them, and how wrong for her to dare dream they'd ever be anything else. She sighed, looking away from him and out towards the sea.

She wanted to stay at Feversham, not only because it would make her work with the Company easier to continue, but also because, in her heart, she could not imagine herself anywhere else. Besides, where would she go with her little chest of gold and silver coins, squirreled away against the future? The captain had been right when he'd said her father would expect to find her there when he returned, and she wouldn't dare disappoint him.

Yet what would it be like to live in the same house with this man—a man this handsome, with moods and a temper as unpredictable as the weather, a man whose authority would pose a constant risk to her and the others in the Company, a man whose charm had already made her drop her careful guard with unsettling ease?

A man who would hold all the keys to her life in his palm, and not even realize it?

"You will, of course, continue with the same wages, as well as the same quarters and entitlements," he was saying, in the brusque voice that she was sure he used for giving orders on board ship. "There is much to be done at Feversham, and at last there will be sufficient hands to do it. That much at least you should find pleasing. You may also find changes in how the house is governed and arranged that may be less agreeable, and I trust you shall adjust. But as you have noted yourself, Miss Winslow, Feversham has always been your home, and I won't have it said that I drove you away."

Her smile was tight and sad, regretting what she could never have. It didn't matter how many brothers he had, or what they'd called him as a boy. He was still Lord Captain Claremont, and she was still a servant, and so it would always be.

"You are kind to think of me, Captain My Lord," she murmured. The kindness and understanding he'd shown her was still there, if not the fleeting, misinterpreted friendship. "I am grateful for the concern you show to me."

"Kindness, hah." He shook his head, as if to shake away the very notion of such a maudlin weakness. "What has kindness to do with any of this? It is the Trelawneys who have tied our hands together, Miss Winslow, those blasted Trelawneys and their confoundedly meddlesome interference. Surely you are sensible enough to see that."

"The Trelawneys?" she asked, surprised once again, something that seemed to happen far too often with him. "The Trelawneys have never interfered in anything to do with Feversham."

Another puff of wind tugged at his hat, and irritably he shoved it down more firmly onto his head.

"They have in this," he answered, "as you would have known if Potipher had bothered to write that infernal letter. The Trelawneys had such regard for your loyalty that they refused to sell Feversham to me or anyone else unless I agreed to keep you on as long as you pleased. There, that's the cold truth of it, and God take me for a simpleton this instant for having signed my name to such a scrap of foolery."

"Then that is the only reason I am to stay at Feversham?" she asked, not wanting to believe what she couldn't deny. "Because you could not have the house unless you took me with it, like any other old kettles and dunnage?"

"I told you earlier, Miss Winslow. I won't have it said that I turned you out from your home." He held his hand out to her. "Now will you come with me back to Feversham?"

She looked at his offered hand, more imperious than gallant, the way she supposed he'd always been if she'd but bothered to see it.

"Thank you, no, Captain My Lord," she said, already turning to leave him, the way she should have done an hour before. "I have my own pony waiting for me. For you see, I won't have it said that I've ridden with you."

With a glass of the fine French brandy he'd found in the kitchen cradled in his fingers, George sprawled in a leather armchair before the grand sweep of windows in his bedchamber, the same windows that had convinced him to buy Feversham. The view of the Channel and everything else he could see now belonged to him, as much as the sea ever belonged to anyone. But this room, and the chair in which he sat, and the rest of the timbers and stone and plaster around him were indisputably now his. This was what he'd wanted, what he'd dreamed of, what he'd had to suffer and survive a great many years of war and hardship and receive a huge dollop of luck to achieve.

So why, then, did it all feel so damned hollow?

"Do that be all for the night, Cap'n My Lord?" asked Leggett, waiting by the door with the tray from supper in his hands. A stout, ginger-haired seaman of indeterminate age from Northumberland, Leggett had been George's manservant since he'd made captain and become entitled to such a personal luxury. Like most seaman turned servants, Leggett was more independent than his landlocked counterparts, and considerably more outspoken, believing it to be his entitlement as a free Englishman to tell his captain what he needed to hear.

And from the way Leggett was now scowling and puffing out his ruddy cheeks, George was sure he was going to exercise that right once again.

"That will be all for the evening, Leggett," said

George wearily, hoping that might be enough to stall the man's comments until morning, for he was in no humor for either company or conversation. "You and the others turn in. We'll begin in earnest in the morning."

"Beg pardon, Cap'n My Lord," said Leggett, purposefully ignoring George's broad hint. "There be one thing the lads wanted me to say."

George sighed, twisting in his chair to face the other man. "Is it your quarters? The food?"

"Nay, nay, Cap'n M'Lord, they all be more than fine," said Leggett hastily. "Fancy beds like them for the likes o' us, eh?"

"Then what the devil ails you, man?"

Leggett gave another contemplative puff to his cheeks. "It be the lady, the one what we saw in the village. She be the same one what lives here, don't she?"

"Miss Winslow has been the housekeeper here at Feversham for some years, yes," said George, weariness sliding into testiness. "Not that she's any concern of yours."

"But she do be our concern, Cap'n M'Lord," said Leggett doggedly. "Everywhere's we look about this house, her mark be there. Womenfolk don't like having their ways changed, and if she be staying here with us, why—"

"I will address that question when and if that happens," said George curtly. "Until then Miss Winslow's likes and dislikes will have no bearing on my orders, or your duty. Do I make myself clear, Leggett?"

"Aye, aye, Cap'n M'Lord." Leggett snapped to attention, the tray still awkwardly balanced in his hands before him as he backed through the doorway, yanking the door shut behind him.

Which was, for once, exactly the response that George had desired, and with a muttered oath he sank back into his armchair, swirling the barely-touched brandy in his glass.

How in blazes could he tell his men what Miss Winslow would do next when he hadn't the faintest idea himself? For what must have been the thousandth—no, the millionth!—time he thought back to that strange, wonderful, dreadful conversation in the burying ground.

Matters had begun badly enough, with no letter from blasted Potipher to ease his way, and making the two of them spit and start at one another like cats there in the middle of the lane, for all the village world to gawk at. He'd tried to make it right with the earrings, and had had that humble piece of gallantry twisted around and tossed back at him. Without thinking, he'd next taken her arm: another mistake, touching her that way, and one she'd soon corrected by vehemently pulling free.

Then, finally, to punish him all the more, she'd dragged him off to stand in the sorrowful center of the burying ground. Wasn't his news likely to be disagreeable enough to her without him having to deliver it surrounded by a sea of ancient graves?

And yet he could not forget how she'd looked when he'd first seen her again, calling to him there in the lane as he'd climbed down from his horse. Her hair had been uncharacteristically disheveled and her cheeks were flushed from the wind, her lips were parted from her haste, and those red gimcrack earbobs were swinging merrily from her ears. Perhaps it had been only a trick of the pale-gray sunlight washing over her face, but once freed of the house, she'd seemed younger, more at ease. She'd also, almost, seemed pleased to see him again.

Until, that is, he'd explained his reason for being there.

Even then the conversation hadn't gone as he'd expected. She'd thought she had to leave, and he'd told her she could stay: fair enough, true enough. But somehow they'd begun speaking of their childhoods, the sort of funny, flirtatious, touching little conversation that he'd never had with any other woman, or man, for that matter.

In that short time, only a handful of sentences, really, he'd learned her name was Fan, not just the formal Miss Winslow. He'd learned she had spent far too much time among adults, just as he himself had been sent to sea and a man's world when he'd still been a boy. He'd learned that she could snap that defensive wall back in place around herself in an instant, and he'd learned—once again—that he still could not speak of his father.

And he'd learned that no matter what clauses the Trelawneys had put into their contracts, *he* was the one who now wanted her to stay on at Feversham, just as she was the one who most decidedly didn't. Not even Brant, with all his much-vaunted experience with women, would be able to make sense of this mess.

Glumly he stared into the glass in his hand. It was all the fault of this wretched, so-called peace with France. If he'd stayed at sea, where he belonged, where he knew what to do and what to say, then none of this would have happened. He would have remained a happy man, plagued only by storms and high seas and enemy gunfire instead of a ramshackle house and a beautiful gray-eyed housekeeper.

So thoroughly was he regretting his carefree past that he didn't hear the first knock on the door to his bedchamber, or even the second. But the third—the third he heard.

"Come," he barked without turning, certain it was Leggett. "It better damned well be important this time, you impudent old rascal."

"It is important, Captain My Lord," said Fan Winslow, "and I promise not to take more of your time than is necessary."

Instantly George lurched to his feet, sprinkling brandy over his waistcoat and the floor.

"Fan," he began without thinking. "That is, Miss Winslow. Yes. That is to say, ah, at this hour, ah, I believed you to be someone else."

"I am only myself," she said. "I've never pretended otherwise."

"Where have you been?" Even George knew enough of women to see she'd been crying, her eyes puffy and red-rimmed. "No one has seen you for hours. I've been concerned, damned concerned."

"Thank you, Captain My Lord," she said, pointedly not answering his question about how she'd passed her afternoon. She held out a large ring of keys towards him. "I've come to return these to you as the new master."

"Hold now, there's no need for that," he said, wincing inwardly at the heartiness in his voice. "You keep those for now."

"Why?" she demanded, somehow still managing to put an edge in the single word even with her face and eyes soft from tears—tears that, he was quite sure, she'd never let slip and shed before him.

"For all the reasons I said before," he said. "Because Feversham's your home. Because you belong here. Because I'll need your knowledge of the house while making improvements."

"Because the Trelawneys' solicitors told you you must."

"Because *I* wish it this way." He reached out and placed his hand over hers with the keys, gently pushing both back towards her. "Because it is right."

She stared down at his hand over his. This time she didn't pull away, and though she was silent, he could sense her warring with herself, fighting her own judgment.

"Because," he said. "Damnation, Fan, because you belong here."

She raised her gaze to meet his, letting him glimpse that same vulnerable, lonely girl he'd discovered earlier in the graveyard, the one that was so carefully hidden behind the guise of the stern, competent housekeeper. He felt her turn her fingers against his, not to grasp the ring of keys more firmly, but to find the comfort of his touch.

"Because you want me to stay?" she whispered, the depth of her daring bright in her eyes.

"Because I want you to stay," he repeated, and to his confused surprise he realized he'd never wanted anything more in his life. No, that wasn't exactly true. What he wanted more was to take her into his arms, to feel the roughness of her woolen gown and the softness of her skin and learn how her hair would come undone and spill over his arm as he turned her face up towards his to kiss her. *That* was what he wanted even more.

But though he was known as a brave man, with medals and gold braid on his coat to prove it, he wasn't brave enough to kiss her that boldly, not now, not yet. Instead he raised her hand, the keys jingling together, and pressed his lips to the back of it, closing his eyes to savor the scent of her wrist there at the edge of her sleeve, to feel the strength and the gentleness of her neatly curled fingers.

That was all, and for this evening that would be enough.

He wanted her to stay, and now she would.

Chapter Five

Sleep did not come easily to Fan that night, and by the time she heard the old case clock in the front hall chime four, she doubted she'd closed her eyes for more than a quarter of an hour altogether. It was not that the newcomers to Feversham had made noise to keep her awake—they were all in bed and asleep long before she'd doused her own candlestick—but simply the knowledge that she was no longer alone in the house was enough to make her toss and turn and worry herself into exhaustion.

Add to that the scene of George kissing her hand in his bedchamber—his fingers cradling hers as gently as if they'd been made of spun glass, his lips warm against her skin, the way he'd murmured her given name—playing over and over in her memory, and she doubted she'd ever be able to find peace in sleep again.

George. A saint's name, the name of kings, and now the name of Feversham's new owner. But oh, when did she begin thinking of him like that, as George instead of the string of his titles? She was his housekeeper, his servant, not his friend and certainly not his lover. To address him with such familiarity would be the one more slippery step downward to her own ruin, with no way ever to climb back.

That kiss on her hand had been another. Why, why hadn't she pulled away with the same decisiveness that she'd mustered when he'd taken her arm in the village? Could she only protest when there were others watching? Or was she so weak that she'd cared more for that shiver of heady pleasure that came from his touch? So weak that she'd welcome his attention even after he'd confessed that he'd kept her here only because the Trelawneys had ordered it?

So weak, or was she simply that lonely?

With a groan of frustration she pushed back the coverlets and rolled from the bed, reaching for the flint to light her candlestick. There seemed little point in trying any longer to sleep, and besides, no matter how early it was, she could always find much to do. She'd squandered yesterday afternoon aimlessly riding Pie along the flat stretch of the beach at low tide, looking for a possible new rendezvous spot of the Company that was off Feversham land and trying to sort her muddled thoughts. But all she'd succeeded in doing was wasting time that she could ill afford to waste, and making herself even more miserable in the process.

She blew the coals in her fireplace back to life, and hooked the kettle over them to heat water for tea while she dressed. With only herself in the house, she'd fallen into the habit of cooking and eating here, in her bedchamber, rather than lighting fires in the enormous kitchen hearth. Her aunt would have been horrified, accusing her of living in one room like some wretched poor cottager, but Fan had found cooking for one below stairs too bleak and solitary, her father's tall-backed chair at the oak table too painfully empty.

That would change now. She wasn't certain exactly how many men George had brought with him, but she could guess that, being men, they would be expecting their breakfast when they woke. It would be a new challenge, no doubt, but she was ready to take it, especially with this early a start on the day.

But she did wish she knew what George liked for his first meal so she'd be able to please him. Was he the sort of gentleman who eased himself into the day with a dish of milky tea and a plate of raisin buns, or did he prefer to make a hearty conquest of his breakfast, with the sideboard laden with meats and pies, pots of butter and marmalade and rafts of toast? She would have to learn his preferences, in this as in everything else.

Swiftly she washed, dressed, and braided her hair while she sipped at her tea, then took the candlestick to light her way and hurried down the back stairs to begin the kitchen fire. A single, mournful *bong* from the tall clock echoed her footsteps: half past four.

Early, yes, but not as early as Fan had believed. Even on the stairs she could hear the sounds of pans crashing together and a man's off-key singing and swearing, one blending seamlessly into the other. She could also smell the scent of roasting meat, and see the bright, flickering light from the fire, a large and wasteful fire, too, from the brightness of it. She frowned, determined to stop such blatant disregard for the cost of wood, and marched sternly into the kitchen.

And stopped abruptly at the sight before her. What

her poor, dear aunt would have made of *this* in her kitchen!

Looming over the hearth was a stout older man with one leg missing below the knee, the stump supported by an elaborately carved wooden peg turned like a newel post at the base of a staircase. The man had no hair left on the top of his head, but from the nape he still could grow the gray queue that hung down the middle of his back, nearly to the strings of the leather apron tied around his barrel-shaped waist. In his hand he brandished a long-handled meat-fork like a kitchen-king's scepter, and beneath his bristling white brows was no welcome for Fan at all.

"What d'ye be gawkin' at, missy?" he demanded.

"And what are *you* doing in my kitchen?" she demanded back, settling her hands on her hips. Not only was the man making free with the hearth and larder, but he'd also changed things that hadn't been changed in Fan's lifetime: the woodbin had been shifted from one side of the room to the other, the ancient black iron kettle with the mended handle had been replaced by one of new copper, and twin rows of new blue-and-white chalkware plates now filled the shelves of the Welsh dresser in place of the familiar battered pewter chargers. "What is your name?"

"I be John Small, His Lord Cap'n's cook and warrant officer of His Majesty's frigate *Nimble,* and twice the man as any you'll ever know," said the man, jabbing his fork at a chicken roasting on a spit over the fire. "Who the devil be you?"

"I am Mistress Winslow, the keeper of this house," she said warmly, giving an irritable little shove at a packing-barrel filled with wood shavings and more new dishes, "and I have no love for ill-mannered old men, whomever they pretend to be. Why are you here at this hour, meddling where you don't belong and waking the house with your blasphemy and caterwauling?''

"I be makin' His Lordship's breakfast, as even a fool in black petticoats could see if she used her eyes for seein'." With the long-handled fork, he turned the strips of bacon sizzling in the iron spider, one deft twist of his wrist that kept the fat from splattering into the coals.

"As for *this* hour or *that* hour," he continued, without deigning to look her way, "why, it be smack in the middle o' morning watch, and if His Lordship's not to go begging for his eggs and bacon, but to have them proper, when he wakes, then *this* be the hour when they gets made."

Fan flushed, for *this* was not how the morning was to have begun. Here she'd contrived a pleasing dream of surprising George with a fine-made breakfast, while this dreadful old man had already done so and better, and in her own kitchen, too, making her feel like a lazy, worthless slug-a-bed in the bargain.

"Now if you wish to make yourself useful, missy," continued Small, cracking four eggs in quick succession into the glossy sheen of melted butter waiting in another pan over the coals, "then there's His Lordship's chocolate still waiting."

"I am not here to take orders from you," said Fan tartly, but still she looked to where he was pointing with his fork. On the table sat a tall, cone-shaped contraption like a pewter coffeepot without a spout or handle, but with a long wooden paddle that protruded through a hole in the lid. Beside it on a trivet sat a pan of steaming milk, and a dish of grated chocolate.

"Get along with it, missy," he said impatiently. "Put the chocolate into the mill, then the milk, slow and easy, to keep out the lumps. His Lordship don't care for lumps in his chocolate, not at all."

Fan studied the chocolate mill warily. No one she knew drank chocolate, not with tea so readily available, and she'd never seen a chocolate mill before this one. Not that she wished to admit that to John Small.

"I don't take orders from the kitchen staff," she said defensively. "As Feversham's housekeeper, I give them."

The man's eyes gleamed. "That don't be it at all," he said, his contempt palpable. "Do it now? Nay, it be that you don't know *how* to make chocolate, do you?"

"Of course I do," she said swiftly, though of course she didn't. She lifted the lid on the mill and poured the milk inside, around the wooden paddle, and then the chocolate, before she snapped the lid down tight. She reasoned that somehow the chocolate must be blended with the milk, and taking the mill in both hands, she gave it a tentative shake.

"Do you be daft, missy, or only pretending to make a righteous idiot of yourself?" Small yanked the mill from her hands and set it on the table. He centered the handle of the paddle between his palms and rolled it briskly back and forth until the milk and chocolate became a frothy, fragrant mixture. "There now, that be how fine London gentlemen drink their chocolate."

"But this isn't London," she protested. "This is Kent."

"Oh, aye, and I be needing you to explain the differences?" He snorted as he deftly flipped the sizzling bacon in the skillet. "I've seen cockle-shell galleys with better kitchens than this. Where's your proper stove, I ask you? Cookin' over a fire like this be well and fine for grannies and cottagers and such, but if His Lordship expects grand dinners for his mates, then a proper Robinson range we must have."

"Perhaps you should be making do with what you have rather than pining after what you don't," said Fan defensively, striving to keep her voice from turning shrill with frustration. She'd no more knowledge of what "a proper Robinson range" might be than of how to operate a chocolate mill, and the more John Small ranted and railed, the more ignorant she felt.

She couldn't deny that Feversham had grown shabby under the Trelawneys, but the kitchen had always been sufficient for her aunt and her mother and a score of other cooks before them, and to hear it attacked now by this one-legged old sailor—why, it seemed disrespectful and wrong.

"Perhaps you shouldn't be looking to change everything just for the sake of changing," she said, "not when—here now, where are you going with that?"

A beardless young sailor with a calico kerchief tied around his head and his arms full of firewood stared blankly at her.

"There's plenty of wood in the woodbin already without you traipsing in here with more," she said. "Besides, dry wood like that costs good money, and we'll not be wasting it keeping a great roaring fire all the day long in the kitchen. Take it back to—"

"Stow it here in the woodbin, Danny," said Small as easily as he'd arranged the breakfast tray. "No use runnin' short o' twigs, is there?"

"No, Danny, don't. Where do you think that wood

comes from, Mr. Small?'' asked Fan, feeling her housekeeper's dubious authority slipping away from her with every word. "Who shall be accountable at the end of the month, when the books show how much wood was wasted in the kitchen fires?"

"Why, missy, I do believe them twigs come from trees," said the cook with a sly wink and a grin. "As for the reckoning, His Lordship will care a hell of a lot more for his chocolate and fresh bread than he will for a few more shillings one way or t'other for the firewood to make them."

"Then I shall ask His Lordship myself." Boldly she seized the tray like a prize away from the cook.

"Here now, you can't take that!" exclaimed the cook, lunging clumsily across the table for the tray.

"I can, Mr. Small, and you cannot," she said, her heart racing at her own daring. "Cook and her—*his*—staff never come above stairs."

But she knew better than to press her advantage, and instead hurried off with the tray before her, up the stairs to George's bedchamber. This all needed to be settled now, on this first day, before matters grew even worse.

Yet with each step both her audacity and her indignation seemed to fade. Most likely Small was right. Most likely his master did care more for his meals and his comforts than for the costs. Why shouldn't he, when he was now wealthier than most princes?

She was the one who, from long habit, felt the need to count shillings and pence. She was the one who seemed so woefully out of place now, the only woman in a houseful of men, the country housekeeper who didn't know how to use the chocolate mill, cast adrift in a sea of hostile sailors.

Yet hadn't George himself asked her to stay? Hadn't he shown her kindness, and laughed with her, and shared confidences, when no one else would? Hadn't he kissed her hand, and spoken her plain given name in a whisper that had made it fit for a princess?

And wasn't she the one who seemed to have lost all sense of judgment where this man was concerned, unable to tell right from wrong, proper from wicked? Everything had become tangled and confused, and she'd no experience to tell her where to begin to sort it out.

No wonder that when she came to stand before his bedchamber door, she was so on edge with doubts that the spoons and forks rattled together on the tray in her hands. He had asked her to stay, and she had believed him because she'd wanted to.

And she'd learn soon enough if he'd meant his request any more than he'd meant that kiss to her hand.

She glanced down at the crack beneath the door, making sure from the strip of faint candlelight that he was indeed awake. She'd no intention of returning to the kitchen with the tray still full, but she'd also no wish to come crashing in on George while he was still asleep. Old Mr. Trelawney had kept to his bed the last three years of his life, and Fan had thought nothing of serving him there or tending to whatever querulous requests his manservant had neglected, but to do the same for George would be an entirely— *entirely*—different proposition.

Balancing the tray against her hip, she rapped her knuckles sharply against the door. Unlike last night, this time his permission to enter came swiftly, and with a deep breath for courage, she unlatched the door and pushed it open.

He was sitting at the long table that he'd turned into a makeshift desk, papers and open books scattered over the top. Unmatched candlesticks of varying heights stood along the desk, some balanced precariously on top of books. The candles' flames wavered in the drafty room, dancing the light and shadows over the walls while the wax dripped and puddled over the papers. But George himself seemed too engrossed in his work to notice, his pen scratching rapidly across the paper before him.

"Set it down wherever you can," he said absently, without looking up. "The floor will do well enough."

"The floor will *not* do!" she exclaimed, scandalized. "You are an English lord and officer of the king. You cannot eat from the floor like some mongrel gnawing at his scraps!"

"Fan!" he said, startled. "That is, Miss Winslow. I did not, ah, expect to see you."

That was clear enough. She seemed unwittingly to be making a habit of this, surprising him by popping up in the place of someone else. But this time, as he automatically rose to his feet from well-bred habit, Fan was equally startled into stammered incoherence at the sight of *him*.

Though she'd found him engrossed in his writing, he obviously wasn't long out of bed. His hair was as tousled as a haystack, his jaw stubbled, and his blue eyes still muddled with sleep, or perhaps the lack of it. But instead of the severe, dark uniform that she'd always seen him wearing before this, he'd barely taken the time to dress at all, pulling on an old pair of threadbare canvas trousers that seemed to hang from his narrow hips—an observation Fan couldn't help but make, considering that he hadn't bothered with a shirt, let alone a coat.

Instead he was wearing some sort of long, loose dressing-gown of dark red silk, open and unbelted, whose details eluded Fan. How could they do otherwise, really, when the shimmering dark red silk seemed to exist only to frame his bare throat and chest and the dangerous, fascinating area directly above those low-slung breeches? The candlelight flickered across the broad, taut muscles and the pattern of dark, curling hair that tapered into the fall of his breeches, the only flaw the jagged, seamed pucker of an old scar: an unintentional display that, even in her inexperience, Fan recognized as intriguingly, flagrantly male.

Startled as she was, she stared only for a single stunned moment before she dropped her gaze to the tray to stare, unseeing, at her reflection in the domed pewter covers over the plates. But the impression of what she had seen was already seared into her consciousness, enough to make her cheeks burn and her whole body feel peculiarly warm.

"Here, let me take that," he said, his voice gruff, almost sheepish, as he lifted the tray away. "I'll make a place for it here on the end. So I won't, as you fear, have to eat on the floor like the old dog that I am."

With his forearm he shoved aside several of the books, clearing just enough to space to balance the tray on one corner of the table.

"I didn't intend to call you a dog," she said quickly, clasping her hands before her to give them something to do. "I meant only that you deserve better than to eat like one, from the floor."

"At least I have obeyed you like a good dog, haven't I?" He smiled crookedly, raking his hands back through his hair with haphazard abandon. Ignoring the tray, he leaned over the papers on the table once again, the red silk of his dressing gown fluttering around him like the robes of a mystical conjurer at the fair.

"This much should please you, Fan," he explained, oblivious to her uneasiness. "I'll grant you that, as calculations go, this sort of ciphering isn't a quarter as interesting as determining a course at sea, but it will determine our course here at Feversham."

She wished he'd tied the sash around that dressing gown. Instead he merely held up the paper for her to see, the sheet covered with unexpectedly tidy rows of numbers.

"This sum shows what I have already spent to acquire this glorious pile of a house," he continued, "and this shows what I have spent thus far on the barest outfitting, for linens and cookpots and such. Ah, Fan, you cannot guess what a favorite I have become among the shopkeepers!"

"No, likely not," she murmured, striving to concentrate on the sheet with the numbers instead of his bare chest behind it. "Forgive me, My Lord Captain, but you—you—it isn't proper for you to call me by my Christian name, any more than I should call you by yours."

He paused, and frowned. "I cannot help it," he confessed solemnly, shaking his head so his dark hair flopped across his forehead. "'Miss Winslow' is far too pompous for you. Fan is your true given name. You told me so yourself, and as names go, it suits you infinitely better. I much prefer it."

She nodded reluctantly. "I should not have shared such—such a confidence with you."

"What, by telling me your name? That was a confidence?"

"What I told you in the burying ground, about my childhood and such—I shouldn't have burdened you with that, My Lord Captain. I forgot my place."

"Place, hell," he said impatiently. "You spoke of your childhood, and I spoke of mine. It was mutual, and it was agreeable, or at least it seemed so to me."

She raised her chin defensively, refusing to be bullied. "I'm speaking of what is improper, not agreeable."

"But matters are already improper enough between us, aren't they?" he asked. "You're more Feversham's servant than you'll ever be mine. You may take your leave of me whenever you please, but I can't dismiss you. Not that I would, but still, there you have it. If that's not one-sided and improper, then I don't know what the devil is."

George smiled, realizing he'd delivered more of a lecture than he'd intended or she'd deserved. He wasn't on his own quarterdeck, and Fan certainly wasn't one of his crew. In a way he rather wished she were, for at least he would have known precisely how to treat her. The Navy's regulations were always useful that way. But with Fan, he felt completely at sea, without a paddle, rudder, or star to guide him.

He could surely use any of the three now. He still could not believe he'd taken her hand and kissed it last night, and the memory of her touch, her scent, had kept him awake most of the night. He'd sworn to his brother that he wished the housekeeper gone from Feversham, but when Fan had said she'd leave, he'd practically begged her to stay.

No, he *had* begged her. He should be honest, at least about that, just as he should be honest about how much he had wanted to kiss her mouth after her hand, and tumble her on her back on that creaking old bed after that: shameful, wicked thoughts for any honorable man to have for his housekeeper. No surprise that he'd determinedly ignored that same bed and set his thoughts to the chilly rigor of mathematics.

It had worked, too, until Fan herself had appeared at his door, his dreams brought to life with the same suddenness that she'd startled him last night. Yet even with her now standing here before him, the hand he'd kissed folded modestly over its mate, he still marveled at the power of her attraction for him. He couldn't explain it except in parts—say, how she'd narrow her gray eyes at him, appraising him through her inky-black lashes, or the curve of her waist in the black gown—but there was so much more that he couldn't understand, let alone put into words.

Especially not now, when she was doing that wicked business with her eyes slanted towards him, skeptical and seductive and none-of-your-nonsense all bundled in one.

"So we can agree that we are properly improper," he said, hoping he sounded as if everything were settled, "or improperly proper, or however else you wish to describe it."

He smiled again, and turned towards the breakfast tray with a certain cowardly haste. As a captain, he was accustomed to having every detail neatly arranged and ordered, but he couldn't help but feel now that matters with Fan were neither arranged nor ordered, nor in the least neat. He lifted the cover from the plate with the bacon and shirred eggs arranged on toast, and sighed blissfully.

"My highest compliments to you, Fan," he said as his favorite scents wafted upward. "This is the sort of breakfast that makes a man rejoice to face another day."

"It's also a breakfast that I did not make, not one morsel, which you know perfectly well." She took the cover and clanged it back over the plate. "Your one-legged cook understands your tastes far better than I ever shall."

"Ah." His bliss vanished as fast as his breakfast had. "You have met Small, then?"

"Of course I have," she said. "He is your cook, and a most accomplished and able cook at that."

He waited cautiously, unsure of what would come next. Like most galley cooks, Small could be prickly and territorial, and while George expected Fan could hold her own, he wished he'd been present to help ease that first meeting between housekeeper and cook.

"Yes," he said finally. "Small does know his way about the galley. His father was a cook for a tavern on one of the stage routes to the north, and Small mastered his cookery before he ran off to sea."

"He also knows how to work a chocolate mill," she said, her unhappiness visibly growing with each word, "which I do not. He knows you prefer your eggs shirred in butter to simmering soft in the shell, and he knows how to cook bacon the way you like it best, which I most obviously do not."

"I'm sure he could show you how," suggested George. "I will have him do so this morning."

It had seemed like a logical enough idea. But bright

pink patches appeared on Fan's cheeks and her chin had risen another fraction, the same that had happened when he'd offered to buy her the earrings yesterday.

And a sure sign, George, my lad, of rough weather ahead.

"Forgive me for speaking plain, My Lord Captain," she said, so curtly that George couldn't help but imagine how exceedingly disastrous that first meeting with his cook must have been. "But I do not believe that your Mr. Small would agree with you, not in the least."

"He wouldn't have to agree," said George. "Damnation, he'd only have to obey."

But she'd stopped attending, frowning instead, with her head turning away from him towards the open door.

"Smoke," she announced. "I smell smoke."

"Oh, blast." He could smell it now, too, faint and acrid: the most ominous scent of all to a sailor on a wooden ship in the middle of the sea, and not much better on the upper floor of a house built of ancient, dry timbers. Swiftly he snuffed all but one of the candlesticks on his desk, taking the one for light as he took her by the arm. "Come, Fan, hurry."

"It's from the kitchen," she explained as they hurried down the stairs. "It's the oven."

"I don't care if it's the devil's own cook-stove," he said grimly, the smoke thickening the farther down the stairs they went. "From this morning onward, I want fire-buckets stowed in every room. I won't be roasted alive in my own house, mind?"

But even if it wasn't the devil in the kitchen, it certainly sounded that way from the crashing and thumping and coughing and swearing coming from the bottom of the stairs. He could just make out Small, flailing a flat wooden peel to clear the air, and his young cook's mate Danny swinging the door to the yard back and forth trying to do the same.

Coughing and squinting as the smoke stung his eyes, George paused to cover his mouth and nose with a handkerchief. Fan didn't wait, fearlessly charging in ahead. Holding the hem of her apron over the lower half of her face, she dodged Small and his peel and hurried directly to the small bake oven built into the side of the hearth. More smoke billowed from the oven's open, arched door, smelling of wood and coals and burning bread. Swiftly Fan took the long-handled coal-rake from the hearth and with one hand thrust it deep into the stove, jabbing it back and forth.

At once the smoke began to thin, then clear, as with obvious experience she flipped the rake over in her hand and one by one drew out the charred, crumbling bricks that had once been loaves of bread. Carefully she balanced each smoking, blackened loaf on the teeth of the rake and carried them through the kitchen, and past both Small and George before she heaved them out the open door and into the yard.

It was, decided George, one of the most efficient and deliberate celebrations of an enemy's defeat that he had ever witnessed.

And he also knew what Fan wanted more than a thousand pairs of garnet earrings.

"If you had but asked, Mr. Small," she said, the rake still in her hands and her smile at once triumphant and disarming as they all stood in the yard to let the air clear inside, "I would have showed you how willful this oven can be. Unless the coals are placed to the back corner of the stove and the door kept ajar a fraction, whatever you put inside will burn, and the coals shall smoke. Unless, of course, you do not know *how* to build a proper fire for baking.''

Small sputtered, his round face streaked with soot and his eyes bright red as much from indignation as the smoke. "If I had a true oven, missy, and not your heap o' witch's stones, why, then I'd—"

"You'd bake as perfect a loaf of bread as Miss Winslow herself would here," said George evenly. "I've been proud to know you many years, John Small, and I know you to be a fair, honest man who'd never fail his mates or his ship."

"Aye, aye, M'Lord Cap'n," said Small cautiously. "No one can say otherwise, true enough."

"And no one shall, either," continued George, feeling more like a judge than a captain, as he bowed slightly in Fan's direction. "Though it is not quite the same as the *Nimble*, this house is my command now, and as Feversham's housekeeper, Miss Winslow is as good as my first lieutenant, with those responsibilities and respect."

Small grimaced, unconvinced. "Aye, aye," he grumbled at last. "If you say so, Cap'n M'Lord."

George didn't smile. "Heed her, Small. She knows this vessel better than all of us together. We need her unless we want to go up in flames the next time you bake bread. Must I continue, or do you understand?"

"Aye, aye, M'Lord Cap'n," Small answered with glum resignation. "Lieutenant Miss Winslow it be."

"Very good, Small." Now George tried not to grin, feeling every bit as wise and clever as old Moses himself. "Now you and Danny go along and clean up this wretched mess directly."

The two men nodded and retreated, doubtless to grumble about the unfairness of their life, but George didn't care. The rosy new sun was just rising clear of the horizon, the air was fresh and chill off the water to clear his head, and Fan—Fan was standing before him with soot on her cheeks and complete wondering amazement on her face.

"So, Miss Winslow," he said. "Must I remind you, too, to be honest and fair, if you wish to keep on as my lieutenant?"

But for Fan the new morning seemed every bit as perfect. What finer sight could there be than to have such a handsome man standing there before her, his head thrown back to greet the rising sun and the red silk whipping around his long, lean body like a scarlet banner? And how nothing, absolutely nothing, could make it better than realizing how amazingly he *understood* her?

"You don't need to tell me anything more," she said, the words coming in a heady rush. "You've already told me more than I ever dreamed to hear, and—and—I thank you, George!"

She laughed, so overwhelmed she was almost giggling. Before she lost her nerve, she leaned up on her toes and kissed him on his stunned, stubbled mouth. His beard was rough, his lips surprisingly warm and soft, his scent undeniably masculine, and she laughed again, giddy at her own boldness. Kissing him like this, using his name as freely as he wanted to use hers, went beyond improper to reckless, and with the panicking realization of what she'd down, she scurried off towards the dairy. With the baking rake still clutched tight her hand, she leaned against the white-washed brick wall and closed her eyes, her breath coming in heady gasps of shock and delight and shame and joy and bewilderment.

She heard a footstep on the slate floor and her eyes flew open with expectation. No one else would come here; though all the buckets and white earthenware bowls remained in place, the dairy had not been used for milk and cheesemaking in years.

"Have you more to ask of me, then?" she asked breathlessly. "Have you followed me for that?"

"Aye, mistress, I have," said Will Hood grimly, "and a good thing it be for the Company's sake that I did. Answers, mistress, that's what I want, honest answers, and I'll not be leaving without them."

Chapter Six

"**Y**ou'll have to ask your questions first, Will Hood," said Fan, trying, and failing, to make herself sound stern and forthright and leader-like, and not just some other giddy, light-heeled country girl meeting her sweetheart in the dairy house. "I can't give you answers without questions, can I?"

"Faith, mistress, I scarce know where to begin." He shook his head, his pale eyes chilly beneath the brim of his hat. Hood had been her most loyal supporter in the Company, but now, for the first time since her father had disappeared, she was no longer as confident of Hood's loyalty or as sure of his trust. How much had he seen, she wondered desperately, what had he heard?

"Then begin at the beginning," she said. She was woefully conscious of the smudges on her apron and the untidiness of her hair, all visible cracks in her usually impeccable appearance. She was also suddenly aware of how very much larger Hood now seemed in the narrow dairy room, looming over her with his famous shoulders and arms strong enough to row to France. "But be swift about it, Will. You shouldn't be here in the day like this, and I've other tasks waiting for me in the house."

"Oh, aye, I'll warrant you do, mistress." He sighed again, sadly, as if the sarcasm had been unavoidable. "You told us this lord captain wouldn't be troubling us. You told us he'd not want Feversham, that he'd choose another house, and now here he is, a hungry red fox plumped down among us poor pigeons."

"He's not like that, not at all," she answered quickly, her voice echoing off the slate floors and marble slabs used for dairying. "I swear I didn't believe he would take the house, else I never would have told you so. But now that he has, he wishes it only for pleasure, a gentleman's retreat from London. He has no eyes for us, nor our trade."

Hood's mouth twisted, skeptical. "But he's a king's man, mistress, a king's man through and through, and he's bound to see things that others might overlook. He's sworn to make things black and white, right and wrong, and straight to the devil with anyone who crosses his path. That's *his* trade, and we'll be nothing more than his quarry for bounty."

"And I tell you, Will Hood," she insisted, drawing herself up straight, "that he took so much of that Spanish king's silver that he has no interest in anything save how to spend it. All he wished to speak of this morning at breakfast was the new roof he is planning for Feversham, and the other improvements he wants to make."

"At breakfast, you say," repeated Hood softly, hearing only the part of her words that mattered to him. "Ah, mistress, what would your poor father make of that? You taking breakfast so cozy with a king's man, making chitchat over the kettle with a duke's son, your own new master?''

She gave a little gasp of outrage. "It isn't like that, Will Hood," she said warmly, "so don't you go spreading tales about that haven't a dewdrop of truth to them. I am the housekeeper of Feversham, and Captain Lord Claremont is my new master, same as old Mr. Trelawney was in his time."

"'Cepting that old Mr. Trelawney was an old bag of bones halfway in his grave," noted Hood bitterly, "and Claremont's a handsome young buck in his prime and without a lady-wife, and rich and titled in the bargain."

She flushed then, unable to help it. Clearly Hood had been watching her and George in the yard, and just as clearly he'd misinterpreted what he'd seen. That quick impulsive kiss had been meant as thanks for George's understanding, his kindness, and for giving her place in the household the authority it had lacked—*that* was the reason why she'd kissed George, and no other.

Wasn't it? *Wasn't* it?

But it had happened once, and, now, with Hood before her as a reminder of how much was at stake— the Company men, their wives, their children—she told herself fiercely, regretfully, that it must never happen again.

She thumped the long handle of the rake on the flagstones with frustration as much as for emphasis. "The Company always comes first with me, just as it did with my father, and his father before him, on and on clear back to when this house was new. *That's* what you can tell the others, Will Hood, the truth, and nothing more—that they should be ready for the run this Friday night, at the time I tell them, same as always.''

"Friday, you say.'' Hood paused, his mouth working hard as he weighed her promise against his trust. "In the same place as always, there on your new master's land?''

"No,'' she said hurriedly, wishing she'd remembered to mention that before he had. "No, but only because I wish to leave nothing to chance, and not because I distrust Captain Lord Claremont. Tell them we'll meet just south of Green Bridge, below Solomon's Hill.''

Hood nodded. "And what shall I tell them about you, mistress, if your word is worth their lives?''

"Because my name is Winslow,'' she said without a moment's hesitation, her voice ringing out in the tiny dairy. "And if any man in the Company is taken and hangs because of Captain Lord Claremont, then I will be there at the gallows beside them.''

George shielded his eyes against the sun with the curve of his hand, critically studying the patches being made to the cracks in Feversham's west facade. At Fan's suggestion, he'd called in the housewright who repaired the plasterwork on every other timbered house in Kent to oversee the mending, and others were busily replacing loose windowpanes, cleaning the chimneys, resetting crooked paving stones, and a score of other such tasks. He relished how the place fair hummed with activity, the same as he'd done with the ships he'd commanded, and already his home was beginning to shed the years, like a still-handsome dowager freshened with a smile and new powder.

His home. He still hadn't grown accustomed to the

sound of that, and he smiled now, thinking of how much that single word was already coming to mean. Five days, that was all he'd lived here, yet in that short time Feversham had become his. No one could take this away from him, the way the Admiralty had seen fit to strip him of the *Nimble*. Rootless and wandering most of his life, he found he was beginning to understand the glow and pride that filled other men's faces had when they spoke of home.

Absently he fished in the overstuffed pocket of his coat for the sketch that the housewright had made earlier, intending to make notes on the margins. He'd been a list-maker from the time he could scribble with chalk on his slate, determined to find order in a life that, in his childhood, had had precious little in it.

But before the sketch his fingers found the round, hard curve of an apple. George smiled, turning the fruit in his hand. This was Fan's doing, he was sure, anticipating that he'd be hungry at the precise moment of the morning that he'd reach into his pocket. She didn't need lists or notes to arrange her life, but somehow she managed to keep every task and detail efficiently in her head. Nothing escaped her. She was a marvel, was Fan, not only as a housekeeper but as a woman as well, and as he slowly bit into the apple, he let himself consider exactly why more of that same marvelousness wasn't shining his way.

Not that she was entirely to blame. He'd claim his due share of whatever it was stewing and brewing between them. Oh, they got along handsomely enough throughout the day, smiling and chatting as they discussed the plans for the house, or which boys from the village would be trustworthy additions to the stable. But two dark squalls clouded this sunny horizon, each so seemingly inconsequential that, if George had heard of it from anyone else, he would have laughed aloud.

He wished he *could* laugh, wished it with all his heart, for what better way to cope with his kiss to her hand, and her own stolen kiss in return? Hell, his brother could manage a full-fledged seduction with less turmoil than those two fleeting kisses had inflicted on his hapless consciousness, and with disgust George bit another chunk from the apple.

He wanted Fan as his housekeeper, his advisor, his companion. That was all logical enough. But he also wanted her as a woman, imagining her lush, pale body freed from its habitual black and sprawled across that enormous playing-field of a bed, her dark hair unpinned and spread across his pillow, the soft moans of pleasure she'd make when he'd wrap those long legs of hers around his waist and drive them both over and over to staggering, delirious bliss.

That was logical, too, but it was also thoroughly dishonorable. Only the lowest scoundrel would go poaching among his own staff, women whose dependency stole their right to refuse, and if he'd any pretense left of being a gentleman, a peer, and an officer, he'd have to train himself to view Fan with only the chilliest of regards.

But the extra twist in all this misery was that he sensed she was just as badly off as he. The way she'd jerk away as if she'd been singed if by accident they brushed against one another, the wistful, longing expression in her eyes when she thought he wasn't watching her, the softness in her smile that seemed just for him, even this apple that she'd taken care to tuck in his pocket—didn't that all point to a greater regard, a greater *interest,* in him than most house-keepers showed to their masters?

Not that Fan could act upon her desires any more than he, not and retain any sort of integrity or reputation. As the lone woman living and working at Feversham, she had to keep herself as free of gossip as Caesar's wife herself, and though it had only been a few days, thus far she'd shown no signs of giving in. They'd even fallen back into the stiff formality of using their titles, especially when others were in hearing.

And so here the two of them were together at Feversham, knotted and bound by respect and behaving as properly as either of them ever could wish, and arriving at the same point of abject misery and frustration.

He thought of what Brant would say, how his brother would howl with amusement until the tears rolled down his cheeks at such a dilemma. With a muttered oath, George threw the apple core as far and as hard as he could into the hedges.

"Ahoy there, Cap'n M'Lord," roared Leggett from the crest of the roof where he perched, mending the chimney's flashing. He pointed down the drive, over the trees towards the main road. "A strange coach an' four, Cap'n M'Lord, bearin' down hard from the east."

Oh, blast, thought George glumly. He hadn't planned on having to entertain guests just yet. Another five or six years would be soon enough for him. "Very well, Leggett," he called back. "Any markings to tell if they're friendly or otherwise?"

"Gentry," called back Leggett succinctly as he

peered off into the distance. "I'll venture no more than that, Cap'n M'Lord."

Of course it would be gentry, thought George crossly. Who the devil else had the inclination and energy to ride about the countryside in a coach and four, pestering their unsuspecting neighbors?

"Fetch Miss Winslow directly," he called. "Warn her to prepare to engage the enemy."

He could see Leggett's grin from the top of the roof as he began to clamber down. "Aye, aye, Cap'n M'Lord! Enemy it is!"

George sighed, wishing he shared the seaman's cheerfulness. He couldn't exactly hide and pretend he wasn't at home, since by now likely every red-faced country squire and lady in Kent knew he'd taken up residence, just as their unmarried daughters likely knew his every move and breath about the county. He'd been their target often enough while in London with Brant, and it amazed him how that hard-won Spanish silver had magically made him more handsome, more clever, more *everything* in the starry-eyed gazes of husband-hunting young Dianas.

At least it had in London, when he was being shepherded about by Brant. Without the charming (if even more elusive) Duke of Strachen beside him, his own appeal might be diminished. He could only hope, and sigh again as he watched the coach come lurching and rumbling along his rutted drive, finally coming to a queasy halt before him.

The driver leaned down from the box, his mouth twisted into an unpleasant snarl, doubtless brought on by considering the fresh damage to his coach's springs.

"Tell his Lordship that Sir Simon Blackerby has

come to call with his ladies,'' the man called to
George. "Go on, sirrah, don't keep your betters waiting!''

George blinked with surprise, then smiled. He'd
dressed in his oldest clothes, the way he always did
on working days at sea or on land, clothes so worn
that the fabric was soft and comfortable and too dis-
reputable for any new stains or spots to show.

And, apparently, so shabby as to fool the self-
important driver of Sir Simon Blackerby's coach.

"Get on with you now, you grinning sot!" said the
driver, raising his whip as a threat. "Go to his Lordship directly!''

"I have," answered George mildly, "and so have
you, too. I am Captain Lord George Claremont, and
so you may tell your master."

"You, sir?" Sir Simon himself thrust his head out
the carriage window, in his haste nearly knocking his
old-fashioned periwig into the drive. "*You* are the one
they're calling the Silver Lord?''

"And you must be the one they are calling the Sir
Simon Blackerby," said George with the slightest,
least encouraging nod possible. "Forgive me for a
sorry host, Sir Simon, but we are thick in improvements here at Feversham, and not ready for receiving
guests."

"For certain you are, my Lord!" A flushed woman
with creaking stays and an overabundance of bows on
her gown pushed her way to the window, applying
her elbows with great vigor and skill. "You see, my
lord, we are not mere ordinary guests, but neighbors—Blackerby Hall lies just over South Bridge, you
know, the shortest drive or ride possible—and you
need not stand on the slightest ceremony with us. I

am Lady Blackerby, my Lord, and I am exquisitely honored to make the acquaintance of *such* a hero!''

With the same vigorous elbows she launched her way through the carriage door just as one of the footman flipped the step down, and landed upon the drive a *whoosh* of underskirts and scarves.

''Besides, my lord,'' she continued coyly, ''a great hero and gentleman such as yourself would not turn two ladies away from his doorstep without so much as a drop of refreshment?''

''She wants to see the damned house,'' said Sir Simon bluntly. ''She wants to see what all that Spanish silver can buy.''

''Do not be vulgar, Simon,'' said Lady Blackerby, her smile sweet for George, and her gaze quite the opposite for her husband. ''We are interested in your progress, of course, being neighbors, and poor Feversham having been in *such* a shambles for so very long, but most of all we wish to make your acquaintance, and offer whatever assistance we can in helping you to acclimate yourself to our little society.''

She stopped just short of winking at George, who was fortunately spared making a reply as the lady had already turned away, back to the carriage door. And there, he knew, was poised the true reason for this visit.

''My daughter, Miss Eliza Blackerby,'' said her mother, beaming so broadly that dusty furrows appeared in her face-powder. ''Eliza, make your curtsey now to Lord Claremont.''

''Honored,'' the girl whispered faintly as she sank rather than curtseyed. With golden hair, milky skin, and enormous blue eyes, she was fair enough to be a belle here in Kent. But even with a good fortune, a girl this meek would be lost in the crush of a London season, and for her sake George hoped her parents would spare her that ordeal.

Though not, of course, at the expense of his own bachelorhood.

"Miss Blackerby, your servant," he said, bowing the precise degree that his brother promised was acceptable for well-bred virgins.

"Ah, my Lord, I see your serving maid is ready," said Lady Blackerby as she pointed towards Fan waiting patiently at the front door in a starched white apron. She jabbed her fan into George's arm, striving to gaze up at him coquettishly. "You are far too modest, my lord, claiming you weren't ready to receive us!"

Eagerly the woman swept up the steps to the house, pausing only long enough to peer up into Fan's face with as little regard as if the housekeeper had been made of wood.

But Fan's composure remained unruffled, even by such open rudeness. "Good day, my lady," she said to the other woman's broad back. "Tea shall be served here, in the front parlor, if you please."

George followed in the Blackerbys' wake, now seeing the parlor through their more critical eyes. In the short time since the house had become his, he'd had time to make only a few changes in here. The ghostly dust-cloths had, of course, been removed from the furniture, and he'd also had the heavy old drapery taken down from the windows to bring more sunlight inside. Everything, too, had been scrubbed and shined and polished to Navy standards as well as to Fan's, and George had added a few of the souvenirs of his voyages that had long been hidden away in storage-trunks: an enormous sea shell from the South Pacific, framed views of the volcano at St. Pierre on the Caribbean island of Martinique, a fragment of an ancient statue from Naples.

But new for this occasion—at least new to George's eyes—was an entire elaborate service for displaying and dispensing tea, arrayed on a table near the chairs, and two trays with sandwiches and biscuits. Clearly Fan, and Small in the kitchen, had interpreted his warning regarding the arriving enemy in a more hospitable light than he'd intended.

They should have listened to him.

"Oh, I say," exclaimed Lady Blackerby with relish. "The Trelawneys did let things go, didn't they? This is most hideous! Eliza, there, take a place on that settee, and pray leave space for His Lordship to join you."

Too stunned to reply, George didn't obey, either, and if he hadn't been so appalled by the woman's audacity—and if Fan hadn't been there as a fellow victim—he would have turned and walked from his own house, and not stopped until he'd found a ship, any ship, to take him back to sea and away from such civilized society.

But Lady Blackerby wasn't finished. She'd scarce begun. Gingerly she tipped one of the chairs back on its legs to inspect the bottom of the seat cushion, wrinkling her nose with disdain.

"Oh, my lord," she said, "you must let me recommend to you the best cabinetmaker in Brighton, so you can toss these dreadful old sticks on the rubbish heap and begin afresh."

But even though the old-fashioned chair was one of the exact ones that he himself had faulted when he'd first been shown the house by Fan, now that this same chair was *his* chair, he didn't wish to hear it abused.

"I'm not about to scuttle these just yet, Lady Blackerby," he said, placing a protective hand on the carved back of one of the chairs. "I'm told they were fashioned of the same Weald oak as the paneling, and there is much to be said for keeping the old ways. Isn't that so, Miss Winslow?"

She stared at him over the heads of the oblivious others, her eyes wide with surprise that he'd remembered, and with pleasure, too. But that shared glance had a shock and pleasure for him as well, a fleeting connection as intense as if she'd touched him with her hand, as if they were the only two in the parlor. The connection lasted only an instant before Fan looked away to return to pouring the tea, yet it was more than enough to shake George.

"But my lord," insisted Lady Blackerby, undeterred. "New furnishings can do so much to reflect and improve one's taste."

"You should know, my dear," said Sir Simon testily. "You have been reflecting and improving our house for years."

But Lady Blackerby had discovered a topic even more fascinating than spending money. As she took the dish of tea that Fan poured for her, she once again stared intently into the housekeeper's face.

"You are most kind to keep that girl in your house, my lord," she said in a loud whisper, as if Fan had left the room entirely instead of merely turned away from her to serve Sir Simon. "Considering her father and all. That old man was quite the wild hare, they say, always in his cups and chasing after Tunford girls half his age. Quite goatish, he was. There were more than a few folk in this county who did not grieve when he disappeared last year, doubtless so drunk he failed to notice when he'd drowned.''

George saw Fan's back stiffen, all the retort that a good servant was permitted to make to a baronet's wife who was a guest of her master.

Fortunately, as master, George had no such restrictions.

"I don't put much weight into village scuttlebutt, Lady Blackerby," he said, not bothering to keep the distaste from his voice. "All I know is that the Trelawneys spoke most highly of the loyalty and devotion of both Mr. Winslow and his daughter, and I have found no reason yet to disagree. Indeed, I cannot imagine Feversham without Miss Winslow's assistance.''

This time Lady Blackerby noticed the glance that he exchanged with Fan, but George didn't care. Let them all be as scandalized as they pleased, he thought. If he were truly lucky, they'd be so scandalized they'd consider him beneath knowing, and wouldn't return to badger him again.

"It is all well and good to be tolerant, My Lord," cautioned Sir Simon, slurping his tea from his dish, "but you cannot be too careful with some of these local men. We have the very devil of a time with smuggling on this coast, My Lord, the very devil, and have since the days of the Conqueror himself. But then I expect you've heard that, being an officer of the king.''

"I was most recently stationed in the Caribbean," said George warily, wondering exactly where the baronet was now steering the conversation. "We heard little of domestic matters here in England."

"Low, thieving dogs, that's what smugglers are," said Sir Simon, his eyes glowing with righteousness as he warmed to this subject. "And it is not a mere domestic trifle, My Lord. Their audacity undermines the safety of all of Britain, and that is the honest truth. What is the good of chasing the French when we've our own native vermin littering our shores?"

George didn't answer. Smuggling was a favorite topic for gentlemen who enjoyed being publicly outraged, and also enjoyed telling the Admiralty how better to do their job. But George would also wager a guinea that, for all of Sir Simon's indignation, there was smuggled French and Spanish wine served at Blackerby Hall, just as somewhere on their beruffled persons, Lady Blackerby and the silent Eliza wore French lace and silk ribbons, and sipped tea that had come from Canton by way of Paris instead of in an English East Indiaman. Even the tea George had found in the caddies here at Feversham was of a far higher quality that would be expected in a country house.

"Consider all the revenues lost to the Crown," continued Sir Simon warmly, "gold that's plucked straight from our pockets. But that is the very least of their wickedness, My Lord!"

"Is it now?" asked George, unwilling to agree with Sir Simon on anything, even a topic as clear-cut as this one.

"Yes, My Lord, the very least, indeed," declared Sir Simon. "Such smuggling gangs are bold as brass, believing themselves above the law and trusting their networks of thievery and intimidation to protect them.

One never knows when they shall come ashore next, rioting in taverns, horsewhipping the excise men, and terrifying poor honest people in their beds.''

But while Sir Simon was doing his best to create a picture of lurid lawlessness, all George was seeing was the blank fear that had unexpectedly drained the color from Fan's face. Standing alone against the wall, forgotten by the others, her mouth was pinched and her hands clasped so tightly together that her knuckles showed white. George had seen enough of what the suffering and pain of war could do to women caught in the middle to realize that the terror haunting Fan's eyes was genuine.

He thought of all the nights she must have spent here alone after her father had disappeared, far from any neighbors but close to the coast and the water. Being young and beautiful as Fan was would only make her more vulnerable.

He searched her face now, hunting for the truth. What fearful memories had Sir Simon's tirade raised for her? Had these same lawless smugglers come one night to Feversham? Had she been one of those honest people terrified from their beds, coerced into offering horses, food, shelter, and threatened into silence?

''Oh, Sir Simon, cannot you see that you are boring His Lordship to tears with your raging?'' said Lady Blackerby, glaring at her husband. ''He has come here to our little corner of Kent for peace, not to listen to you rant on about smugglers and pirates and goodness only knows what else. Civil discourse and genteel conversation is what a fine gentleman expects from his acquaintance. Isn't that so, my lord?''

With his thoughts turned towards Fan, George was

only half listening, and let the baronet's wife over-whelm any semblance of genteel conversation with a note-by-note description of the latest piece Eliza had learned for the pianoforte. But at last even Lady Blackerby could sense his disinterest, and the family made their farewell amidst countless invitations and promises. Finally their carriage began the long rumble home, and George quickly returned to where Fan was collecting the cups and tea-dishes.

"We shall do better next time, My Lord Captain," she said apologetically. "With so little notice, I couldn't do more than—"

"Do you think I give a damn about that?" Gently George rested his hands on her shoulders, so she'd no choice but to look at him. "Fan, talk to me. Tell me about the smugglers. No matter what they told you, you don't have to protect them any longer. Have they come here to Feversham, when you were alone?"

In an instant the fear returned to her face. "I never said that."

"You didn't have to, lass," he said gently. "I saw it on your face when Blackerby was talking, and I see it there again now."

"You said yourself you pay no heed to village gossip," she said, pulling free to turn away from him and back to the tea dishes. "Why did you listen to Sir Simon and his prattling nonsense?"

He watched her fuss with the cups and plates to avoid his gaze, her gestures agitated and disjointed and thoroughly unlike her. Something *had* happened here; he was sure of that now.

"Fan, please," he said. "All I wish is to help."

"Then ask no more such foolish questions," she said, gathering up the tray for the kitchen. "Questions will only bring trouble and grief, mind? This close to Romney Marsh, wise folk will no more speak of the smuggling companies than of the devil himself. If you care for yourself—for all of us!—you shall do the same.''

She turned and hurried away, nearly running in her haste to leave him, and for now he let her go. But the dread in her face haunted him, determining what he'd do next. If it was at all in his power, she would never be afraid like that again.

Chapter Seven

With the small knife she carried for the purpose, Fan snipped the heavy thread that stitched the top of the bag closed. The bag's rough linen sides sagged open, releasing the heady Oriental scent of the tea into the damp night air. As Captain Markham and the others watched and waited, Fan solemnly plunged her bare arm deep into the tea and drew out a fistful of the shriveled black leaves. By the lantern's light, she crushed them gently between her fingers, gauging the texture and the density of the leaves as much as how quickly they crumbled, then held them to her nose. The men around her stood in silence, awaiting her judgment of this last bag as patiently as they had the first.

"'Twill do," she said at last, purposefully nonchalant. With her approval, her men quickly tied the top of the bag once again closed, and slung it over the back of the final waiting pony, ready to be taken to the waiting customers. Fan dusted her hands together and smiled at Captain Markham, as brisk and businesslike as she could, considering she'd been awake for nearly twenty hours straight.

Markham touched the front of his hat. "You are a discerning woman, Mistress Winslow," he said, his words showing as faint clouds in the chilly air. His face had a colorless, washed-out look to it, as if he seldom saw any daylight, his laugh a dry, perfunctory bark. "That never changes, does it?"

"Nor do you, Captain," said Fan. She always took care to keep her own men close by, just as, by her orders, they kept their pistols at hand. Her father had never entirely trusted Markham, saying the man had spent too much time among the French to be truly reliable. Fan agreed: there was something too silky, too smooth, about Markham.

Now he nodded. "Then all that remains is our usual conclusion, mistress."

Fan reached into her pocket and unpinned the fat pouch of coins from the gathers of her petticoat, there beside the pistol she wore tucked into her belt. "The same fee as always, eight pence a pound for seven hundred pounds of black China tea."

Markham took the pouch, tossing it lightly in his palm as if he could tell how much was inside by the weight alone, and for all Fan knew, he could. "The same fee, Mistress Winslow, but alas, the last."

"The last?" Uneasy, Fan frowned. "We have an agreement, Captain Markham, one that is favorable to us both."

"But the conditions have changed, haven't they?" His smile widened, not reaching his eyes. "I've heard you've taken a new lodger at Feversham, the captain of a frigate. I do not like frigate captains, Mistress Winslow. They are bold and brash and ambitious, and make life very difficult for poor sailors like me."

"But this captain no longer has a command, let

alone a frigate,'' insisted Fan, her heart racing as she remembered the conversation she'd had earlier with George, and how much it mirrored the one she was having now. "I do not know what you have heard, Captain Markham, but Captain Lord Claremont is not your usual Navy captain. He has come to live at Feversham as a gentleman in the country, not as a customs-man intent on hunting you."

"Then perhaps you can persuade this country gentleman to take his lodgings elsewhere," said Markham, an unpleasant edge to his voice. "Surely, for the sake of our agreement, you can do that much."

"No." She took a deep breath. There was no point in lying about this; he'd hear the truth soon enough elsewhere. "He's not a lodger, Captain. He has bought Feversham outright, and he has no plans to leave."

"Bought Feversham?" Markham grunted with surprise. "Ah, who would have guessed there'd be such a fortune to be made in following the king? I am only a poor sailor, you see, mistress, with only myself to answer to. You will understand my concern, I am certain."

"But I can assure you that—"

"*Assure* me? Of what, mistress? What kind of assurance can you offer me that will carry any weight when your own men are speaking of how you yourself have changed your gang's meeting place from Feversham lands, for safety's sake?"

"A common enough practice," she said quickly. She could guess which one of her men had let that slip. Most likely it had been Bob Forbert, who was now studiously gazing away from her. "Every sensible company switches their meeting places to help confuse the customs officers.''

''Or to avoid crossing the path of your pet frigate captain.'' Markham waved for his men to join him at the boat. ''When next we meet, Mistress Winslow, the price of this black China tea will be a shilling a pound instead of eight pence.''

''A shilling!'' cried Fan, stunned. Quickly she did the reckoning in her head. A shilling would mean that with the next run, that little pouch of coins would need to hold a hundred crowns. ''That is half again what you ask now! A shilling a pound is beyond reason, beyond sin!''

''And what shall you do to protest, Mistress Winslow?'' asked Markham with a careless shrug as he tucked the pouch of coins into his own pocket. ''Haul me before the customs officers for deceitful trading? No, Mistress, I fear you must agree to share my risk this way, or else find another vessel to replace the *Sally.*''

She had no other choice, and he knew it, and worse, *he* knew she knew it as well. She couldn't afford to pay her Company men less, and risk losing them and their tenuous loyalty. Not that she'd fault them for it, either. The majority had wives, children, and aging parents, and they relied upon the money they earned to support their families, just as they'd always relied upon the Winslow Company. When Father returned, he'd expect her to have done whatever was necessary to keep the Company together, and to provide for the Company's people. Her only option was to pass Markham's increase on to her own buyers, and pray that, because it would still be more reasonable than the price of legal tea, they'd accept the new price.

It wasn't fair, not in the least, and she couldn't help but believe that Markham wouldn't have raised his fee if her father had still been the one making the arrangements. For that matter, if Father had been the one to show Feversham to George, he would also have been sure to contrive that George wouldn't have even considered buying the house, and Markham wouldn't be making his ridiculous demand now.

And she herself would not be in this sorry, tangled mess with George Claremont, telling him such a crafted and scrupulous version of the truth that open lies would have been more honest.

Her nod was curt and final, still that of a leader. "Very well, Captain Markham," she said. "You'll have your hundred crowns, but not a farthing more."

Yet her heart was heavy with trouble and foreboding. Honest lies, and lying truth, and the heavier weight of a bag filled with gold: no good could come from this, no good at all.

From the height of Caesar's back, George scanned the dark horizon for the shadow of a sail or the gleam of an uncovered sternlight.

"Not a glim, Cap'n M'Lord," said Leggett on the horse beside him, his disappointment echoing George's own. "We'll not be snaring any smuggling bastards this night, leastways not on Feversham sands."

"No," said George with a sigh. His little band of followers had been eager for the hunt, the six men he'd brought with him from the *Nimble* impatient with housekeeping and spoiling for a fight more in their line. But despite the muskets across their saddles and the pistols in their belts, their patrols along the beach these last two nights had come up empty. "As much as we might wish it, Leggett, we can't go prowling about on another's land. We'd be as likely to be shot as the smugglers themselves, trespassing like that."

"Aye, aye, Cap'n M'Lord," agreed Leggett sadly. "But couldn't we rig out some neat little craft, a pinnace, say, and sniff along the shore that way?"

"And how long could we keep a secret like that on this coast?" George shook his head again, and breathed into his cupped hands to warm them. There was a dangerously fine line between protecting one's own property and becoming a vigilante, especially for military men. "For now we're watching over Feversham's shore, and no other."

He was sure it was only a question of timing. He'd stumbled across the proof yesterday, a small, overgrown barn with a sagging roof that he hadn't realized he owned. Close to the water, the barn had outwardly looked abandoned, but once George had pushed open the door, he'd discovered the evidence of smugglers' visits. The smoky marks on the timbers from recently lit lanterns along the walls and the fresh hay waiting for the horses who'd not long ago been tethered to the rails inside showed the old place had often been used for rendezvous, doubtless a gathering place for a local band. Tomorrow morning, when he'd more time, he'd return there himself and see if he could discover any more clues.

Again he remembered the terror in Fan's eyes when Blackerby had spoken of the smugglers. Now he knew for certain they'd dared to use Feversham when there'd been no strong master to deny them, though he still could only guess what they'd done to her while they'd been here. All he could do now was make sure it would never happen to her again.

"Remember what I told you all," he said softly, mindful of how easily voices carried on a lonely beach. "The man who lets this slip to Miss Winslow will answer directly to me. I'm doing this to put her mind at ease, not worry her afresh. Our only task is to catch the scoundrels at their thievery, then turn them over to the magistrates. Do that, and we'll make Miss Winslow the most grateful woman in Kent."

The eastern sky was just beginning to pale as Fan parted from the others in the Company, and began the last part of her ride home across Feversham lands. At least Pie knew the path without any guidance from her. The extra time Fan had had to spend dickering with Markham had made the night stretch out much longer than usual, and now she was too exhausted to do more than hold the reins, the weariness in her limbs matched by the weight upon her conscience. She couldn't wait to wash the heavy scent of the tea from her skin and to shed the clothes that were covered with black flecks of it, infinitesimal reminders of what she must do in her father's name.

As she led Pie into the stable, both her father's fat old bay and George's chestnut gelding thrust their heads over their stalls to nicker a welcome, or more likely, being male, to request an additional ration of oats for their breakfast.

"Hush now, you two," she said softly, unsaddling Pie and beginning to brush her down. "The last thing

I need tonight is having the pair of you telling tales on me.''

The horses whinnied again as if to answer, and Fan smiled. She wasn't yet accustomed to having the third horse here in the stable, and such a grand horse as Caesar, too. At least George had not yet hired grooms or stable-boys, and she could still come and go through the stables as she pleased without being noticed.

Navigating the house would be more of a challenge. Because none of George's men seemed to bother with the nicety of using the back stairs, she could go up that way without being seen, then come back down only to announce that she felt unwell and would be returning to her bed for another hour, not to be disturbed. No one would question her, even if to her own conscience it seemed like a measly, idle excuse. Men always grew squeamish about any sort of women's ailments or illness, one of the more dubious advantages of being the only female at Feversham.

One hundred crowns. With a groan, Fan closed her eyes and rested her forehead against Pie's warm side. Father had dealt with Markham for as long as she could remember, and she wouldn't know where to begin to find another captain to replace him. But how she hated the thought of carrying that much hard money on her person, as much a temptation to her own men as to Markham and his!

And what was to stop Markham from asking for more next month? Any excuse would do now, or even none at all. She'd still be helpless to refuse him, or risk losing her supply of tea altogether. On and on it would go, with no end in sight, and as Fan's despair deepened, she realized she was thinking what, before this, she'd always dismissed as unthinkable.

What would she do if Father never returned?

The horses whinnied again, but this time she didn't open her eyes. Another moment here to rest, she bargained with herself, just another moment, and then she'd have the strength to go into the house.

"Fan?" asked George with obvious surprise. "You're up with the sun, aren't you?"

Her eyes flew open, and her head jerked up to stare at him over Pie's back.

"Why are *you* here?" she blurted out. "That is, here in the stable, at such an hour?"

"For Caesar," he said evenly. "I couldn't sleep, and thought an early-morning ride might clear my head. Besides, he could use the exercise as well."

Of course that was why he was here. She'd only to look at how he was dressed, in polished boots, light leather breeches, and a dark riding frock coat, to see that for herself.

She, of course, as housekeeper had no good reason at all for being in the stable at this hour. Her day in the house should have already begun. Certainly Small would be at work by now in the kitchen.

"So it is with me," she answered quickly. With Pie standing between them as a screen, she prayed he wouldn't notice the crumbs of tea still clinging to her skirts and cloak. "I could not sleep, either."

"There is a great deal of not sleeping at Feversham these days, isn't there?" He smiled. "Or rather, these nights."

"Both, if you are to be truthful," she said, wincing inside at her choice of words. Hadn't he always been truthful with her, while she had been the one playing games with words to twist their meaning? "Night into day, that is."

"And day and night." He glanced over his shoulder as if to marvel at the rising sun, showing in the doorway behind him. "This is your pony, then?"

She nodded as he came forward to stroke her horse's shaggy neck, and wondered uneasily if he even knew that Pie was hers. "I know it is unusual, Captain My Lord, for a servant to keep a horse in the same stable as the master's, and I know we have not discussed it, and if you wish, I can shift her to the stable in Tunford."

"Don't be ridiculous," he said. "She's company for old Caesar here. What do you call her?"

"Her name is Pie," said Fan, watching how comfortable he was with her rough little horse. "She is not much to look at, I know, but she is fast and true-footed."

"Never apologize for a humble-born horse," he said with mock sternness. "They're generally the best of the lot. Aren't you, my bonny girl?"

Pie whinnied in return and pressed her velvet nose against George's arm, making him chuckle.

"Can I coax you back out with me?" he asked. "I'd wager Pie here is game. You can show me where you ride yourself."

Oh, yes, thought Fan grimly, *the way where all paths lead to the gallows.*

"We are done for the morning, Pie and I," she said, leading the pony to her stall. "I was just going inside when you came out. I have much to do."

"You are certain?" he asked, clearly disappointed. "You cannot be persuaded to change your plans?"

"I am sorry, My Lord Captain." She smoothed her

hair back with her palms as best she could, striving to look more like a proper housekeeper. Riding in the damp night air loosened her hair, and made a fuzzy halo of tiny curls spring up around her forehead at the edge of her cap. "I have many duties to attend to, and I'm late beginning as it is."

"Let them wait," he said softly, turning from the pony towards her. "There's no good reason they can't."

She swallowed, searching for a resolve she wasn't sure she possessed. "Is that an order, Captain My Lord?"

That crooked smile again, wildly disarming because it was so unconscious. "No, not an order, not to you. More of a request, I suppose."

"A request." She sighed, troubled. "You make my position here at Feversham difficult to understand, My Lord Captain. Am I still your housekeeper, or—or something else?"

"You are my *responsibility*," he said firmly, no doubt or hesitation in his voice at all. "I want you happy, content, and safe. You cannot doubt that, can you?"

"I do not know what to doubt, Captain My Lord," she admitted forlornly. Happiness, contentment, and safety were such modest needs, and so far beyond her own reach! "What to doubt, or think, or believe, or expect. I cannot answer for any of it."

"Poor Fan," he said gently. "Life is a muddle, isn't it? It's no better for me, you know. Here I thought I'd marked out my place in it as well as any man could. I had my command, my ship, my crew, my officers and orders, even an enemy I'd sworn to destroy. But with a single treaty signed and delivered by men whose names I don't even know, everything was stolen away. Peace, they call it, and hail me as one lucky bastard for coming home with my pockets stuffed with silver.''

"You could have been killed instead," she said, realizing how glad she was that he hadn't been, "and that wouldn't have been lucky at all."

"I almost rather I had," he admitted wryly. "At least I wouldn't have been reduced to running Feversham as if we were all still aboard the old *Nimble*."

"And where's the sin in that?" she asked, ready to defend him. "Look at how much you've already done. You've brought more order and life into this house in a week than others did in the last century!"

"Ah, I do that without a thought," he said sheepishly, rubbing the back of his neck. "I went to sea so young that the Navy marked me forever with its ways. I must put everything to rights, shipshape and Bristol fashion, whether it's a tangle of lines aloft or a squabble between gun-crews. But why am I burdening you with all this, Fan? I've never made any other woman suffer so. Why should you have to listen to my quirks and follies?"

"I like to listen to them," she admitted shyly. "'Tis no burden at all, for your stories interest me. Your life has been so different from my own, in so many ways."

He grinned, suddenly boyish. "You shouldn't encourage me like that, lass, indeed you shouldn't, or you'll find me rambling on like the most tedious old salt between decks."

"I do not believe that is possible," she insisted. "Go on now. Tell me more."

"Well, then," he continued, clearing his throat

self-consciously. "A happy ship is a sort of family, you know, with everyone dependent on everyone else. A captain generally has good reasons for giving his orders, and he expects to be obeyed without question. If one man chooses to disobey, or neglects his duty, however slight, then everyone is put in peril. In a storm, or in a battle, disobedience can mean death."

"So that is how you see me, then, Captain My Lord?" she asked. "An unruly cabin boy who must be brought into line?"

"Not at all," he said, and not laughing the way she'd expected, either. "You're the reason I cannot sleep, Fan."

She gave her head a swift little shake, trying to defuse the tension that she could feel pulling them together.

"And so I am a responsibility, and a reason," she said, hearing the tremor in her own voice. "Though neither a cabin boy nor a housekeeper."

"Hush, Fan, and listen," he said, taking another step closer to her, close enough now that she could smell the scent of the soap he'd used for shaving. "When those wretched Blackerbys invaded Feversham yesterday, the way they spoke of you and your father as if you were not even there, as if you were dirt beneath their vile, undeserving feet—"

"But that is a servant's lot, Captain My Lord," she protested, even as she blushed. She'd never had anyone champion her like this, especially not someone like George, and even if it was wrong of him to do so, she still found the experience almost unbearably wonderful. "We are supposed to be invisible."

"Damnation, not like that," he said sharply, "and not you."

"But why not me?" she asked, bewildered. He was not only an officer, but an aristocrat, a peer, accustomed from birth to understand and embrace the differences that separated class and rank. "What else is a housekeeper if not a servant?"

"Because you are part of Feversham," he said with great deliberation, "and Feversham is my home. Because no woman, servant or otherwise, deserves to be treated with as little regard as Lady Blackerby showed you. And because most importantly to me, Fan, you are *you*."

She caught her breath, stunned. "Captain My Lord, I do not—"

"George," he said. "For this moment, if no other between us here, call me George. Just George, mind?"

"Just George," she repeated softly. "Just...just George."

He smiled, his pleasure so genuine that his whole face relaxed, and looked years younger. She smiled shyly in return, forgetting every warning her conscience had tried to tell her.

Oh, Fan, Fan, you are in treacherous waters now! The old stable was already a warm and suggestive place, all musty sweet hay and warm animal smells and the shadows mixed with slanted beams of new daylight, with the three horses their only company. For any girl bred in the country, stables always meant forbidden trysts in a pillowy loft and the sweet abandon that followed, as much a place for dalliance as a new hayrick at harvest. In this barn, she and George could almost be guaranteed of their privacy, for no one from the house would think to come looking for either of them here.

But for Fan, the lure went far beyond that, the way it always did for her with George. When he spoke to her of his past, it seemed as if they'd always known each other, as if their lives had magically twined together without them realizing how. How could he know that his confidences could mean so much to her?

With the Company slipping from her control and the danger increasing, with her father's return growing more unlikely with each day, George's kindness and understanding were a sanctuary to her, a place she did not want to leave. It seemed she had been strong all her life, and now he was offering her the chance to share and halve that impossible burden, even only for a short time.

He smiled at her, and she longed to tell him everything. He told her she would be safe at Feversham, and she wanted to spill out all her troubles with Markham. He said he wanted her to be happy, and she came perilously close to confessing how loveless and lonely and empty her life was in all the ways that mattered.

Until, that is, he'd come into it, and changed everything forever.

"I must go," she said softly, though she made no move to leave him. "To the house, I mean."

He smiled as if he didn't hear her. "Look at you, Fan," he said, pretending to scold her. "You're covered all over with leaves and twigs. Did Pie toss you into a thicket of brambles and blackberries?"

She looked down at her skirts to hide her dismay, pretending she was only noticing the tea for the first time, and praying, too, that he wouldn't smell it for what it was.

"Bramble Fan," he teased softly, reaching out to brush her cloak clear. "What's to be done with you, eh?"

Still looking down, she laughed, from giddy exhaustion, from the foolishness of George's teasing, from the ridiculousness of her position, having scraps of black China tea brushed from her cloak in a barn by the son of a duke.

She was so very tired, and if she slipped forward just a little, just a little more, his arms would be there waiting to catch her....

She shivered when he touched her cheek, not from surprise, but from the inevitability of it, and instinctively she let her eyes flutter shut to heighten her other senses. Gently he traced the curve of her cheek, his fingers warm, slightly rough. The ruffled cuff of his shirt brushed over her skin, the pressed Holland linen carrying the faint scorched-iron scent mingled with starch and bluing: a gentleman's scent if ever there was one.

"Bramble Fan," he said again with fondness and an odd sort of wonder, too. "Perhaps we should just fall off this horse together, eh?"

He turned her face up towards his and kissed her then. His lips were warm, sure, surprisingly soft—ah, everything was surprising to her, this being all so new!—and though she guessed it wasn't quite right, she smiled in the middle of it from purest delight. His mouth moved over hers, leading her, his newly shaved beard was the merest rough bristle as he let her grow accustomed to this much. Finally he parted her lips and deepened the kiss, enough to make her catch her breath. Instinctively she slanted her lips against his, exploring this unexpected world of new sensations, of the feel of his tongue playing against hers, of a taste so different from her own, rich and deep and masculine and infinitely complex.

And desire, too: with this first kiss he was teaching her desire and longing and passion, or maybe she was simply learning it for herself. She could feel the heat spreading through her whole body, curling and licking like a lazy flame through her limbs, and when George's hand slipped into the opening of her cloak to find her waist, she shifted to one side, making it easier for him. His hand spread around the curve of her waist, following the bones of her stays beneath her gown as he drew her closer, arching her back over his arm. She raised her hands, curling her arms around his shoulders and letting the ripples of pleasures intensify as his body leaned more neatly into hers. Her heart was racing, singing in her blood.

Make this last, she told herself with fierce joy, *make this last so I can remember it for always!*

And then, abruptly, it ended.

"What in blazes," muttered George as he broke the kiss. "Fan, what is this here—a *pistol?*"

"Yes, a pistol," she said defensively, grabbing at the gun tucked into her belt as she struggled to pull free. How had they melted together so effortlessly, only to become so awkward and tangled in the long folds of her cloak as they separated? "I—I always carry that when I go out alone."

He stared at her, incredulous. "You *always* do? To market, to the village—you are carrying a pistol like that?"

"Yes, George, I do." She raised her chin, feeling oddly near to tears. They'd been so magically close for a handful of minutes, yet what more cruel reminder of her other life could there be than that wretched, inopportune pistol? "I've told you before, I'm accustomed to looking after myself."

Her body was still wantonly on edge, her senses raw and unfulfilled, and to her shame she could tell from the black look in George's eyes that he felt much the same.

"But not like that," he said grimly. "You shouldn't carry a gun unless you know how to load and fire it."

"I do," she said, self-consciously resting her hand on the pistol's well-worn wooden butt. Though the gun was old and nothing fancy, it still fired true, and she would never go to the beach to meet Markham or the others without it. "Father taught me."

George's expression grew darker still. "A lady doesn't know such things."

"I never claimed to be a lady, George," she said, turning on her heel so he wouldn't see the angry tears that burned in her eyes. "It's only you who saw me as more than a housekeeper."

With quick, furious steps she hurried across the yard, her shoes crunching on the white crushed shells and the unfortunate pistol knocking heavily against her hip beneath her cloak. She'd thought when she'd left Markham that the day could grow no worse, but how mistaken she'd been!

"Hold now, Fan, wait!"

Of course he'd follow, determined to set her life to rights, too, tidy and neat in a way it was never destined to be.

And of course she quickened her steps, equally determined to resist him, even as he easily matched his long strides to hers.

"It's the smugglers, isn't it?" he demanded. "You fear them returning to Feversham, and feel you must defend yourself. Damnation, Fan, look at me and tell me that isn't the reason you're walking about armed!"

"All you wish to see is smugglers!" she said, staring steadfastly ahead. "What of all the other men in this county? What of hired day laborers from the fields who've drunk up their wages at the Tarry Man, and the soldiers from the garrison up the stream, and the stable-men at the stage inn, and the sailors, too, particularly their officers who believe that any unprotected, unwed woman is fair and panting game for their amusement?"

"Fan, so help me, I'll see to it that you're never frightened again," he said. "Trust me, Fan, please, trust me and—"

"Cap'n M'Lord!" Leggett ran towards them from the house, his weather-beaten face bursting with excitement. "At last we've found you, Cap'n M'Lord! Everywhere we've been huntin' for you, but here you are now, and just in time, too!"

"In time for what?" demanded George. "Speak up, Leggett, and stop nattering on like an old woman!"

"Why, in time for *him!*" said Leggett, scarcely able to contain himself. "Already he be waiting for you in the front room, almost as patient as any regular man. It be your brother, Cap'n M'Lord, come a-visiting, His Grace the Duke of Strachen here at Feversham!"

Chapter Eight

"So this is it, then?" asked Brant, standing at the window beside George. "This is what convinced you to buy this ancient pile of out-of-fashion rubble? A view of the same grim gray water where you have spent most of your life?"

"It's neither grim nor gray, especially not on an evening as clear as this." George sighed, wondering why he ever tried to explain such a distinction to his brother. "If you had been the one sent to sea, Brant, then you would understand."

"No, if I had been the one banished to sea at such a tender age, I would most assuredly be dead, and for a good long time, too," said Brant philosophically, sipping at the brandy in his glass. "And if you had had the joy of being born first, to the title and the debts that came with it, then the estates would by now be completely bankrupted, and you would be living in genteel squalor in Calais. No, I must admit that Fate and Father did conspire to arrange some things correctly to favor our respective talents."

"I'm not sure Revell would agree," said George. In his opinion, the youngest Claremont brother had received the worst lot, being shipped off with the East India Company, to make his fortune among the heathens and fevers.

"Oh, I believe Rev would swear otherwise," said Brant easily. "He demonstrated a great talent for surviving in a vile climate, speaking Hindi to bandits, and, of course, being able to coax sapphires and rubies to drop from the mountaintops and into his palm. And recall that in Calcutta he also found himself a delightful little wife to bear his name and his children, something neither of us seems to have been able to do here in England."

George grumbled wordlessly and flung himself into his armchair. As orphaned boys, they had pledged to one another to make their fortunes in the world and restore the honor to the much-tarnished family name after their father had done the tarnishing. It had been a very grand and glorious pledge for three boys to make, especially as young and frightened as they'd been, and through various paths they'd managed to succeed remarkably well.

But as Brant had pointed out, only Revell had been blessed enough to find love along with his fortune. George had met Revell's wife Sara, who was small, dark, bookish, and quiet, and wildly in love with Revell. She was also quite different from the women that Brant fancied, or at least the ones that George had met: voluptuous and fair, with acres of creamy skin and golden hair, and seemingly very empty heads. As for George's own tastes in women, the choice was hardly a choice at all.

Fan, his Fan, all spirit and spark and gray eyes that missed nothing and promised everything. His Fan who went riding before dawn, caring more for the feel of the wind through her dark hair than the twigs and leaves that clung to her skirts. His Fan, who had kissed him with a passion that had made his head spin and his heart race like no other woman ever had.

His darling Fan, who also carried a pistol worthy of a highwayman tucked into the folds of her petticoats.

Not, of course, that he was going to reveal any of that to Brant in the middle of a conversation regarding wives, and especially not after that disastrous encounter this morning in the barn. The less he shared with his brother regarding Fan, the better.

"Is this the reason you've come to bedevil me?" he asked, grumbling still. "So that we can sit here, dry, wizened old bachelors, wondering why no decent women will have us for husbands?"

Brant laughed, settling comfortably into the chair beside George's. They both had every reason for being comfortable, for they had dined on one of Small's exemplary dinners and had also drunk a good deal of the excellent wine that Brant had brought with him as a house-warming gift. If only George's conscience wasn't so busy plaguing him over Fan and the stable, then he, too, might be feeling as relaxed and content, and chuckling like some simple-minded idiot.

"Since when," continued Brant, "does one brother need a reason to visit another?"

"Since that first brother shudders at the thought of leaving London for any other less worthy place," answered George, "by which he means the entire rest of the country, including the remote home of the second brother."

"But it is *your* home, George, however remote," said Brant evenly, stretching his legs before him, "and as your wiser, older brother, I wished to see how you've tossed away your good fortune."

Moodily George swirled his brandy in the glass. "You don't like Feversham, do you? What was it you called it? 'An ancient pile of out-of-fashion rubble'? You think I'd have done better walking to the edge of the sea and heaving the money directly into the waves."

"What I think is that you have found a home that suits you to perfection," said Brant, his smile genuinely fond. "You could no more live amidst the marble, gilt, and looking-glasses of Claremont Hall than you could on the moon. But this house will be your home, George. I could tell that from the drive, before I'd even come inside. My only hope is that you have time to enjoy it as you deserve."

"Why the devil not?" Instantly George forgot his grumbling, all eagerness as he leaned forward in his chair. "What have you heard, Brant? What are they saying in London?"

Brant shrugged with a true courtier's understatement. "Nothing definite, no true words to pin your hopes upon. But the whispers do fly about like butterflies, everywhere one goes."

"'*Butterflies*'?" exclaimed George incredulously. "Damnation, Brant, tell me what they're saying. Tell me if I have half a chance of being called back and given a ship before I'm old as Methuselah!"

"Oh, I should venture before that," said Brant. "They say that Addington's days in power are dwindling. They say that neither side of his coalition has faith in the other. They say Pitt stands just off in the shadows, waiting and smiling like the tabby ready to steal the cream. But the rumors that should mean the greatest to you come from France, where Napoléon Buonaparte is still slicing away at his own government, as if no peace were ever signed.''

"Buonaparte." George sank back in his chair, letting the impact of his brother's news blossom and grow. Brant knew everyone in London that was worth knowing, and while his rumors could have just as readily have come from an actress at Drury Lane as an acquaintance in the House of Lords, they were generally more reliable than many other men's sworn facts. If Brant had heard that Buonaparte was disregarding the Treaty of Amiens, then he was.

It was as simple as that, and as complicated. If the peace ended and Britain returned to war, the fleet would be the first service mobilized. The last time they'd been at war, the Navy hadn't been permitted to deal Buonaparte the final blow that he deserved, and now, at last, would come their chance to finish the task.

George was ranked high enough on the captain's list to be among the first called back, and he was certain to receive a command, a good command, too, based on his record. Given his success with prize money, he'd have his pick of crewmen as well. It might damned well be as close to perfect as the Navy could make it. His orders could take him anywhere, to the Caribbean again, the Mediterranean, the Baltic, and George realized now he was the one grinning like an idiot.

"I thought this would be happy news to you," said Brant quietly. "Though God knows I'm hardly as eager to see my brother go back to war."

George shook his head, knowing that this, too, was another thing he'd never be able to explain to his brother. "I'm not some bloodthirsty savage, Brant. I've seen too much killing to treat death lightly."

"I didn't say you were." He sighed softly, his regret palpable. "We each found new worlds, new lives, to replace the ones our dear bastard of a father stole from us, and yours was the sea, and the Navy with it. I'll even grant you that the Admiralty has served you with more kindness than our father ever did. But this time will be different for you, won't it, Georgie? Because this time, when you sail, you'll have a home of your own—*this* home—to leave behind."

Home. Slowly George glanced around his bedchamber, from the sweep of the window to the old-fashioned bed, to how he'd arranged his books and papers and journals exactly the way he wished them on his table-turned-desk. Brant was right. He would miss Feversham, and for the first time in many years he'd sail away with a yearning to return home, because, at last, he'd a home that would be waiting.

But with an odd twist in his chest, he realized that Feversham meant more to him than the house alone. It meant Fan, the two so closely intertwined that it was impossible to imagine one without the other. He had never before gone to sea with a heart burdened by a tearful farewell from a sweetheart, and he'd never gone into battle or a storm with last thoughts of a special woman waiting ashore for his return. This time for him would be different, because this time he'd be carrying the memory of Fan's face with him, her kiss, how she'd felt to hold in his arms....

"So where is your fair housekeeper, George?" asked Brant lightly, pulling George abruptly from his thoughts. "All I've seen here has been your usual pack of unruly rascals."

"You mean Fan," answered George without thinking, until he saw the satisfied smile cross his brother's face. "She sent word earlier that she was feeling unwell, and has kept to her rooms for most of the day."

"That is her name, eh?" asked Brant. "Fan? A sweet name, doubtless for a sweet lady. No wonder you'll regret leaving her behind when you sail."

With a grumbling sigh, George knew better than to try to deny it. He'd never been able to keep secrets from Brant. Too often it was as if he'd written his thoughts on his forehead, there plain as day for his brother to read.

"Yes, I shall miss her when my orders come," he admitted, still choosing his words with care. "She has been most useful to me in arranging Feversham."

"Then I wonder why doesn't your face take on the same mooncalf glow when you speak of, say, your steward?" mused Brant, running his fingertips around the rim of his glass. "Certainly he must be of equal use in arranging your quarters for you as Miss Fan."

"Stow it, Brant," ordered George. "Now, before you venture on to say things we shall both regret. The, ah, the connection between Fan Winslow and me is of no concern to you, mind? None."

Bemused, Brant regarded him over the edge of the glass. "You would thrash me for the sake of this woman?"

"If it came to that, yes," said George deliberately, and he realized he meant it, too, his fingers tightening on the arms of his chair. "Don't test me, Brant."

"I shouldn't dream of it," said Brant easily. "I've no doubt you'd blacken both my eyes and leave me

groveling for mercy. I concede the field of honor entirely to you, my dear bellicose brother, and shall vow
to say not one word further of your housekeeper. All
that's left for us now is to do honor to this excellent
brandy, and drink to the swift confusion of old Mon-
sieur Buonaparte.''

Lying on her bed with the paper propped against
her knees, Fan tallied the figures once again, making
sure they were right. Unlike many of the larger smuggling companies that took their tea directly to mer-
chants in London, hers still catered to individuals,
selling the bags of tea to a list of regular customers,
inns and coffeehouses and even to the kitchens of
several grand houses in the county.

The deliveries were begun as soon as Markham's
shipments were unloaded; only in rainy weather was
the tea kept longer in a warehouse. Then, on the following night, with Will Hood as her escort, she would
follow the same route as the deliveries had taken,
make the usual small conversation, and collect the
payments.

But tonight would be different. Tonight she'd have
to slip unnoticed from a house still in an uproar over
the arrival of the duke, and tonight, too, she'd have
to tell each of her customers of the increase in tea's
price.

She put aside the paper, rubbing her temples with
her fingertips. As exhausted as she was, she hadn't
been able to sleep, and now her weariness was com-
pounded by an aching head. How foolish she'd been
to believe even for those few minutes in the stable
that there could ever be anything special or lasting
between her and George! The kiss they'd shared had

been magical—more than magical!—but then he'd discovered her pistol, and the magic had vanished as quickly as the dew at dawn.

He was an officer and a peer, sworn to serve the king, while she was common-born as could be, his servant, and devoted to picking that same king's pocket. What kind of future could they ever build together with so much between them?

She slid her hands over her eyes and bowed her head over her knees. But she would not cry: not for George, not for herself, not for the passion and love and life they'd never share.

She would *not* cry.

"Miss Winslow? Are you within, Miss Winslow?"

"A moment, if you please." She didn't recognize the man's voice through the door, but given all the people who'd arrived with the duke this morning, that wasn't unusual. But for him to come here to her room to summon her after she'd left express word not to be disturbed could only mean some genuine catastrophe must have happened below stairs.

Quickly she sniffed, and swiped her eyes with the hem of her sheets before she slid from the bed. She shoved the paper with her figuring beneath her pillow and, on second thought, put her pistol there as well. Next she pulled the coverlet from the end of the bed and flung it over her nightshift, padding across the floor on bare feet to open the door.

The man was standing away from the door, his face indistinct in the shadows of the hall, but she could make out enough to know he must be one of the duke's men, and not George's.

"Yes?" she said with her best haughty housekeeper's voice. "Is there a problem downstairs that requires me?"

"So you did in fact take to your bed," said the man, not bothering to answer her question, "and by yourself, too. Ah, what joy to find a woman both honest and honorable!"

"And what a trial for me to find a man who is neither," she said irritably. The fellow definitely was one of the duke's people. Not only did he speak with a London accent to ape his betters, but his manner carried a London cockiness to it as well, taunting her about being honorable and honest. "Tell me your business now, else I'll have you turned out in the morning for your insolence, see if I don't."

The man laughed, amused. "You truly have no notion of who I am, do you?" he marveled. "How barbarously ill-mannered of me, Mistress Winslow, to keep such a secret! I am the Duke of Strachen, and I do pray you won't turn me out in the morning."

Finally he stepped forward into the light from the open door, and she could see the undeniable resemblance between George and his older brother.

"Oh, my," she said faintly. "You *are* the duke, aren't you?"

"I am," he said with a graceful twist of his wrist. "Although 'Good day, Your Grace' is the more customary greeting."

"Forgive me, Your Grace," she said, ducking into the required curtsey. Insolence from a duke held a somewhat different color than the same ill manners in a footman. "But since your visit here to my rooms like this is far from customary, the customary greeting flew straight from my head."

He laughed again, not at all irritated with her reply.

"You are every bit as prickly as my brother said you were. 'A dish of nettles', I believe is what he said, and every bit as prickly as he is himself."

"Nettles," she repeated, perplexed. She'd always thought of herself as practical, straightforward, with no patience for folderol or nonsense. Admirable qualities, she'd always thought, not...*prickly*.

"And of course you are most handsome, even in your shift," continued the duke, looking her up and down in frank appraisal, and approval. "Honest, honorable, handsome, and prickly, every attribute that George would seek. No wonder he is so besotted with you."

"George—that is, Captain Lord Claremont—is not besotted with me," she answered quickly, stunned that his brother would even suggest such a thing. "Not in the least."

"No?" said the duke. "I have known him far longer than you, Miss Winslow, and I can assure you that he is more thoroughly besotted with you than I have ever seen him before with any other woman. Might I come in? If we are to discuss George's besottedness, then we should do so with more privacy, and besides, this hallway is deuced drafty."

She opened the door further to let him enter past her, still too preoccupied with what he'd just told her to argue. Besides, she doubted a worldly gentleman like the duke would be much impressed to learn that, other than her father, he was the first man, highborn or low, to be invited into her rooms, especially so late and with her in her nightclothes.

He stood poised before one of the two chairs, respectfully waiting for her to sit first. It was a small nicety she hadn't anticipated, and enough to make her blush as she scurried to the second chair, plopping down in an ungainly tangle between the coverlet and her bare feet.

He, of course, had no such tangle, flipping aside his coattails as he sat with perfect masculine grace. He was more classically handsome than George, his features more regular and less weathered on account of spending his life in drawing rooms instead of on board a warship, and his hair was a neat shock of burnished golden blond instead of George's unruly dark waves. But what she noticed most was the guarded sadness in his eyes, almost as if he didn't quite trust his own elegant facade and cleverness. If this was the opposite of what he called "prickly" in George and herself, then she'd gladly claim the nettles.

"You wish to speak of your brother with me, Your Grace?" she asked, self-consciously straightening her back against the spindles of the chair. "To be sure, there is little enough to discuss. Captain Lord Claremont is the owner of Feversham, and I am Feversham's housekeeper."

The duke made a small tent of his fingers, pressing the tips together over his chest. "Oh, you are far too modest, Miss Winslow. Look at what you have done! With your plain black gowns and country ways, you have accomplished what the very cream of this season's belles have not. You have quite captured my brother."

"I am sorry, Your Grace, but no." She shook her head fiercely, denying her own feelings as much as his assertion. "No, no. That cannot be true. It *isn't* true."

He shrugged carelessly. "But it is, whether you

believe it or not, and also whether you act on it or not. More prickliness, perhaps?''

Abruptly he screwed his face up into an odd scowling frown, before he smoothed it with a smile.

"Did you know I am unwed?" he asked. "I have no duchess, and therefore no legitimate son. George is my heir, the second eldest brother. Has he mentioned that to you? If I unwisely stumble on those stairs out there and break my neck, then he becomes His Grace, and I am reduced to a mere bushel of unlamented old bones and nothingness.''

"Oh, Your Grace, no!" she exclaimed, taken aback. "That would be most dreadful! Not only are you far too young to die, Your Grace, but Geor—the captain would be miserable. It would be an utter disaster for you both.''

"You believe George would regard becoming the seventh Duke of Strachen a disaster?'' he asked, watching her closely. "To sit in the House of Lords, to be received by His Majesty, to be master of all the Claremont houses and lands? Most gentleman would consider such a change in their status to be a great gift from heaven.''

"But not your brother,'' she answered firmly. "He would feel cursed by it, and burdened beyond measure. He would do his best to be a good duke, because he believes in responsibility, but what he loves is the ocean and the Navy and this house, too, not London and court life. Why, most days that he has been here, he has worn such clothing that you would guess him to be any other farmer or sailor, scarce a lord and great hero!''

Gently the duke bounced his fingertips together, considering what she'd said. "You realize that, as affairs stand now, George will receive no inheritance of his own. All he has, or will have, must come from his own hand, from prize money and such.''

''Which I'd warrant is exactly how he prefers it,'' she said, nodding for extra emphasis. ''He welcomes challenges, Your Grace.''

''You sound remarkably confident regarding my brother's happiness,'' observed the duke, plucking idly at the lace along his cuff. ''Especially given that you are, as you say, no more than his housekeeper.''

''And if, as *you* say, Your Grace,'' countered Fan warmly, ''you know your brother as well as you claim, then you would already have understood all of this, without asking me. You taunt me about being honorable and honest, as if such things count for nothing except for mockery. Perhaps in London, that is so. But here in Kent, they still matter, and I can say— I *will* say!—that Captain Lord Claremont is the most honorable and honest gentleman ever I have met, and that, Your Grace, is all the further I have to say of your brother.''

She rose to her feet, clutching the coverlet tightly around her. She was determined not to say another word. Likely she'd already said more than she should have, anyway, but she wasn't going to let George go undefended, no matter what had happened between them earlier in the stable. Besides, she needed the duke to leave so she could slip away from the house herself, and meet Will Hood at Green Bridge.

In response the duke slowly rose as well. His earlier smile returned, and the easy charm with it.

''So here you are,'' he said, ''turning me out after all.''

Cautiously she smiled back as he headed to the

door. She'd seen enough of men to know that, duke or not, this one was the kind who would make either a most loyal friend and ally, or a most dangerous enemy. Now she could only guess which he'd be for her.

"Good night, Your Grace," she said, and this time managed to remember a curtsey, albeit one made lopsided by the coverlet around her shoulders. "Now I have it right, Your Grace, don't I?"

He paused at the door, his hand on the latch and his expression purposefully unreadable.

"Yes, Miss Winslow," he said at last. "I'd vow you now have everything exactly—*exactly*—as it should be."

Slowly George climbed the dark back stairs, questioning his sanity with every step. Although Feversham was his, he'd never been to this part of the house before, consciously avoiding it because he knew Fan's rooms were here.

Not that he didn't try to imagine what those rooms were like. Did her bed have posts and curtains, he wondered, or was it small and narrow? Had she added the little luxuries to make her quarters a home, cushions on the chair, a soft wool coverlet, an earthenware tea service, and a handful of novels for company, to keep away the loneliness when the wind blew and the rain dashed against the windows? In those two rooms, he knew she slept, and washed, and dressed, and undressed, and picturing even one of those simple but intimate acts was enough to make George groan.

He told himself he was coming here now to see if she felt better, or if there was something he could send to ease her discomfort. Any thoughtful master would do the same with one of his people, the same way he'd visit the sick bay to look after his ill and wounded crewmen. If he also found the opportunity to apologize for how he'd behaved towards her in the stable, well, then he would do that, too.

And if in her gratitude for such a noble apology, she decided to invite him to linger in her rooms with him, to show him exactly the kind of bed she did have, to kiss him again, of course he'd—

No. He wasn't going to her rooms for that, and bitterly he swore at himself for letting his thoughts once again roam back to this morning. Hell, hadn't he spent nearly every blasted second reliving that kiss as it was? He'd never experienced anything remotely like it, because he'd never known another woman remotely like her. She'd made his heart pound and his blood turn hot with desire, and before their lips had even touched he'd been hard and ready in his breeches for her.

With another oath, he struck the banister hard with his fist and continued up the stairs. Only a minute; he'd stay only a minute, and then he'd leave.

At the last landing, he saw the soft candlelight from the end of the hall. He frowned, quickening his steps. There shouldn't be a light here, not unless Fan had left her door open. Then he heard her laugh, soft and low, unmistakable, followed by the deeper rumble of a man's voice.

At once George stopped, riveted to the stair. He'd thought what he'd found with Fan was special, just between them. Yet here when he'd been so damned gentlemanly about coming to her rooms, clearly there was some other bastard who'd made the climb before him, and at her invitation, too, from that seductively soft laugh of hers.

The door clicked shut, taking the wash of light with it, and the stranger's footsteps came down the hall towards George. They'd have to meet on these stairs; there was no other way down, and George set his candlestick on the windowsill, determined to have both hands free for whatever came next.

What came next, humming a haphazard scrap of an opera's theme as he began down the stairs, was Brant, his expression as happily satisfied as a man's could be.

And in an instant, all of George's frustration spilled into the shock of learning he'd been betrayed by his own brother.

"What the hell were you doing with Fan?" demanded George, so angry he could barely put the words together. "You couldn't even let one day pass before you went after her, could you? Not even one blasted *day!*"

Abruptly Brant stopped, too, three steps above his brother. "Whatever are you saying, George? What are you implying, anyway?"

"I'm not *implying* a damned thing," said George furiously. He reached up and shoved his brother, shoved him so hard he staggered back. "And I'm through talking, too, because you never listen."

"That's because you don't have anything to say, you bloody idiot," snarled Brant, shoving George in return. "Go ask Miss Winslow yourself. Go ask her, and she'll tell you what—"

But George's anger finally exploded, his fist squarely catching his brother's handsome chin and sending him flying back against the wall. With a grunt

Brant scrambled to regain his footing, then threw himself at George, knocking him down the last two stairs and to the landing, the two of them rolling over and over as they struggled to hit the other. They hadn't fought like this in years, but the old boyhood tactics came rushing back, driven by anger and resentment and ancient competition.

Until they heard the gunshot, the ball whistling close enough over their heads that they both felt the splinters of flying wood as it struck the wall.

"What the devil," growled George, instinct driving him now as he pushed free of Brant to turn in the direction where the shot had come.

"What the devil, indeed!" cried Fan, completely dressed and standing at the top of the stairs in a fading cloud of pale gunpowder, the pistol still clutched tightly in her hands, and more a vengeful fury than a woman who'd just dallied with a lover. "Behaving like a pair of mongrel dogs, you two are!"

"Fan," said George, breathing hard as he sat upright. "Fan, I cannot have guns firing in my house. You could have killed one of us."

"Not if you'd killed yourselves first, falling down the stairs and breaking your overbred necks, just like His Grace said would happen!" she declared, her own anger spilling over. "If you won't have gunfire, I won't have fighting, either, and unless you two begin behaving like the gentlemen you are, then I shall turn you *both* out into the yard with the other animals, see if I don't!"

She turned with a final disgusted sigh and a flurry of black skirts, and marched back to her rooms while Brant and George watched wordlessly in something close to awe. For a long time they sat there still on the landing, catching their breaths and patting gingerly at their new bruises.

"What a vastly amazing creature," said Brant finally, wincing as he smoothed back his hair. "Ah, George, George, you have met your match at last, and there's none more perfect for you in all Creation."

Chapter Nine

John Small watched Fan set the master's tray for breakfast, wearing his curiosity as boldly as he did the spotted kerchief around his head.

"So do it be true then, mistress?" he asked finally, his thumbs tucked into the ties of his apron while his mate Danny listened intently. "Did you fire a gun at the two merry Claremonts last night?"

Fan sighed. Living alone for so long, she'd forgotten how fast exciting gossip like this could fly through a house.

"Yes, I did," she announced, knowing there'd be little use in denying such a thrilling truth, especially with the proof of it still buried in the paneling in the back staircase. "Not that it's any of your affair, Mr. Small."

"Oh, aye, but it do be my affair," he said with relish, coming to stand beside her. "It be all our affairs among the *Nimble*'s people here at Feversham. We've each one of us bound our fortunes to Cap'n Lord Claremont, sure as sure, he's that good a man. But what would become of us if you'd've killed him outright, I ask you?"

"But I didn't," protested Fan. Why couldn't any of these men have faith in her skill or accuracy? Father had insisted that there was more danger in carrying a gun that you didn't know how to use than in not carrying one at all, and he'd made sure she'd practiced until her aim was sure, especially at night. "I'd no intention of killing your captain, or his brother His Grace, either. All I wished to do was startle them out of their tussling before they broke their necks falling down the stairs."

"Aye, now that would be a pretty mess, wouldn't it?" Both Small and Danny shook their heads solemnly. Yet for the first time there was an undeniable admiration in Small's gaze, something Fan had never expected to see. "The duke and the captain, mashed together in a pulp of blood an' gristle at the bottom of the stairs."

Fan wrinkled her nose as she spooned the marmalade into the silver pot, wishing he hadn't been quite so descriptive with the same gory delight that the duke himself had favored. "I suppose I'm glad you understand, Mr. Small."

"Oh, I understand." Sagely he tapped a finger to the side of his bulbous nose. "Even lords an' officers need a thrashing every so often, to keep 'em honest and agreeable. But if we'd've been at sea, by now you would be in irons an' charged with mutiny for what you done, and facing a dangle from the yardarm as your reward."

"Then how fortunate that we're at Feversham instead," she said, carefully picking up the tray to carry it upstairs. At sea she'd be faced with hanging from the yardarm for mutiny, while here it could be the gallows for smuggling; neither seemed a more pleasing prospect than the other.

"Ah, but you still do be a rum one, missy," said Small, beaming with approval. "A right rum one, and don't let anyone tell you otherwise. Else you'll take your blunderbuss to them directly, eh?"

He and Danny laughed, but all Fan could muster was a weak smile as she left the kitchen with the tray. She'd no intention of causing such a fuss when she'd fired the gun over the heads of the two brothers last night. They'd left her no choice, really. At first she'd tried shouting at them to stop to no avail, and had finally used the pistol only when it seemed her last recourse.

Not that it had even seemed that drastic at the time. Her father had never been afraid to use his gun to get the attention of the Company men, and she'd done it herself, too, when they'd fallen to fighting among themselves.

But there were several grave differences about last night. First of all, they'd been indoors, and the gun had caused damage to the old paneling. Next, the men she'd fired over were both lords, and one was also the owner of the house where she lived and worked. That was bad enough. But then there was also the perplexing matter of her having kissed George in the morning, and aimed a pistol—the same pistol he'd deemed hideously unladylike—over his head at night.

Who could guess what would happen now?

When she entered with the breakfast tray, George was already at his table writing letters, the way he usually did this time of day, and though he smiled at her when she entered, she sensed a definite wariness about him this morning. She could hardly blame him. After last night, she was feeling a bit wary herself.

"Good day, Fan," he said, rising to clear aside his papers so she could put the tray on the table between them. "I, ah, I wasn't certain I'd be seeing you this morning."

"No?" she asked, surprised, and wondering if he'd expected her to be halfway to Scotland and fleeing a charge of attempted murder. "Whyever not?"

"Because you were unwell yesterday," he said, looking surprised himself. "You still look somewhat, ah, pale."

And no wonder, too, she thought, since she'd spent most of the night traipsing across the countryside, delivering the grim news of the increased prices to her customers. Three hours' sleep could make anyone look pale.

"And because after Brant arrived," he continued, "I didn't see you again until—ah, until later."

"Yes." She clasped her hands before her, determined to plunge ahead as she'd planned. "Later, it was. I wish to speak to you of that, George."

He smiled warmly. "There's no need to apologize, Fan, not to me or to Brant. We understand."

"But you don't," she said, perplexed. "I'd no intention of apologizing because I'm not sorry for what I did. I wished to stop you from risking your lives by fighting one another on the stairs, and though I know you believe women should not handle firearms, I was glad I did what I did. I won't apologize for it, any more than I shall apologize for having the pistol in the first place."

"You won't," he said, a statement, not a question, and equally perplexed.

"No," she answered as firmly as she dared. "What I wished to say was that I expect you to take the cost for repairing the wall from my wages. Shall I pour your chocolate?"

"Yes, please," he said, though he didn't sit back down in his chair. He hadn't shaved yet, his jaw rough with stubble and his hair still unruly from bed. "But the truth is that I wasn't planning to have the wall repaired at all."

"You weren't?" she asked uneasily, pausing with the pot in her hand. She'd always thought that his being a gentleman, clean-shaven and well-pressed, had been much of his appeal to her, but seeing him this way, gravelly and sleepy-eyed before his breakfast, was more dangerously intimate, more intriguing, especially with the unmade bed behind him. "I thought you always wanted everything shipshape and tidy."

"Not this time." He smiled proudly, clearly pleased that he'd surprised her. "I'd rather leave the ball where it struck as a reminder. One more fantastical story for Feversham's history—the night Mistress Winslow tried to shoot the duke!—to be recited along with Sir William Everhart and his sixteen matching chairs in the parlor."

"As you wish." It wasn't exactly the story Fan would have chosen to be remembered by, but the house was his, and if he wished to leave the hole unmended, it was his right to do so.

"Yes, indeed. Yes." He cleared his throat self-consciously. "Then I suppose it is my turn to apologize, Fan. For yesterday morning, when I—"

"There is no reason for you to apologize for that," she said swiftly, her cheeks burning at the memory.

"There most certainly is," he said sternly. "What I did was unforgivable, Fan, both as a gentleman and as an officer, and I—"

"No apologies, and no forgiving, either," she said, setting the chocolate pot back down on the tray with an indignant thump. "*You* kissed me, George, and *I* kissed you."

"But I *am* the master," he insisted, in his best—and worst—captain's voice. "Because of my position, I took advantage of you."

"And perhaps because of *my* position, I also took advantage of you." She sighed unhappily, wishing she could make him understand. "Oh, George, can't you see? You're making this sound as if I had no choice in the matter, as if all I did was stand there like an unfeeling block of wood!"

He frowned. "I would not kiss a block of wood, Fan."

"And I would not have kissed you had you been only the master," she said, troubled. "I don't think of you like that, George. I don't believe I ever have, not since you first came to Feversham."

"How much better for us both, then, if I'd never come at all," he said, his frown deepening. "Better if I'd left you as you were, and gone to another house."

"It would not have been better for me," she said quickly. "How could I wish never to have met you, or for what has happened to be otherwise?"

He looked up at her so sharply she felt her heart race and her palms grow damp. "You have no regrets?"

"I don't regret what I cannot change," she said,

and she meant it. "The past is done, and it's only the future that's still mine to make different."

"Then you do not believe in kismet, Fan?"

"Kismet?" she repeated uncertainly, the word new to her. "I do not know what that is, let alone whether I believe it or not."

"Kismet means that everything in our lives is predetermined," he explained, his voice low, confiding, as if telling a special story just for her. "That you and I were fated to meet, to kiss, even to stand here now, with my chocolate growing a chilly skim across the top. Kismet has already decided the smallest detail of every one of our days, and we miserable mortals are helpless to do anything but follow along the charted course. It is a notion much favored among the Turks and others in the East, and my brother Revell learned of it when he lived in India."

"But not for here!" she said, scandalized. "What a heathen, barbarous notion, that we can choose nothing in our lives for ourselves!"

Another man would have turned her objection into teasing about her country ways, but George didn't. "Very well, then, no kismet," he said almost solemnly. "But if you believed so strongly in determining your own fate, Fan, what kind of future shall you wish for yourself?"

"My future?" She hadn't expected that, and the simple question made her pause. She couldn't answer it with entire honesty, at least not about the part of her wished-for future that would include him: that was too farfetched a dream to confess aloud, especially to him.

"Why, what would be expected, I warrant," she said instead, hedging. "I would want to remain here at Feversham, because it is my home. I would wish to be useful all my days, to have my health and my wits, and not to want."

"That is all, Fan?" he asked incredulously. "A humble sort of future you want, and a lonely one, too. Don't most women wish for a husband and children?"

She flushed again, even as her chin rose defensively. "You asked for *my* future, George, not for anyone else's. But I could turn your question back upon you, and make you tell me what you wish for yourself."

"My own future, you mean." His smile was uncertain, almost shy, but his eyes held her gaze with an intensity that only increased the warmth that had flooded her cheeks. "Very well. I wish for another command, another ship, another chance to serve my country and my king with honor. That much has been the same with me for years. But now there's more."

"More?" she echoed breathlessly, her heart beating wildly in anticipation not only of his confidence, but with what she knew would surely follow. This was such a dangerous game for her to play, with every sensible impulse to grab the tray and flee back to the kitchen overwhelmed by having George stand so close.

She'd come here only intending to bring him his breakfast, and to offer to pay for the damage she'd caused. But the more time she spent in his company, the more she had to admit that the real damage hadn't been caused by her pistol. As soon as the duke had said George was besotted with her, she'd realized the foolish word applied to her as well.

Besotted, and befuddled, and bewildered, that was

her, she thought miserably. No matter how futile and ruinous such an attachment was bound to be—the housekeeper and the lordly officer!—all her heart remembered was the joy she felt each time George smiled at her, or touched her, or, most blissful of all, when he'd kissed her.

Oh, yes, she was besotted, and worse, more than halfway to being in love.

"More," he repeated, oddly echoing her thoughts as he reached for her. "Now instead of dying gloriously for my country, I find I'd rather selfishly prefer to live to a ripe old age, and die peacefully in my bed. *This* bed, in fact, here at Feversham, if I've any choice in the matter."

"Now how can that be selfish?" she asked, her laugh suddenly nervous as he mentioned the bed, still so invitingly unmade and perilously convenient. "What is the use in being a dead hero, when a live one would serve just as well?"

"Blasphemy," he said mildly. He slipped his arm around her waist to draw her closer, and made her completely forget the chocolate pot and the tray and the safe haven of the kitchen and instead focus all the more on that enormous tumbled bed. "The Admiralty would have your head for such talk, and then take mine, too, for inciting such unspeakable mischief."

"They wouldn't dare," she scoffed, looking down at his chest to avoid his gaze. Lightly her fingers played along the front of his shirt, feeling the warmth of his skin and hard muscles through the linen. One kiss, she bargained with herself as her heart raced in anticipation: there'd be no sin in a single kiss, and the memory would be one she could treasure the rest of her days.

"You're a good, brave, fine gentleman, Captain Lord Claremont," she whispered fiercely. "If I could tell that to His Grace last night, I'd hardly be afraid to speak the same to a fleet of old admirals."

His dark brows arched with surprise. "You defended me to Brant?"

"I did," she declared proudly, "and he believed it, just as you should, too."

His chuckle slid into a groan as she slipped her arms around the back of his neck and arched against him, her breasts pressing heavily against his chest. He settled his hands on either side of her waist, his fingers spread, and gently slid them up along her sides, letting his thumbs tease the curve of her breasts through her stays. Her body was tightening until it ached with longing, and he hadn't even kissed her yet. "You would test my powers of belief that sorely, sweetheart?"

"*I* believe it, George," she said, her voice fading into a whisper breathless with excitement. One kiss, one kiss and no more. "I wouldn't say such things about you if I didn't believe them."

"You cannot believe in kismet, but you do believe in me," he marveled as she turned her face up towards his like a spring flower towards the sun. "Ah, Fan, what have I done in this life to deserve you?"

She closed her eyes just as his mouth came down upon hers, making her gasp with surprise and pleasure. Eagerly she parted her lips for him as he slid his hands lower, possessively holding her closer against him. Here again was the delight she remembered from their first kiss in the barn, the fascinating male taste and texture of him that was so unlike anything else she'd ever experienced.

But this time was different, too: this time there was an urgency to his kiss that her body seemed to know how to answer even as her conscience balked with uneasiness. She was infinitely more aware of how much bigger and stronger he was, yet how she still held the power to make him groan with desire—desire she found she was just as ready to explore, hungrily deepening the kiss he'd begun.

She was so lost in the rush of sensation that she didn't realize he was easing her backwards until she felt the edge of the table behind her. Without breaking the kiss, he easily lifted her up and onto the table, and now as he pressed closer, her knees parted for him, her skirts sliding up her legs past her garters and bare knees. This morning he'd find no hidden pistol in her petticoats, but it was her turn now to discover the hard, hot length of him inside his breeches as he pushed against her. Her poor lost conscience struggled to remind her that only a few layers of linen and wool were keeping her from complete ruin, but the rest of her wanted only the man in her arms.

"Ah, George, George," she murmured as he broke their kiss to trail his mouth along her jaw to find the pulse on the side of her throat. She buried her face in the dark silk of his hair, just as he untucked the modest kerchief from her neckline and pushed her bodice lower and the shift beneath it as well. Deftly he freed her breasts, spilling them out over the top of her stays, her nipples already taut and waiting for his mouth. She gasped as he teased her with his tongue, then cried out as he drew the tender flesh into his mouth, scarcely noticing how his hand was stroking delicious little circles on the inside of her thigh, and oh, this was all so much more than the single kiss she'd promised herself and yet she could not stop, not George, not herself, not—

"Ah, my dears, forgive me, pray," said a voice that, to her horror, Fan recognized as the duke's. "I seem to be intruding at a most inopportune time, don't I?"

Shocked and shamed, Fan gasped as she flew apart from George, her hands fluttering to cover her wickedly bared breasts, swollen and red-tipped from George's kisses. She felt trapped, ambushed, not so much by the duke as by her own wantonness.

But as fast as she scrambled away, George moved faster still, stepping forward to shield her from his brother and giving her the privacy to pull her bodice and kerchief back into place.

"'Inopportune', hell," he thundered, his hands knotted into fists at his sides, his legs widespread as if he stood on his own quarterdeck, ready for battle. "What in blazes are you doing here, Brant?"

But the duke only smiled, and instead of leaving, he sauntered into the room and dropped into the other armchair, crossing his legs neatly at the knee. He was in half undress for day, with a long silk dressing gown patterned with fighting silver dragons over his breeches and shirt.

"I have come for breakfast, brother dear," he said, making a little tent with his fingers. "And at your invitation, too, if you can but recall. How was I to guess that we weren't to be *en famille?*"

"Forgive me, Your Grace," said Fan, her eyes downcast and her cheeks flushed as she ducked around George, intent only on reaching the door. "I am leaving, Your Grace."

"No, Fan, you're not," ordered George curtly, catching her arm to hold her back. "You're staying."

She gasped with wounded surprise at his tone, and at once he released her arm. He gestured towards the armchair, offering her the seat as if she were a lady, instead of a housekeeper to be ordered to stay.

"Please," he said belatedly, his gaze now filled with remorse as he struggled to control his temper and frustration and a score of other emotions, all warring together on his face. "Please stay."

For his sake, she slowly sat, but only on the very edge of the chair, her hands clasped tightly in her lap. The tensions between the three of them were far too charged to do anything else.

"Shall you order me to leave now, George?" asked Brant wryly. "Is it my turn to go, or to sit?"

But George couldn't share his brother's amusement. "Blast you, Brant," he said, wheeling around to face him. "Consider if I'd done this same low bastard's trick on you!"

The duke's mouth curled into a bemused smile. "You mean if you'd blundered in upon me with a woman in such a situation? Why, being brothers, I would have asked you if you'd wished to share her favors, of course, and—"

"Enough!" roared George, lunging towards the duke.

But this time it was Fan who jumped up to grab his arm with both her hands, pulling him back and to an off-balance stop.

"No, George, don't, not on my account!" she cried, horrified by the hostility that had escalated so rapidly. As flattering as at might be to have George as her champion, she didn't want it at such a cost. "I won't have two brothers fighting with me in the middle!''

"But you heard what he said about you, Fan!" said George furiously, though instead of trying to pull away from her grasp, he covered her hand with his, reassuring her. "Didn't you understand what he meant?"

"I heard," she said miserably, slipping her hand free, "and I understood the rest. But I won't be caught between you and His Grace, not over such foolishness as this. I told you before, George, and I meant it. If you try to treat me as if I've no mind or will of my own, so help me, I *will* leave, not just this room, but Feversham as well."

The words had scarcely left her mouth before she wished them unsaid. She had never believed in idle, empty threats, any more than she believed in making promises not in her power to keep, and to her shock she realized she hadn't changed now. Before this, leaving Feversham and the Company had always been next to impossible, but in this instant she suddenly understood that, to save her heart and herself from George Claremont, the impossible had now become very possible indeed. She had money enough to start over, and both the wit and abilities to make a new life all her own in a place where no one knew her: Brighton, London, or even America.

George shook his head, clearly not wanting to believe her. "You would not leave Feversham."

Or me: he left the last two words unsaid on account of his brother, but Fan understood just the same, and the longing and sorrow in his blue eyes were nearly enough to make her relent. Already she loved him too much, cared too deeply. ˙

You would not leave me, Fan, would you?

"I would," she said, her voice barely above a whisper. "If you test me, I will."

He shook his head again, desperation stealing the edge from his anger. "But I cannot let my brother speak of you with such blatant disrespect, Fan."

"Yet I never did speak of Miss Winslow in such a manner, not by name or person," said the duke mildly. "I was referring to the slatterns and harlots, both low-bred and high, that constitute my regular company. You asked what *I* would do if caught *in flagrante*, George, and *I* replied as to my own circumstances. I intended this most honorable lady no disrespect, and apologize if I caused her any."

He rose from the chair to bow elegantly to Fan, enough to make her blush all over again as she thought of what he'd witnessed earlier and how much of her he'd seen. She didn't want this apology any more than she'd wanted George's, and if she'd any spirit, she should be on her knees to the duke, thanking him for interrupting them when he had.

George took a deep breath, then another, and Fan could feel him laboring to calm himself. "Damnation, Brant," he said finally. "You should not provoke me like that."

"It's nothing new, brother dear," said the duke as he poured himself a dish of chocolate. "You possess precisely the same fraternal gift for provoking me, and always have. The only difference is that now, I believe, you've found something worth a true fight."

He smiled at Fan as he bit into a triangle of toast, just in case she'd somehow missed his meaning, and in her confusion she looked down, away from both men.

"If you please, Your Grace, Captain Lord Clare-mont," she said, the ring of keys at her waist jingling softly as she dipped a curtsey. She'd always been proud of those keys, the symbol of her position in the household, but now their weight seemed as heavy as a prisoner's manacles, trapping her mercilessly in a rank and station so far below George's. "Pray excuse me, for my duties wait for me below stairs."

She left then, her back straight and her eyes brim-ming with tears. The duke could say all the pretty things he wished about George being willing to fight for her, and George had already proved that he would.

But no matter how he defended her or how won-derfully, perilously close they'd come to being lovers, she couldn't afford false hopes about her lasting place in his life. She was a passing amusement, no more. She knew that. When he'd told her his hopes for the future, he'd been sure to include Feversham, but not her, unless he meant to include her among the fur-nishings. Not that she'd any right to more. She was only a country-born servant, bound to serve all her life in the same house where she'd been born. What else could she hope for?

Yet tomorrow Captain Lord George Claremont could sail from her life as blithely as he'd sailed into it, and the world would not fault him if he left a score of broken hearts in his wake. In fact the world would wink and chuckle and praise him for being all the more gallant with the ladies.

And she would be the only one who'd truly suffer, because the broken heart would be hers.

"Go after her," said Brant as he and George watched her go. "You're a damned idiot if you don't."

"No." Deliberately George made himself lift his cup to his lips. The chocolate was cold, worse than cold, but he'd so little interest in it that the chill scarcely mattered. He'd revealed enough to his brother, and he'd no intention of making himself any more vulnerable where Fan was concerned. And as for Fan herself—ah, he'd blundered into such a wretched mess with her this morning that he doubted she'd ever speak to him again. "I'm sure she would prefer time apart from me."

"And I say she wouldn't." Brant reached for another slice of toast, his appetite undeterred. "She's a woman, and she's your mistress, and as such—"

"She's not my mistress," said George sharply, then sucked in his breath, determined not to lose control again. He'd already done that once this morning with Fan, and then again with Brant. Considering how he'd always prided himself on being an officer able to master his emotions, twice was definitely two times too many. "We enjoy one another's company, that is all."

Brant snorted derisively. "Oh, yes, and the moon rises in the morning and the sun sets at the dawn. What kind of jackass do you take me for, George?"

"The meddlesome sort who sticks his nose into affairs that do not concern him."

"But you are my brother," said Brant, "and therefore your affairs most definitely do concern me. And I do believe I've the right to meddle in Miss Winslow's affairs, too, even if you insist on pretending I don't. She may have been born common as clay, George, but she deserves better from you."

"I don't need you to lecture me," said George bitterly, all too aware of what he'd done, and not done, with Fan. "I know how rare Fan is, and I don't need one more blasted word from you, mind?"

But Brant shook his head, undiscouraged. "If Miss Winslow isn't your mistress, then she's a damned close approximation, given exactly how you were enjoying her company earlier."

"She's not my mistress," insisted George. Fan had absolutely nothing in common with the mistresses that Brant so happily indulged, spoiled, tawdry mercenaries in bed and out. Instead Fan was the most honorable woman he'd ever known, a rare, noble beauty who didn't realize it, strong and brave and passionate, and not a minute passed when she wasn't in his thoughts.

He wanted to be with her, to laugh with her, to listen to her dreams and sorrows and to share his own, and he wanted to protect her however she needed protecting, whether from gossip, loneliness, or the villainous smugglers along this coast. If he must go back to war, he wanted to know she was here safe, waiting and praying for his return. He even held a bewildering admiration for her independent streak, for the way she'd stood up to both him and Brant. He didn't understand it, true enough, but he could still admire it, just as he admired nearly everything else about her.

But that was only the beginning of what he felt for Fan. When he remembered how eagerly she'd responded to him this morning, her mouth open and yielding and impossibly sweet, her breasts full in his hands, the quivering skin along her inner thigh the softest thing he'd ever felt, her breathy little moans of delight and anticipation enough to make him hard again at the memory alone. No wonder he'd treated her with such shameful abandon, instead of the respectful distance he'd intended. There was something about her—about the two of them together—that turned his best resolutions to driest tinder.

"So, then, Captain Brother," mused Brant softly. "The fair Miss Winslow is not your mistress, but she is also clearly far more than merely your housekeeper. It's only a question of how much farther, isn't it?"

A question, yes, and George, to both his sorrow and his joy, already knew the answer.

Chapter Ten

Fan paused on the steps to the apothecary's shop, tucking the packet with her purchase deeper into her basket for safekeeping. Danny, the cook's young mate, had been complaining of the toothache, and before he made the ominous trek to the surgeon in Brighton to have the tooth drawn, Fan had offered to make a poultice to ease his suffering with less dire consequences.

Besides, she welcomed the chance to trade Feversham for Tunford, if only for a few hours, and on this balmy afternoon, the sun warm on her back and the meadows beginning to turn green with spring, she could even forget the wretched morning in George's bedchamber.

She glanced up at the sky, gauging the hour. She just had time to stop at another shop for a new pair of cotton stockings before she began the ride home to oversee the evening meal—a considerably more elaborate process with the duke in residence. She tightened the ribbons of her hat beneath her chin and turned towards the lane, and very nearly into the barrel-broad chest of Will Hood.

"A word with you now, Mistress, if you please," he said, though the way he was blocking her path left her little choice.

"Not here, Hood," she whispered urgently, smiling for the benefit of anyone who might be watching. She saw him so seldom by day that he seemed almost like a stranger, his face pale and lined beneath a grizzled shadow of beard, and uneasily she thought of the gun and the knife that were surely hidden beneath his long homespun coat. "You know there's no business between us like this."

"And you should know, mistress, that I'll not go again to Feversham, not with your bloody Navy-lord living there, ready to take me for the price on my head." Pointedly he spat against the wall beside them. "This be quick, anyways. Tonight, by the churchyard, and we'll ride together to Caddem's."

"Not tonight," she said, glancing nervously over her shoulder to make sure no one could overhear. "On Thursday, three nights from this, the way I decided when we parted last."

"Tonight," countered Hood. "None o' us can see the use in waiting, 'specially not with a rascal like Caddem. Your father always said Caddem's the biggest catch in the Company's net, mistress, and there's no good reason for leaving him be after you've told the others last night."

Fan hated it when Hood invoked her father like this, just short of out-and-out defying her. The reason she didn't wish to go to Caddem's tonight was that she was, quite simply, too tired after catching so little sleep here and there. She'd need all her wits about her to deal with John Caddem, and now those wits felt as dull as an old knife. Not, of course, that she could use that as an excuse to Hood or the others.

"Thursday night," she said firmly, refusing to back down. "Not before."

Hood narrowed his eyes, tugging the cocked brim of his old hat lower over his forehead. "The men won't take to this, mistress," he warned ominously. "They won't like—ah, 'tis your damned Navy-lord!"

At once Hood hurried off, hunching his shoulders and looking downward in a way that, to Fan, only seemed to make him look more furtive rather than less so. Not that she had much time to consider it, for George was even now striding resolutely across the lane towards her, his black brows drawn together in fierce concern. He was wearing his undress uniform, the spring sunlight glancing off the polished brass buttons and gold braid, and all he needed was a snow-white charger to look the part of the rescuing hero.

Not, of course, that Fan felt as if she needed either a hero or to be rescued, except perhaps from how her heart was racing so foolishly at the sight of him.

"Was that rascal bothering you, Fan?" he demanded, looking past her towards the corner where Hood had disappeared. "I know a scoundrel when I see one, and that man was—"

"He's an old friend of my father's," she said quickly. Could there be a greater disaster than having George chase after Hood on her behalf? "He may look like a scoundrel to you, My Lord Captain, but he means me no harm."

George looked at her sharply as she addressed him formally, but there were other people within earshot, and here she had to be as careful, as proper, with him as she had been with Hood.

"Then why the devil did he bolt away like that?" asked George. "There's no more sure sign of guilt than that."

"It's your uniform, My Lord Captain," she said, almost painfully aware of how handsome that same uniform made him to her. She glimpsed their reflection in the glass of the store window behind them: he, tall and splendid and commanding, while she in her habitual black seemed as common and forgettable as a little crow. "You forget you're in a little harbor village in Kent, not some grand port like London or Portsmouth. Navy captains are precious rare here."

"And precious unwelcome, too," he said, shaking his head at such a preposterous notion, "if even half the tales I've heard of smuggling along this coast are true."

"But there are the press gangs, too," she reminded him gently. As dangerous as it might be, she still could not let the Company go undefended. "They've done their share to make the Navy unpopular, stealing men away from their families. And mind that in this county, smuggling's not seen as an evil, but as a way for common folk to make ends meet in hard times."

"It's also a way that will lead them to the gallows if they don't watch themselves," he grumbled, though the fire had faded from his argument as he looked down at her. "You left my rooms deuced sudden this morning, Mistress Winslow."

Heat flooded her cheeks. She hadn't forgotten why she'd left, no matter how handsome he might be in that blue coat with the brass buttons. "Yes, My Lord Captain, I did leave. But there seemed no real reason for me to stay."

"I wanted you to," he said. "Or isn't that reason enough?"

She lifted her chin, and the ends of the bow tied beneath it fluttered up against her cheek. "Is that only a reason from you, My Lord Captain, or an order?"

He paused uneasily, rubbing the back of his neck. "No order, Fan—that is, Mistress Winslow, not for you, not like that. Oh, blast, I'm not good at this, not like Brant."

"You *are*," she said fervently. "You're even better. Go on, pray, go on."

He nodded, his gaze intent upon hers. "Very well. I did not intend to give you an order. Rather a wish. I *wished* you had stayed with me. I wished you hadn't left. I wished you'd always stay at Feversham, where we both belong. There, I'm done."

Swiftly she looked down, away from him, at her black skirts ruffling back and forth over the toes of her shoes. It was as close to an apology as a gentleman like him would ever make, and far more than a woman like her could reasonably expect, let alone deserve. Yet was it enough to pin her heart, her life, her whole future upon?

"Was I as bad as all that?" he asked, trying to tease, and failing miserably. If they'd been anywhere other than the middle of Tunford, they both knew he'd have kissed her instead. "I warned you I'd no gift for fancy poesy."

"You did fine," she said softly, without looking up from her toes. "His Grace your brother could not have done better if he'd tried all night."

"Good for us he didn't have to try." Self-consciously he cleared his throat. "So did this friend of your father's have any news for you?"

"News?" she repeated, stalling, and now she quickly looked up to search his face for his meaning. Had he somehow overheard her conversation with Hood? Had she revealed so much of her sympathy towards smugglers that he had guessed the rest?

"Of your father." He smiled crookedly, as if the answer were so obvious she must be jesting. "Has this man heard something fresh of your father's fate? Is that why you've come to the village?"

"No," she said, faltering at this, the second time her father had been mentioned in the last hour. "I— I came to Tunford for the apothecary. And no, no, there is nothing new regarding Father, although I expect to hear any day."

"You will, lass," he said with conviction, and with kindness as well. "Surely your loyalty will be rewarded, yes?"

She nodded, not trusting her voice to answer. She'd always tried to be both loyal and honorable, true, but where exactly did her loyalty now lie? With her father, and the Winslow Company, and all the people here that depended on her leadership in her father's absence? Or with George, a man so vastly different from herself in so many ways, a man she now realized she loved?

"Ah, here comes my own reason for journeying to Tunford this day," said George, unaware of her thoughts as he waved at his brother. "You cannot keep Brant anchored in one spot for more than a day at a time, even if the alternative is only a little village like this one."

"Ahoy there, Captain Brother," called the duke as he crossed the lane to join them. "And ahoy to you, too, Mistress Winslow. You see—or rather *hear*—the nautical airs I have acquired in my brother's company. I am glad to see you looking more like your charming self, thanks no doubt to the salubrious airs of fair Tunford.''

He grinned wickedly, stopping just short of winking at her. So much of what he did seemed calculated to mock the rest of the world, or perhaps simply being a duke made him immune to worrying about what others thought or said about him, the faces peeking curiously from open windows and the passersby with marketbaskets on their arms slowing to catch the spectacle. Surely he didn't give a fig about the attention he was drawing to himself now, ahoy-ing away and grandly taking Fan's hand to bow over it as if she were a duchess herself.

Yet all Fan could think of was how fast the duke's playacting would be relayed to Hood and the others in the Company, and how many heads would be shaking in Tunford over Mistress Winslow being so familiar with those two lordly brothers. And her father—her father would have had her head outright, and demand to know why she hadn't shot the blue-blooded idiot where he stood.

But Fan had already done that once, with decidedly mixed results. Instead she pulled her hand free of the duke's, and curtseyed stiffly as a proper housekeeper should.

''You've lost your gift, Brant,'' warned George. ''Can't you see your antics don't amuse the lady?''

''That's because she's so bedazzled by your antics, dear brother, that she's scarce had a chance to admire the glory of mine.'' He smiled, smoothing the linen ruffles on the front of his shirt. ''You haven't told her yet, have you?''

At once Fan looked at George, questioning. There were far too many secrets between them without adding another.

"It's nothing worth a long face," he said, smiling to reassure her. "Quite the opposite. I have decided to host a gathering at Feversham in a week or so, supper, music, dancing, the usual folderol. It is high time I met my neighbors in the county, you know, and Brant shall be my attraction for all the local young ladies and their mamas, eager for a chance to bring a duke into the family."

"Just as all the gentlemen shall come from miles around, hoping that some of the famous Silver Lord's heroic glory might rub off upon their unworthy shoulders," noted Brant, thumping his brother's own shoulders for good measure. "You shall have them clamoring in droves before your house."

"But Feversham isn't ready yet!" exclaimed Fan, her uneasiness growing. "A grand entertainment such as you propose would take weeks—*months!*—to prepare!"

Yet George only shrugged, unconcerned. "Oh, I think not. Small and the others will help you however you please. And remember that Small learned his trade in a tavern before he went to sea. He's quite adept at cooking for great numbers, whether a ravenous ship's crew or my guests."

"But the supper is the least of it," she protested, shaking her head. She hadn't forgotten the awful visit from the Blackerbys, how they'd tittered at Feversham's crooked old rooms and stiff-backed chairs. While George had done much to shore up and repair the aging structure, the interiors were still shabby and peculiarly old-fashioned by modern standards, and

Fan dreaded more county gentry coming to poke fun at the ancient house she loved as her home. She also worried about her own abilities to oversee such a complicated event; Mr. Trelawney had never entertained company, and she'd no experience with ordering so much food and drink, or with marshalling a small army of hired musicians and extra servants, especially not with a duke as the guest of honor.

But there was another, more threatening reason as well. At any gathering of gentlemen in Kent, the talk was bound to turn to the smuggling and ways to stop such an infernal, illicit trade, and the last thing Fan wished was for them to come to Feversham to recruit George. Rich, well-bred gentlemen were always looking for ways to crush those who hadn't the same blessings, indignantly planning and plotting to destroy the smuggling companies. In their virtuous opinions, to imprison, try, and hang a poor man for smuggling was purest English justice, no matter if the poor man's wife and children were left homeless and starving.

Once, when Fan had been a girl, her father had taken her to see the results of such justice with her own eyes, the rotting, eyeless corpses of men they'd known, now hanging in chains at the crossroads near the harbor as a warning for other smugglers. She'd retched in the street at the sight, shaming Father, but she'd never forgotten what she'd seen, either. Given George's boundless loyalty to his king, she could unhappily guess whose side he would choose if the county gentlemen asked for his help, and it wouldn't be hers.

But George, of course, could know none of this. "I have endless faith in you, lass," he said. "So long as the wines flow, no one will be critical. Besides, I will be depending upon you to act as my lieutenant. I'll need you to stand by my side that night and identify everyone properly for me.''

''At your side, when you receive your guests?'' she asked, surprised by his unusual suggestion. She could do it, of course, for the local gentry and other fine folk likely to be invited led public enough lives that, by asking about, she could learn whatever she didn't know already. But George granting her such an important and prominent position was sure to offend guests like the Blackerbys, and cause no end of difficulties for them all. ''You would wish your housekeeper there beside you, as if I were your equal?''

''I wouldn't have asked if I didn't,'' answered George gravely. ''I'd like you by my side the entire night. You possess the information that I don't, and shall need, unless I wish to make a bumbling ass of myself. I've told you before, Mistress Winslow, I judge a man—or a woman—by ability, not reputation.''

Fan's thoughts were already racing ahead. If her place was at George's side for the entire evening, then while she was whispering a lady's husband's name, or that an elderly gentleman had served with the army in Nova Scotia, she could also be gently guiding George away from the men known to be most vehemently against smugglers. She hated being dishonest like this with George, especially when he was so willing to trust her, but the alternative could be as grim, and as fatal, as the gallows that her father had shown her so long ago.

''Very well, My Lord Captain,'' she said, lowering her gaze as much to hide her shame as from respect.

"I shall do as you wish, and serve you as well as I can."

And oh, George, my love, my love, forgive me whatever I must do....

"I am heartily glad to be through with him," said Fan to Will Hood as they rode away from John Caddem's tavern three nights later, the darkness swallowing them up. "He's the only one who balked at the increase, but no matter. We won't miss them. I can sell their portion of the next shipment to the White Horse instead."

She'd almost expected Caddem to refuse to pay more for tea, for he was a mean, tightfisted man, disagreeable even when she didn't come with unpleasant news. No wonder he'd been the last customer she'd told of the increase in the Company's price, and no wonder, too, that she felt more relieved than angered that he'd tartly ended their relationship tonight because of it.

"'Tis not what your father would've done, mistress," said Hood, steadfastly looking over the head of his pony as they turned down the dark-shadowed lane. It would not be long until dawn, and both of them needed to be home before then. "That wasn't his way, not at all."

Fan frowned, urging her pony Pie to keep pace with Hood's. She'd thought Hood's arguing was done when he'd joined her tonight as they'd first planned. The wind was sharp across the fields from the water, full of salty bite as it tugged at her skirts and tossed Pie's rough mane across her hands. "Nothing was lost. The profit's the same."

"Your father wouldn't have settled for that, mistress," said Hood doggedly. "Letting a customer of ten years' standing like John Caddem wriggle away neat as a greased eel! Your father would've done different for certain."

"Very well," said Fan, too weary to be truly impatient. Why should she, when Caddem's last payment was sitting in her pocket? Everything was even and fair, as it should be. "What would Father have done that was different? How would he have settled with a man as stubborn and cross as old Caddem?"

"That be easy, mistress," said Hood promptly. "He would've told Caddem he'd burn his barn if he didn't agree, and then your father would've kept his word and done it."

Incredulous, Fan stared at Hood. "Father would have set fire to the man's barn over this?"

Hood nodded. "Aye, mistress, he did what he must. Joss Winslow wasn't a man who shied from such things."

"Isn't," she corrected unhappily. "My father *isn't* a man who *shies* from such things."

"As you please, mistress." Hoods tugged his hat lower over his forehead. "But burnings have always been part of the trade. Barns, shed, hayricks, whatever be necessary, mistress, whatever—"

"I know," she said, cutting him off before he said more. "I know the trade."

She knew it, yes, but wished she didn't, and worse, she'd tried to pretend otherwise. Just because their company was a small one compared to others along the coast didn't mean they could afford to be soft. Caddem would find another source for the tea he served, and even if he had to pay more for it, he'd still boast to anyone who'd listen of how he'd gotten the better of the Winslow Company. As soon as Father heard of it, likely he'd set fire to Caddem's barn anyway, just on principle.

That is, he would after he'd thrashed Fan for being so meek and cowardly as to let Caddem go in the first place.

"How much longer, mistress?" asked Hood.

"How much longer?" repeated Fan, jerked from her own thoughts. "Why, you know that as well as I, Hood. We've only to cross the stream and the wizened oak at the crossroads, and then—"

"Nay, mistress, not that," said Hood, still not meeting her eye. "I meant how much longer are you going to keep with the Company?"

Sharply Fan drew Pie to a halt, forcing Hood to stop, too, and double back to where she waited.

He swore softly when he saw the pistol in her hand, the long barrel glinting dully in the moonlight.

"I've always thought I could trust you, Will Hood," she said, holding the gun steady with one hand clasped over the other. "You know I'll use this if I must."

"'Course you would, mistress," said Hood with grim resignation. "They're talking all over the village that you nigh killed the duke up at the Hall. Why then would you balk at peppering the likes o' me?"

"Not when you question me," she said firmly, "and now you've done it twice. I can't have that happening in the Company, Hood, not even from you."

"I'm not challenging you, mistress," argued Hood, twisting the reins more tightly around his hand. "I'm only saying the same as the others are, excepting I'll do it before your face and not to your back. Things be changed since your father went. There's Markham's raising his price for the tea, and this business with Caddem, and that high-bred king's man buying Feversham, having you live on there with only his men for staff, and him putting us all at risk—''

"Captain Lord Claremont has nothing to do with any of this, or with any of you!" she cried, lashing out desperately for George's sake. If he suffered on her account, if they tried to harm him because of her, she would never, ever forgive herself. "You don't touch him, mind? Not one hair!"

"Nay, mistress," said Hood carefully, not needing to say anything more than she'd already said herself. "I won't. But I can't answer for all the others, can I?"

"But you can tell them," she said, her voice rising with urgency. George was a large, strong man, a brave man who'd spent nearly all his life at war and would know how to defend himself. But she also knew he was also given to long rides along the beach in the early morning, when the fog and mists could hide another with a musket until it was too late. "Captain Lord Claremont has been occupied with his own affairs and with making Feversham his home. He has done nothing, *nothing,* against anyone here!"

But Hood only sat there on his horse, offering none of the assurances she wanted to hear in return.

"This all be a powerful burden for you, don't it, mistress?" he said finally. "A powerful great burden, and more than I'd want for my wife or daughters."

"It's not more than I can bear," said Fan, though the tremor in her voice told otherwise. "For Father's sake, I can. I *will,* because he'll wish it that way."

Hood only shook his head, the expression of his

eyes lost in the shadow of his hat's broad brim. "How long has he been gone now, mistress?"

"Eight months and a week," she said, wishing the words didn't sound so hollow and final. "Truly, not long at all."

"Long enough without word from him, or of him," he answered, his voice turning rougher. "More than long enough if he still lived, mistress."

"But we never found a body!" she insisted, refusing to admit such a possibility to Hood. To say it out loud would be disloyal; to say it out loud might make it true. "Not Father's, nor Tom Hawkins's either!"

"Last anyone saw, they went a-walking towards the water, drunk as stoats," said Hood. "You've lived on this coast all your life, mistress. You know as well as anyone that the sea don't always give back what it takes."

"But I'm doing this because Father would want it so!" she cried, her anguish so real that Pie whinnied in restless sympathy. "I've told you that before, haven't I? I'm keeping the Company for him, for when he comes home again!"

"Then mayhap you can stop your keeping, mistress," said Hood, his pony inching closer, "because I believe your father's done with wanting, leastwise in this life."

"No!" She raised the pistol a fraction, steadying it, refusing to let him judge her soft again. "I don't believe that, Will Hood, and if you had any regard for my father as your leader and your friend, you wouldn't, either!"

Hood went very still. "Then mark a date that you will be ready, mistress. If you hold your father's memory dear, as a daughter should, then you must decide when to mourn him proper, and when to let the Company pass to another's hands.''

To let the Company pass to another's hands. The idea was as unthinkable as accepting her father's death, but at the same time, it was traitorously seductive as well. To be spared the danger and the endless responsibility, to stop deceiving George and the others, to end the meetings with dangerous men like Markham, even the uncommon luxury of sleeping the night through safe in her own bed—all could be hers if only she'd agree. She would be free to leave Kent if she decided, or simply live out her days at Feversham without fear of meeting a violent end. For the first time in months, her life would again be her own.

But in return she would have to admit that she'd never again hear her father's laugh, or smile at his teasing, or be able to rest her cheek against his shoulder and know her world was safe, the same as she'd done since she'd been a tiny girl in his arms.

"Think upon it, mistress," warned Hood. "Already there's men in the Company, Forbert and others, who speak of seizing your place for themselves."

She gasped, not so much from what he said but that he'd dare say it to her. "They would not dare!"

"They would, mistress," he answered firmly, "and you know it. Why else would you be pointing that pistol at me now, eh?"

He was right, and in her heart she did know it, too. She wouldn't have been nearly so quick to draw the gun if she hadn't sensed the growing resentment and restlessness among the men, even ones as trustworthy as Will Hood. And why else would she have felt such a cold stab of fear for George's sake? How they'd delight in a chance at a Navy captain, especially if they could justify it as self-protection!

If she wasn't careful, if she tested their patience too far, both she and George were just as liable as Caddem's barn to meet with a lonely, violent end, and the possibility made her tremble at her own vulnerability. It was too late for her father, and if she didn't act soon, it could be too late for her, and for the man she loved.

There was, she thought bitterly, no real honor among thieves.

"One more run, then," she said at last, each word dragged from her soul. "If my father has not returned, I'll leave it to you and the others to choose a new leader among yourselves. The company shall be his, to do with what he pleases with no meddling from me, and so I'll tell Markham myself next week."

Hood nodded, approving. "That be the brave thing to do, mistress, and true to your father and your blood. Will you be finding yourself a new place then, too, instead of staying at Feversham with that black bastard of a lord?"

So much was being left unsaid, yet Fan heard it all: how the talk around Tunford was that she and the lord captain were closer than they should be, how no respectable woman would remain alone in that house of sailors and king's men, how her most private affairs had become the righteous concern of every other person in the county. No wonder she craved something more from her life.

"I'll make my way," she said carefully, "and I'll do what's best for me."

"Good girl," said Hood, exactly as if she'd been

a stubborn mare who'd finally been subdued. "Now best we head for home, eh?"

He turned his pony towards Tunford, confident that she would join him. He would be the new leader of the Company; she didn't have any doubts of that. Which of the other men would dare challenge him? Yet as Fan watched him go, she knew that her father would have had no qualms now about shooting his old friend in the center of his broad back and leaving him to die on this lonely road, a message to every other Company man with traitorous thoughts.

But Fan was neither brave nor true as Hood had said, but only a meek, hopeless coward that shamed her father's memory and that of every other Winslow before him, and with a lonely little sob for her own wretched failure, she uncocked the pistol, and followed.

Chapter Eleven

Impatiently George swept aside the day's crop of neatly written replies to his invitation, and reached instead for the newspapers that had just come down with the post from London. He already knew the replies would all be acceptances, composed with varying degrees of hysterical anticipation and gratitude, or at least so had been the case with every other scrap of cream-colored writing paper that had been delivered this week, and all better left for Fan and Brant's pinch-faced secretary Tway to sort out between them. The real surprises for George would come in the news-sheets, and he didn't even bother taking off his mud-flecked riding boots before he began scanning the long columns of print for word of a coming war.

"And a fine good morning to you, too, brother," said Brant, joining him in the hall. Although his man-servant had seen that he was properly shaved, combed, washed, and dressed to face the new day, the grumpiness in his heavy-lidded eyes showed he'd prefer to have been in his bed still. "How appalling that you insist on keeping sea-hours here in the country."

"They are the hours that most of the world outside

of London does keep," noted George absently, without looking up from his reading. "You're not obligated to follow if you don't wish to, you know."

"No, I'm only obligated to listen to you pontificating about the joys of country life," grumbled Brant. "Where's Fan?"

"Fan?" That made George look up, instantly on guard. "I don't know. Below stairs, I suppose."

"Don't dissemble with me, George," said Brant crossly. "You damned well know where that woman is every blasted minute of the day."

George's expression darkened. Last week he *would* have known Fan's whereabouts, but ever since the day they'd met in Tunford, Fan had kept her distance from him, or made certain that they were never alone together. Now Danny was the one who carried up his tray with breakfast, and Leggett who brought him his letters on the round silver salver. Her excuse was that she was occupied with planning and plotting the coming party, that she was closeted away with Small and Tway and the devil only knew who else, but George was certain the change was deliberate, her wish to try to undo everything that had happened between them.

Yet all the wishing in the world wasn't going to make him forget the kisses they'd shared, nor could she put it aside, either. The double-charged memory of their passion was always there between them, refusing to go away, and simmering below the surface of every polite question about the order of supper courses or the musical selections.

And although George told himself this was for the best, the honorable, responsible path, he was unhappy and frustrated and as short-tempered as the village bull. He didn't want only memories, and he didn't want to be honorable.

All he wanted was what he couldn't have, and that was Fan.

"You can believe me or not, Brant," he said curtly, tossing the newspaper onto the back of a nearby chair. "At this time of the day, Fan will most likely be in the kitchen or the pantry with Small, planning the day's meals. Not that her whereabouts should matter to you, anyway."

"But it does," said Brant, "and it should to you, too."

He stepped closer, lowering his voice even though they were alone together, with no one to overhear. "Even if you want to slaughter me for telling you this, George, you must hear it, and better from me than anyone else. You swear that the fair Fan Winslow doesn't share your bed, but can you swear as well that there's no other man claiming her favors instead?"

Outraged, George's fingers closed into a fist. "By God, Brant, if that kind of slander is—"

"Listen to me first, George," ordered Brant, raising his own hands, palms open. "You go riding every morning. Have you ever passed Fan on your way, on a little piebald pony?"

"She keeps the pony for her own use," said George, relaxing his fingers. Fan's dawn jaunts on Pie were hardly worth this measure of suspicion. "I've never seen the harm in that. She occasionally goes riding in the early morning, too, just as I do."

"But she's never gone in your company, has she?"

"No," admitted George, fighting his own uneasiness. He'd trusted Fan from the start, and she'd never given him any reason not to. Instead he'd always thought her among the most loyal women in the world: to her father, to Feversham, to her neighbors here in Kent, and, he'd hoped, to him. "But that's because she goes out earlier, before her duties here in the house begin."

"Not always." Brant sighed, troubled. "Late last night, long after Fan had told us she was retiring to her bed, I saw her from the window. She was riding out on her pony, George, hard and fast, the way one does when there's somewhere to go, someone to meet."

"Fan would ride like that," insisted George, trying to forget how Pie had been already been rubbed down and blanketed and returned to his stall when he'd come into the stable this morning, the little horse obviously tired from a hard ride. "She's not about to mince along like some fine lady on a sidesaddle."

"So why insist she was going to bed when she wasn't?" asked Brant with maddening logic. "Why should she creep down the back stairs to the stable? Why behave as if she's something to hide, if she doesn't?"

"Enough of your riddles, Brant." Once again George's fingers knotted into a fist, and so, too, did his stomach. "What the devil are you saying?"

Brant glanced down at George's fisted hand, well aware of the likely consequences, but continued anyway. "There's only two things that will make a woman leave her home at such an hour. The first is a sick child, and the second's a lover. Amuse yourself however you please, George, but if the woman's faithless, then for God's sake, don't let yourself get entangled."

But not Fan, thought George defensively, never his Fan, with her solemn gray eyes and lips made more red with kissing and brambles from the marshes scattered over her dark skirts. Fan would have a third reason for riding alone into the night, a good reason, too, no matter what his brother was trying to prove.

"Damnation, Brant, I do not need your—what is it, Leggett?"

"A Madame Duvall and her assistants, Captain M'Lord, come down from London at your request," announced Leggett from the doorway, his gaze straight ahead and all too uncomfortably aware that he'd interrupted. "I put them in the front parlor to arrange their dunnage for showing."

"Oh, hell." Three days ago, when his relations with Fan had been less complicated, George had invited the fashionable mantua-maker to Feversham as a special surprise for Fan. Now, in his present humor, the last thing he wished was to have his front parlor filled with fussing false Frenchwomen and their trunks of overpriced female fripperies. But could there be a better way to show his brother—and himself—that he still believed in Fan's honesty, her innocence, her loyalty, even, God take him for a fool, her love?

He took a deep breath to compose himself, to present a show of calmness he didn't at all feel. "Leggett, pray tell Madame Duvall that I shall join her shortly. And ask Mistress Winslow to join me there, too."

Leggett bowed, leaving him once again with only his brother's questioning company.

"You are sure of this, George?" he asked softly. "Heed your wise old brother's experience in such matters. Lavish gifts upon a lady, and everything changes between the two of you.''

"Stow your infernal experience," said George, though without any real anger left. How could there be, when Brant was so close to being right? Everything *had* changed between him and Fan, though lavishing gifts would be the least of it. No, everything had changed for them both the moment Fan had first opened the door to Feversham, and while he'd never wish it otherwise, he could only hope that she'd agree.

"Short, brisk strokes—*that* is how it's best done to dislodge the dust and dirt." With her sleeves rolled high over her elbows, Fan demonstrated to the small circle of doubtful, pigtailed sailors, sweeping her broom efficiently back and forth across the floorboards. There was a great deal of dust and dirt that needed dislodging, for the ballroom had been empty and shut up for at least a generation. "I want every inch of the floorboards swept twice, so clean that there won't be a speck of dust left to soil the young ladies' dancing slippers."

"Beggin' pardon, mistress," said Small with his thumbs tucked into the front of his leather apron, present more to supervise the others than to contribute any actual labor. "But I should think a good holystone would do the task a sight better'n any little bundle o' twigs such as that."

"Holystones." Fan sighed her contempt, and shook her head. She might not know the latest London fashion for doing things, but she did understand how best to clean a floor. "I am sorry, Mr. Small, but I do not share your seafaring love of holystones, and holystoning. Perhaps it is better to scratch away at a ship's deck with a block of rough stone, but it will never do for the floorboards of a house.''

"But a holystone scours a deck clean as new snow!'' protested Small, as scandalized as if Fan had maligned the Bible the stones were named for. "There be nothing like it!''

"Nothing like it for sanding wood away to a worthless sliver, either,'' answered Fan firmly. Feversham was her command, and she'd brook no mutineers, not even Small. "No, 'tis far better to sweep first with a clean broom. Then we shall strew the green herbs, here in the basket, over the floorboards, and rub them gently with a sprinkling of spring-water into the boards with those short brushes. Tansy, mint, balm, and fennel. *That* will make these old oak floors gleam like polished mahogany, and give a wondrous fresh scent to the room that even—what is it, Leggett?''

"Captain Lord Claremont wishes you t'join him in the front parlor, mistress,'' said the servant, hovering just inside the doorway to make sure he wouldn't be drafted into sweeping, too. "He says there's company waiting, and he says it's most urgent for you to come quick.''

"Company? At this hour?'' Fan frowned, tapping the bristles of her broom on the floor. There had been a steady stream of footmen bringing notes of acceptance to the house since the invitations had been delivered, but it was unusual for an invited guest to bring his or her reply in person, and rarer still that Fan's presence would be required as well. "You are certain, Leggett?''

Leggett's brows came together in a wounded, sorrowful arc. "'Course I'm certain, mistress. He wouldn't've sent me if he didn't wish you to come to him, and handsomely, too.''

"Very well. I'll be back as soon as I can to see how you're all faring." She handed her broom to one of the men and followed Leggett, smoothing her hair and then her apron as she hurried along the hallway after him. She couldn't imagine what George wanted her for, especially when he must know how much remained to be done with his party only four days away.

At the door to the parlor, she paused, barely remembering to unroll her sleeves over her forearms. Though she could not make out the words, she could hear the high pitch of a woman's voice from inside the room, followed by George's lower rumble. That made her hesitate another moment, both wondering and dreading what she might be interrupting. George didn't entertain ladies, especially not so they'd laugh and trill like the one now was in the parlor. Yet he was the one who'd ordered Fan to come at once, and with her head high she rapped her knuckles on the door, heard the reply, and entered.

And gasped aloud with amazement at what she saw.

The parlor was one of the oldest rooms in the house, with its dark, heavy chairs arranged in a somber row along the tapestry-hung walls, the same room that had inspired Lady Blackerby to such high rudeness. But magically, since the morning when Fan opened the shutters, the parlor had been transformed into a shop filled with costly ladies' wares.

The tall-backed old chairs had been drummed into fresh service displaying ribbons and plumes, garters and stockings, while the long sideboard now served as a parade ground for brightly colored silk slippers. On the floor were the trunks that had held so many wonders, their lids propped open to show off the gloves and laces and pocketbooks that still remained inside.

An exquisitely gowned older lady stood with her hands spread before her and one slippered toe extended from the hem of her dress, as if waiting to begin a dance, while two younger ladies, dressed less extravagantly but with no less style, held a pair of elegant, costly gowns draped over their arms.

They were beautiful women, surrounded by beautiful things, and more than enough to make Fan feel hideously aware of the faded old gown she'd worn today for cleaning, her skirts mussed and daubed with white spots from soap suds and her hair coming unpinned in messy wisps beneath her cap. She might know everything there was to know about sweeping a floor, but she knew nothing—worse than nothing—about silks and muslins, and these other women had realized her ignorance the moment Fan had opened the door.

She could feel her spine stiffening, her shoulders drawing back defensively, and she would have gladly faced down a whole ship's worth of revenue officers if in turn she might be spared the scrutiny of these three sharp-eyed women of fashion.

But perhaps this was some sort of extra fillip for his lady-guests, a benefit at parties that, in Fan's inexperience, she hadn't known existed. Perhaps every host and hostess also included a makeshift shop along with the extra powder, hair combs, and scented soaps in the ladies' withdrawing room.

"This is the lady in question, Your Grace?" purred

the older woman with a winning smile for the duke, and none for Fan.

"The very one, Madame Duvall," said the duke, standing beside George. "This is Mistress Winslow, Feversham's housekeeper, captain, and queen. Mistress Winslow, this is Madame Marie Duvall, come clear from Bond Street in London to turn you out properly."

Fan gasped again, too stunned to reply. This was the garnet earrings all over again, only a thousand times more sinfully *wrong*.

"Now you should know, Mistress Winslow," continued Brant, misinterpreting her gasp as pleasurable surprise, not outrage, "that Madame Duvall dresses all the most fashionable ladies at court, and it's only on account of my brother's heroics and heartfelt invitation that she's agreed to grace this benighted corner of Kent."

But George wasn't looking particularly heroic right now. Instead he was standing off to one side, tugging at his coat's cuffs and steadfastly looking out the window instead of watching the scene before him. Everything about how stiffly he stood betrayed exactly how uncomfortable he was with this fashionable, feminine invasion of his parlor.

And yet his attitude made no sense. This *was* all George's doing, wasn't it? He was the one who wished to treat her like—like his mistress, buying her favors with parasols and handkerchiefs. Hadn't the duke just said that Madame Duvall and her assistants were here only at George's express invitation?

"*Mais oui,* we shall do our best with your housekeeper, Your Grace," said Madame, studying Fan as she glided forward with pitying amusement. "She shall be our greatest challenge, eh?"

But Fan didn't want to be a challenge, pitiful or amusing, and she wasn't going to let this mincing Frenchwoman humiliate her for the sport of it. And *blast* George for putting her in such a position!

"No, thank you, M'dame," she said as proudly as she could, folding her arms in their rumpled sleeves across her chest. "I am sorry you have come such a distance for no reason, but I'm perfectly content with how I dress myself respectable-like, and not pretending to be some strumpety London harlot."

"But dressing yourself respectably is the entire point!" declared George so forcefully that every head in the room turned his way. "Why the devil should I wish you to be rigged out like a strumpety harlot, when you aren't one? You are Feversham's housekeeper, and yes, the household's captain, as Brant noted."

Furiously Fan shook her head. "But that still doesn't mean I must—"

"Hold now, Fan—mistress—and hear me," he interrupted, cutting her short as he sliced his hand through the air. "When you stand by my side to help me greet this infernal pack of guests, I want you to look worthy of your position in this house, a woman who is honest and just and intelligent—a woman I trust with my affairs and my property. That is why I have asked Madame Duvall here. What you wear now does well enough when it's only us, but before others I wish you to be well clothed, as befits your responsibilities. And I ask you, Fan, where is the sinfulness it that?"

"*Absolument,*" said Madame, lightly clapping

her hands in agreement. "There is nothing sinful in dressing well. Now come, permit me to show you what has been chosen especially for you."

But Fan wasn't listening, her mind still trying to sort out what George had just said—no, what he'd *declared,* to her and everyone else in this room.

"You wish me to wear finer clothes as a sign of respect, and not the other way around?" she asked incredulously. "You wish to buy me gowns as a way of *honoring* me?"

"Damnation, yes," growled George, but his smile was meant only for her. "Why is that so blasted hard to understand?"

Because it's me, she thought but didn't say. *Because no one has ever thought so much of me to make such an offer, or pay me such grand compliments for all the world to hear. Because if they'd been alone, she would be in his arms now. Because he was Captain Lord George Claremont and he cared for her as she was, and wished to protect her, and let her dare wish and dream for more….*

"I understand, My Lord Captain," was what she finally said, though the words sounded breathy and odd to her own ears, as if she didn't quite trust them. "On account of your explanation, that is."

His smile widened, and she felt the warmth of it across the room, enough to make her feel like butter left in the sun.

"Consider a new gown rather a uniform," suggested Brant. "Just as George trusses himself up in gold lace and buttons to do battle with the enemy, so must you."

"Enemy, ha," said George with a groan. "When

you meet Sir Simon and his villainous wife, you'll see how truly you speak.''

"But with the proper armor," said Brant with an easy wave of his wrist, "our Fan will take the day. Now run your paces for Miss Winslow, Madame, and mind, she is to have whatever pleases her. Come, George, and let us leave the ladies to it.''

"*Vite, vite,* quickly, quickly," ordered Madame, clapping her hands again to hurry her assistants into action. "You have heard His Grace. We must please this lady, and we've little time to do it.''

Longingly Fan looked after the brothers as they left, and watched them through the window as they walked across the rough lawn, their heads bent in some deep discussion. She'd been foolish to fear she'd come between them; even with the great differences in their lives and personalities, their bond was deep and lasting, and wistfully, she'd always envy them that. How much she'd rather be with them now with their scuffling and mock insults, outside where the familiar salty wind would be blowing from the water, than in here with these women, where she so obviously didn't belong.

"Sit, sit, *s'il vous plaît,*" ordered Madame as one of her assistants held out a chair for Fan to take a seat. On the long table before her were already arranged oversized books that Madame opened facing Fan. Each page featured illustrations of one or two elegantly attired women, showing not only the stylish cut of their gowns, but also the details of their hats and headdresses, fans and muffs and gloves—possibilities and choices bewildering enough to make Fan's head ache.

"First we shall decide upon what fashion, what colors, what lines, shall suit you best, mistress," continued the Frenchwoman, "and then proceed with measuring. We must cut this day and stitch tonight, so that we can fit you tomorrow, with the gown complete for Captain His Lordship's ball the evening after that. *Vraiment,* it is most costly to work with such haste, but when a gentleman insists, eh, we oblige, *oui?*"

Especially, thought Fan, if the gentleman was willing to pay too much for such service.

"One gown," she said firmly, wanting to make sure the mantua-maker understood. "Only one. I'm sorry you brought so much else with you for no reason."

But the Frenchwoman only shrugged, and smiled coyly. "When a gentleman is being generous, most ladies discover there is more that they require than they first thought. It is wise for me to anticipate their desires."

"Perhaps with other ladies," insisted Fan, "but not me. I am not by nature greedy."

Madame clicked her tongue, as if the very notion of mercenary greed was unthinkable. "One gown, *oui,* but even one gown needs the proper slippers, stockings, a fan, ribbons for the hair."

"Perhaps," admitted Fan reluctantly, for even she could see that her sturdy buckled shoes and thick thread stockings would be out-of-place. "But no more than is necessary, Madame."

"As you wish, Mistress Winslow," murmured Madame, but there was an unmistakable gleam of anticipation in her eyes as she turned the pages of the big book. "Captain His Lordship will be in his dress coat, *certainement,* a deep midnight blue. You must contrast with brightness. You should not wear white, no matter the fashion. You need the strength of color. Unless, forgive me, you are wearing this black for mourning?"

"Oh, no," said Fan quickly, trying not to think of her father. Her severe black gowns with the long sleeves had nothing to do with him, for it seemed she'd always worn black or dark gray. *That* had been her uniform, with a dark green apron over it. Her aunt had deemed it the proper color for housekeepers, carrying a somber authority with it, and besides, it was practical and didn't show soil. "It is by my choice."

"Then it is a wrongful one," said the mantua-maker severely, appraising Fan with a frown. "It is not becoming to you, and hides your beauty. Color, that is what you need, a rich shade to set you apart from all the others who will be in white."

Rapidly she flipped through the book's pages, searching for an example. "Your figure is straight and handsome, without any ill features that must be disguised. That is an advantage, *vraiment.*"

She paused, studying Fan again so closely that Fan blushed, as if the woman had looked clear through her clothes.

"You still wear the old stays, don't you?" asked Madame, faintly accusing. "Stiff, stiff, and so very ugly! We must at once put those aside, mistress. You must be graceful, *élégante,* like sweet Venus herself. You see, here, this picture, how the true curves of the body are revealed. Maryanne, fetch the plum Italian lutestring, and the peacock green shot sarcenet to show Mistress Winslow."

Appalled, Fan stared at the illustration Madame was showing. The gown certainly did reveal the true curves of the body, along with a good deal more: the waist was raised very high and the neckline cut so low that that the bodice seemed no more than a strip of straining fabric that scandalously covered only half the breasts. Tiny gathered sleeves clung to the tops of the shoulders and went no further, leaving the arms almost entirely uncovered, and the skirts were so narrow and worn without petticoats that the shape of hips and bottom and even the legs were shamefully apparent. There would be no security in dressing like this, let alone decency, and Fan shuddered to think what would happen in such a low neckline the first time she bent over to adjust a fire or retrieve a dropped spoon.

"I cannot display myself in such a manner," she protested, all too easily imagining what would be said of her in Tunford and in the Company if she did. And her father—Father would be most direct of all, saying she looked like a Brighton whore. "'Tis neither modest, nor decent. And I should also be quite cold."

Once again Madame clicked her tongue, almost scolding. "But it is both modest and decent, mistress, especially for evening, for ladies of fashion. His Grace and Captain His Lordship would agree. And if you fear a chill, we have the softest, the warmest of cashmere shawls. Not—what was it you said?—nothing slatternly."

As if prearranged, one of the assistants draped an oversized cashmere shawl around Fan's shoulders, as soft as a new kitten. She'd never in her life felt anything so seductively luxurious against her skin, but she refused to be seduced.

"This is Kent, M'dame, not London," she insisted, "and what's proper there is different from here. Recollect that I am not a lady of fashion, but only the housekeeper here at Feversham."

Madame only smiled knowingly. "If my eyes do not mistake the signs, you are a great deal more to Feversham's master than only his housekeeper, a good deal more. I see many gentlemen, mistress, and I can see how they regard the women they hold most dear. Love, Mistress, love makes gentlemen forget which is a lady, and which a housekeeper."

Unhappily Fan looked down, her fingers twisting in the ends of the cashmere shawl. "That cannot be so, M'dame. That—that would take a miracle."

"All I can do is dress you so that he will forget every other lady in the room," said Madame gently, reaching out to pat Fan's arm. "But the miracle—ah, mistress, that you and your handsome lord captain have already made on your own."

Chapter Twelve

Carefully Fan twisted the spermaceti candles into the final wall sconce, then climbed down from the wide cushioned bench, rubbing the stickiness from the wax onto her apron and slipping her shoes back on her feet. She wouldn't trust anyone else with such costly candles—she'd gasped aloud when she'd seen the reckoning that had come in the box from the London chandler—but the duke himself had assured her expansively that only spermaceti candles would do for such a grand gathering, and the cost was nothing compared with knowing such candles would neither smoke nor drip down upon the guests. She wanted everything exactly right for tomorrow, everything perfect for George.

She'd waited until this last night to put the candles in all the sconces and chandeliers in the ballroom. Though the effect would surely be different tomorrow night when the eight dozen candles would be lit instead of the single lantern on the floor at her feet, the silent room already seemed to be alive with anticipation.

And in a way, so was she. Madame Duvall had

delivered her finished gown this afternoon, and now it hung waiting in her room like some elegant visitor come to call. Madame had had her way with the color, a brilliant shot silk sarcenet that the mantua-maker had called peacock, a shade that shimmered from blue to green as Fan moved, and made her pale skin glow and her eyes bright in a way that plain black wool never could. Along with the gown had come insubstantial slippers in matching silk with beaded flowers on the toes, fragile thread stockings the color of rose petals, and yellow ribbon garters because, as Madame had wickedly warned, a lady never knew when a gentleman might wish one for a souvenir.

There was, of course, only one gentleman in Fan's life who'd any such right, and Fan smiled, every bit as wicked as Madame as she tried to imagine George's reaction to discovering that incongruously bright yellow garter. She'd scarcely seen him at all these last days, and never without the duke in tow, and though she liked Brant, she couldn't help looking forward to the time when it would once again be only her and George at Feversham.

Tomorrow night would be like that, the two of them together, side by side, despite the crowds around them, and her smile widened in anticipation. It would still be a challenge, and the other guests would likely still be as shocked by her presence as she'd first feared, but the preparations had served to make her feel confident and assured, and the gown had done the rest. Now, as hard as she'd worked this week, as late as it was now, she doubted she'd sleep at all from purest excitement, and humming to herself, she gathered her skirts in one hand and swept with giddy enthusiasm across the wide, empty dance floor.

Her shadowy image skipped with her, reflected and fragmented over and over in the lantern's light across the rows of tall windows like some fairy-wraith from the marshes. And why not, she thought wistfully. The entire evening ahead, from the gown to the candles to even George himself, would be as unreal and short-lived as any fairy-magic, to be enjoyed before it vanished except for the dearest of bittersweet memories.

The notion sobered her, and she stopped before the window, hugging her arms across her chest as she stared out across the lawns. The dew had fallen, twinkling in the lantern's light on the grass closest to the house. No moon, no stars, and patches of hazy damp drifting from the water: a perfect night for smuggling, and that hard, unforgiving reality flattened the rest of her lighthearted anticipation.

But she was almost done with that part of her life, wasn't she? Soon the moon would be the moon and nothing more, and stars would be only for wishing....

The tap on the glass startled her, making her jump and catch her breath.

"Mistress Winslow!" mouthed the boy silently on the other side of the window, and she hurried to unlatch the door that opened to the lawn. The boy entered warily, sliding sideways through the door, his gaze darting around the empty ballroom as he pulled on the sides of his knitted cap. Matthew Carr was no more than twelve, and small for his age at that, but he'd been a part of the Company for years now, carrying messages and standing watch for the others on the beach.

"I tried th' kitchen first, mistress, same as regular," he said, wiping his nose on the sleeve of his jersey, "but it be all full of them Navy-men, crashing an' swearing about, with you nowhere in sight."

"That's right," said Fan, keeping her voice low even though they were alone. "There's to be a grand party here tomorrow night, and they're working to make ready. Now what's brought you here, Matty? What's about?"

"Markham," he said succinctly. "Thursday night, same as always."

"*This* Thursday?" asked Fan, surprised. "He's not due for another week."

Matthew sniffed again, visibly wounded. "That be the message, mistress, coming through the fishing boats same as ever. You know I always tell you true, don't I?"

"Yes, yes, you do," she said quickly, reaching into her pocket for a shilling that she pressed into his palm. His father, another Company man, had died of consumption last winter, and while his mother did odd sewing and mended fishermen's nets to make ends meet, Matthew prized himself on contributing to her support, and the coin was instantly tucked inside his pocket for safekeeping. "You always tell me true, Matt. It's just that I didn't expect Captain Markham to return this soon, especially this week when we've so much to do here at Feversham."

It wasn't only her responsibilities here at the house that would complicate matters, or the fact that the closer she became to George, the more difficult it would be to slip away unnoticed. There was also the higher fee that Markham would be expecting, and uneasily she wondered if coming early was his way of pressuring her for even more. She was in no position to begin accepting a shipment every week instead of every two, or even three; her customers simply did not consume that much tea, and she would be left with the difference, a dangerously incriminating hazard that would, somehow, have to be hidden away, and a whole village made to keep the secret.

Yet by Friday dawn, she'd be done with it. One more run, and generations of her family's leadership would glide forever from her fingers, and she would be free. One more run, and it would all be someone else's puzzle to sort out, not hers.

"But the Company's trade always comes first," said Matthew stoutly, and with the absolute certainty of his age. "That's what Father said, t'put your trust in the Winslows and the Company, for they'll never sell you wrong."

So Will Hood had kept her intentions secret; she was grateful, if surprised, by this one last act of loyalty. Soon none of them would speak of her with such respect. None would know that she'd given up the Company to save her own life, and George's with it. Most likely none of them would ever deign to speak to her again after such a betrayal. But her father, if he'd lived, would call her selfish and cowardly and a traitor and worse, far worse.

"Tell the others to be there Thursday," she said. "Tell them what you've told me, that Markham has changed his sailing date. And tell them to gather a quarter hour earlier, for I've something I must—"

"Who's that?" demanded Matthew uncertainly, already backing away towards the door. "Someone's calling you, mistress!"

Fan turned, listening. The second time she heard it, too: George calling her name, and coming closer as he did.

"Hurry, Matty, away with you!" she whispered, but the boy had already fled, racing across the dewy grass. Swiftly Fan closed the door after him, turning the latch just as George entered the room.

"Here you are," he said, smiling as he joined her. "Small said he thought you were here."

She smiled nervously, wondering if he'd heard the boy. "I was setting the candles for tomorrow night. I cannot remember a time when there were so many. What a blaze of light you'll have for your guests!"

"We will at that." Though he'd sensed her nervousness, he'd misread the reason for it, and stopped apart from her, his hands clasped behind his back and without the kiss of greeting she'd expect. "You've done a splendid job with your arrangements, Fan. The secret of any success always lies in mastering the details, doesn't it?"

She nodded proudly. "I can't prepare for everything that might happen, of course, but I do believe your guests will be most pleased." She pointed up to the sconces. "Even down to the proper candles."

"We'll need every one of them if it's another gloomy night like this one." He cleared his throat and looked past her, out the window. "Not a star in the sky, is there?"

"But I like a dark sky," she protested, hoping he'd keep looking up for those stars and away from the footprints that the boy had left in the wet grass. "It's more mysterious this way."

"Oh, yes, it's mysterious enough, wondering who or what's hiding in it." He nodded sagely, the lantern's light playing over the sharp planes of his face. This late in the day, he'd loosened the neckcloth around his collar. The dark shadow of stubble had softened the line of his jaw in a pleasingly intimate way, and she caught herself wishing he had kissed her after all.

"A night like this is what a captain prays for," he continued, "especially when he wants to creep along the shore unnoticed, or catch another ship with its watch sleeping. That's how most captures are made, you know, not with all guns a-firing and mighty heroics, but by playing cat-and-mouse surprise, with false colors and calls in another language. Not that you'd think like that, of course. To you ladies, fog means mysterious tumbledown abbeys and other Gothic nonsense."

"Not all ladies think that way," she said, thankful he'd never know how similar her thoughts had been to his own. A night meant for smuggling could also be one that benefited the king: she had to admit she'd never considered that, thinking of fog and starless nights as her Company's ally and no one else's. "Leastways, I don't."

He smiled without turning back towards her. "That's because you're not like most ladies, and a precious good thing that is, too."

"Hah, it's a good thing I think like a gentleman?"

"More that we seem to be cut from the same bolt of cloth," he said easily, leaving her to guess if he was teasing or serious, or perhaps a bit of both. "We suit one another, in the best possible ways. And you can be sure, Mistress Fan, that no one will ever mistake you for a gentleman."

She laughed softly, accepting the compliment. He did make her feel more feminine—not as a weakness, not as a failing, which was how she felt too often when dealing with the Company, but in a way that left her happy and desired and glowing with contentment. And he was right: they *did* suit one another.

"Very well, then," she said, copying his manner. "Tell me, pray. What do tumbledown abbeys have to do with fog and starless nights?"

He shook his head, still gazing up at the overcast sky as he tapped his fingertips lightly against the glass of the window. "Not a blessed thing, as far as I can see. So who was the boy in here with you, Fan?"

"The boy?" she repeated, startled. She couldn't deny Matthew had been here, but she couldn't very well tell George the entire truth, either. "Yes. That was Matthew Carr, a boy I sometimes hire for work about the house. He's too small to be of much real use, but his father is dead and his mother not well. She relies upon what Matty can earn, and I'm willing to make sure he always brings home something in his pocket."

That much *was* true, with nothing in it for George to doubt or question, and he didn't.

"Then he should come to me," he said firmly, "and we should see what can be arranged on a more regular basis. There's always a place in the Navy for an enterprising boy, especially one with a widowed mother to keep. When I'm given a new command, I'll put him on my ship's list, and keep an eye on him for you. If he's as promising as you say, he'll make his own way in no time."

"That is kind of you, George," she murmured, unfortunately aware that Matthew and his mother, who shared the local contempt for any authority that served his majesty, would likely spit in the eye of such a golden opportunity. "But I do not believe his mother is willing to part with him just yet."

"Ah," he said softly, a lifetime of his own regrets and losses wrapped in that single syllable, and Fan remembered how orphaned George had been sent to sea at a younger age than Matthew. "Then perhaps we can find work for him with Small below stairs until he's grown to size. But tell him to present himself like a man, at the door, and no more skulking about Feversham in the dark like a little thief. I've heard the smugglers have lately grown more daring, and I wouldn't want him running afoul of those rough bastards."

"No," she said unhappily, knowing she could hardly undo what had long ago been done. "His mother wouldn't want him to come to harm, either."

"You're kind to worry over them both." He turned towards her, reaching out to touch her cheek. "The world is full of widows and fatherless boys, and most people manage determinedly to look the other way. But not you, Fan."

"They're my people," she said simply, turning just enough to rub her cheek against his fingers. She loved being touched by him, how he could turn the most innocent brush of his hand into a caress. "My responsibility."

"Because you choose them to be," he said, sliding his fingers into the sleek wings of her hair, gently loosening the strands from the tight knot at her nape. "It's in your nature."

She smiled, and when he pulled her cap away and dropped it to the floor, she didn't protest, instead letting him slowly pull each pin from her hair, one by one by one, until the heavy coil uncurled and fell down her back.

"I am no different from you, you know," she said

as she shook her now free hair over her shoulders. "I doubt there are many other captains who look after their crewmen like you. Mr. Small, and Danny, and Leggett, and the others—they'd gladly follow you to the ends of the earth."

"They already have," he admitted, gathering up her hair and letting it slip like silk through his fingers. "Though a frigate's crew is not quite as vast a responsibility as your entire village."

"Not all of Tunford," she protested, chuckling as she came closer and rested her hands upon the broad wall of his chest. "Only a small part of it."

"Only a part," he repeated as he drew her closer, letting her feel his body against hers in a way that seemed both protective and seductive. "The most fortunate part, I'd say. But then who looks after you?"

"I look after myself," she said, striving to sound proud of her self-reliance. But even she could hear the uncertainty in her voice, a forlorn little tremor that made this sound more like a confession than a bold declaration.

"The pistol," he said, frowning down at her with concern. "I've told you before that that's a false sort of confidence for a woman alone, Fan, even for you. The world is full of rogues and scoundrels who'll think nothing of twisting it right from your hands to use against you. For my sake, if not for your own, I wish you to take more care."

"But I shall be fine," she insisted, toying with the buttons on his waistcoat to avoid meeting the question in his eyes. Soon she could give him that assurance and mean it, for once she parted with the Company, she intended to spend every night safe and snug beside her own hearth, in her own bed. "And I never journey farther than Tunford."

"Tunford." He rolled the village's name in his mouth in an ominous growl, curling the long strands of her hair around his hand. "So is that where you go riding alone at night? Is there some special rogue that you go to see there?"

Instantly Fan froze, the warm, teasing mood between them broken. She should have guessed this would come; she should have known that what she shared with George could not last, not with so many differences between them.

"Is it a secret, then?" he asked, his voice turning grim and the tension building with each second she hesitated. "Hell."

"Oh, George," she said unhappily, her heart more full of sorrow than fear. "As much as I wish I could tell you, I cannot. It is a secret, a very grave secret, but it's not mine to share with you or anyone else. There are others who would not wish it, others that I have promised, and now—now likely I've already said more than is wise. But I cannot tell you more, George. I—I cannot."

"Cannot, Fan?" he asked roughly, still holding her steady with his hand tangled in her hair so she could not look away. "Or will not?"

"I *will* not, George, because I choose not to," she declared, her heart racing in her chest. Oh, God help her, this wasn't a choice at all. She didn't wish it to end like this, with him suspecting her of a sin she hadn't committed, but to tell him the truth and defend herself was impossible. "But I *can* not because I am loyal to those who have trusted me with their secrets and their lives!"

"Double blast it, Fan!" he exploded, jerking his hand free from her hair so quickly that she lost her balance and stumbled back. "I'm trying to trust you, too, but you make it so damned hard I'd be a fool to do it!"

"Then be a fool," she challenged angrily, rubbing the side of her head where he'd pulled at her hair. "Because I'm already a fool to trust you, if this is how little you value my trust, yes, and me with it!"

Anger had turned his eyes hard and fierce as a hawk in the marshes, and set his jaw with determination. She'd always thought of him as a gentleman, the son of a duke, and yet suddenly here was this other side of him she hadn't seen: intensely male and forceful, the ruthless warrior, the fighting captain that earned and demanded the respect of hundred rough sailors.

But not from her, not now. "Is that what you believe, then, Fan?" he thundered, his voice echoing against the windows in the empty ballroom. "That I have no regard, no affection for you?"

"I do not know what to believe," she answered furiously, too angry and too on edge to rein her emotions in. "First you tell me we are two of a kind, that we're cut from the same bolt of cloth, and God knows what other pretty-talk claptrap meant to befuddle the ladies, and then you say you cannot trust me because I won't confess every last confidence that's been made to me!"

"Don't question my word, lass," he warned, stepping closer to her. "I'm not a liar. I say what I mean, or I don't speak at all."

"Then tell me what you *do* mean," she countered defiantly without backing away, and as soon as she'd spoken she realized how long she'd wanted to ask him exactly that. She also realized she was daring him, a dare that tempted sanity as well as fate. But her father and the Company had long ago taught her that recklessness could bring its own kind of freedom, and what greater dare was there in life than love?

"If you live so much by truth alone, George," she continued, "then tell me all these ways that we are so much alike!"

"You do not know?" he asked, his voice dropping low, incredulous. "You, Fan?"

"I wouldn't ask if I did," she answered, still challenging, though the shiver that raced up and down her spine betrayed something else entirely. Not that it made any sense. She was furious with him for doubting her, just as he was furious with her for not answering, but neither fury made for an explanation of why she kept looking at his mouth and the little peppering of the day's beard over his upper lip and thinking of how wickedly, how wrongly, much she wanted to kiss him.

"Damnation, Fan, we're tacking in circles over the same patch of water here," he grumbled, but his manner seemed to have shifted, too, the anger itself fading while the passion of it remained, the way the flames of a fire die down only to leave the greatest heat waiting below in the coals.

"Then tell me, and be done with it," she demanded in a rough whisper, impatiently shoving her unpinned hair back from her face. "Tell me *now*."

"Blast it, Fan, you know already," he muttered hoarsely, watching as she lifted her arms to fuss with her hair, his gaze sliding down to how her breasts shimmied above the top of her stays. "We wouldn't be fighting like this if you weren't suited to me."

"We're not fighting," she said, and licked her lips which had, quite suddenly, gone dry. No regrets, she told herself fiercely, no regrets at all. "You'd know it if we were. Now tell me."

"Damnation, Fan, I'm a sailor, not a poet," he said. "I can't tell you why we belong together, or how, or—oh, blast, how can I explain this?"

George didn't give her any warning as he pulled her into his arms, nor did she seem to expect any. More likely both of them had been expecting this moment for days, or weeks, or maybe even from that first morning when she'd opened the front door to find him on Feversham's step.

God knows he had. He kissed her now, marveling at how she knew the exact angle to tip her head back for him, and marveling, too, at how readily she answered his kiss, not turning squeamish or shy the way some women would, but meeting his tongue with her own. He could taste her passion, her desire, until he couldn't tell where her mouth began and his ended, enough to make him groan aloud from wanting the rest.

And the rest was there, too, as eager as he was himself. He could tell by how she was arching against him, her breasts pressing into his chest when he circled her arms around the shoulders, the touch of her fingertips on the nape of his neck sending delicious chills down his backbone. Somehow—he couldn't recall exactly when—the white kerchief she'd tucked into her neckline for modesty had pulled free and disappeared, leaving the twin mounds of her breasts temptingly uncovered except for the shifting curtain of her hair.

He'd asked her flat-out where she went at night in Tunford, the way Brant had wanted him to, and she hadn't answered. She hadn't even tried, only asking him to trust her. Trust wasn't an excuse, and didn't come close to being an explanation, yet because it was Fan, trust her he would. If that made him a fool, then so be it. At least they'd be fools together, for however brief a time the Admiralty would allow them.

He slid his hands from her waist over her hips, feeling the richness of her curves even through the layers of petticoats. He loved that magical place where the unyielding whalebone in a woman's stays gave way to her flesh alone, how the contrast made the flesh seem that much softer and more lush and so fascinatingly different from his own, and he slid his hands lower, relishing how her bottom filled his hands. He pulled her closer, against the hard, insistent proof of his desire, doubtless lifting her feet clear from floor in the process. But he needed her to feel exactly how much he wanted her: how much he wanted her *now*.

"George, ah, my own George," she murmured, her words ragged and her lips damp as she pressed them against his throat. She was fumbling blindly with his clothes, impatience making her clumsy, or perhaps she was simply as befuddled by male fastenings as he was with stays and petticoats. Then, finally, she managed to find her way beneath his coat and waistcoat and tug his shirt free of his trousers. Her hands snaked up along his back, her touch warm, demanding, on his bare skin, making him gulp for air, just as he tugged down the front of her gown to free her breasts, making her gulp in exactly the same way.

They suited each other, all right, he thought with whatever part of his brain remained able to think as his hand cupped the sweet, heavy weight of her bared breast. How could she ever doubt it, even for an instant? She was the first woman he'd ever met who was every bit as damned independent as he was himself, and he wouldn't have her any other way.

She was looking up at him now through her lashes, her gaze slightly, charmingly out of focus, her mouth red and swollen from his kisses and her breathing catching as he teased the taut crest of her nipple.

"You—you're making me dizzy, George," she whispered, clinging to him for support, her smile wobbling with wonder.

"You're doing the same wicked business to me, lass," he said hoarsely, surprised, really, that he could manage to say that much as he kissed her again. Over her head he had a fleeting glimpse of their shadowy selves reflected over and over in the tall windows and looking-glasses, and crazily he thought of how this was something Brant would do, not him. And then Fan shook her tangled hair back from her face and slid her hand around to the flat of his belly.

"*Fan.*" His voice was strained as he struggled for self-control. Though he wasn't Brant, he wasn't some green boy, either, and he'd had enough experience with enough women scattered around the world, that he shouldn't be this close to being unmanned.

But this wasn't all those other women in his past. This was Fan, his Fan, and this was now, and with a wordless groan he swept her backwards, onto the broad cushioned bench along the wall. She leaned up on her elbows, all creamy pale skin and black hair, dark skirts and white linen against the striped cushions.

As she watched him yank his arms from the sleeves of his coat, her eyes were enormous by the light of the lantern on the floor behind him, yet there was not a breath of shyness or reluctance as, finally, she linked her arms around his shoulders to welcome him and draw him down, over her, onto her.

They were past words now, past anything but the rawest sensation, their movements driven by urgency. Swiftly he shoved her skirts over her knees, above her garters and the tops of her stockings to discover the softest skin imaginable, there along the insides of her thighs. She was trembling, yet still she eagerly eased her legs farther apart for him, and as he slid his hand higher, he realized he was shaking, too. She was wet and hot, arching against his fingers, instinctively trying to draw him deeper.

With her little breathy gasps filling his ears, she couldn't wait much longer, and neither could he. He tore at the fall of his trousers, heedless of the buttons he sent skittering across the floor, and settled himself over her. As gently as he could, he entered her, feeling her tightness gradually yield to him, groaning as he found the heaven that was her body. She stiffened beneath him, curling her legs around his waist and as he began to move, she gave a small cry that was halfway between a sob and a laugh.

Instantly he stopped, realizing now the truth he'd been too bullheaded to understand. "You are— were—a virgin, weren't you, Fan?" he gasped, the blood still pounding. "Are you all right?"

"Oh, yes—yes," she managed to whisper raggedly. "It's not that it hurts. It is only—only different than what I expected."

He grunted, not exactly sure what that meant, but deciding to take it for permission to continue. Slowly he moved again, and this time he was rewarded with a sigh that could only be one of pleasure. Tentatively she began to match his rhythm, finding her own pace as her confidence and pleasure built. Soon their movements grew more and more urgent, more demanding, as the tension spiraled higher and higher between them until, with one final thrust, he brought them to a release that left them both shuddering and spent.

Mindful of the width of the bench, he carefully lifted his weight from her, shifting to his side and bringing her with him, their arms and legs still intimately tangled together. He smoothed the dark tangle of her hair back from her face to kiss her, and saw the tears that streaked her face.

"Oh, lass, I'm sorry," he said with gruff but genuine remorse. "I should have known you were—well, what you were. I never wanted to hurt you like this."

"But you didn't," she said, trying to smile even as she sniffed back her tears, "and I'm not, not at all. I'm only crying because it was so—so much *more*."

"Ah," he said cautiously, not beginning to understand. He'd never experienced anything as bone-shatteringly amazing as what he'd just shared with her, but he didn't think that was what she meant. "Yes."

"Yes." She sniffed again, but her smile seemed more steady as she shyly traced her finger along his jaw. "And I'm not sorry, either, not at all."

"But you deserved more, Fan," he said. Damnation, she meant so much to him, yet he couldn't help but feel he was making another righteous mess of all of this. "Better, anyway. There should have been roses and champagne and a feather bed instead of this wretched bench in a drafty great room, and all the rest that ladies deserve in such, ah, circumstances."

"But I'm not a lady, George," she said with a wistfulness that tore at his conscience, and his heart. "You always forget that."

"What you are, Fan, is the woman I love," he said firmly. "That's more than sufficient for me, and I'm not bloody likely to forget it, either."

"Love?" she repeated, clearly too stunned to venture more.

"Yes, love, because I love you," he said, surprising himself as much as her. Not because he didn't mean it, of course, but because he *did*, more than any words he'd ever spoken. The surprising part was that he'd never before said those particular three words, in that significant combination, to anyone else in his life. "I love you."

At once she pressed his fingers over his lips. "Don't say such things, George!"

Gently he pulled her hand aside, turning it so he could kiss her moist little palm. "I told you before, Fan. I'm no liar, especially about this."

But she shook her head, her eyes troubled and pleading as she drew her hand away from his. "Please, George. Don't make promises you've no intention of keeping once we leave this room."

"Then stay with me after we leave it," he said, the idea immediately appealing. "Upstairs, to my rooms, to my bed, and we'll watch the dawn come together."

She sighed, and sat upright back on her heels and away from him, pulling her bodice back into place.

"I do not know if that is such a wise plan, George, not for either of us."

"The devil take such wisdom." He sat, too, impatiently rebuttoning whichever buttons still survived on his trousers. "Fan, listen to me. I could receive my sailing orders from the Admiralty tomorrow morning, even tonight, and then be shot to pieces by some French bastard a week after that."

"For men it is war, for women childbirth," she said softly, sadly. "Death is too much a part of life."

"True enough," he said. Tonight he'd put her at risk of bearing his child, a responsibility he'd also accept with the rest of her. "And knowing that makes me not give a damn what the world will say or think or do about me, Fan. I answer to my king and the Admiralty, but beyond that I'm only accountable to myself and my honor."

"But Brant says you could become duke next because he has no children," she said, her unhappiness palpable. "He says you must be mindful of that in every—every connection you make."

"And I say my brother should be mindful of his own damned business." He reached for her, drawing her forward and into his arms, where, as far as he was concerned, she absolutely belonged. "I love you, Fan Winslow, and only you have the right to tell me if I'm a bloody fool for doing so."

"You know I won't," she said, dashing the heel of her hand against the tears that had again spilled down her cheeks. "I won't because I love you, too. Blast you, George! So now we must be fools together? Is that how it shall be?"

He chuckled, much preferring to have her swear at

him like this than weep. "We've made such a good start of our foolery that I'm not about to quit now."

"Haven't we just." She narrowed her eyes at him, and while this time her sniff had less to do with tears, it was more than enough to make him laugh with happiness.

"Two fools together," he said. "I told you, Fan. We just might suit each other after all."

Chapter Thirteen

Fan woke slowly, hovering pleasantly in a drowsy haze. She opened her eyes just far enough to see that the room was still midnight-dark, time enough for drifting back to the blissful world of sleep. Dawn and her responsibilities would come soon enough, and with a contented sigh she pulled the coverlet up a little higher over her shoulder. The pillow beneath her cheek seemed as soft as a duckling's down, the mattress like drifting upon a cloud, the warm weight of the man's arm curled over her bare hip was both comforting and protective, and—

The man's arm? At once the drowsy haze vanished, and she jerked upright, now pulling the coverlet higher over her thoroughly naked self. That male arm now resting on her thigh belonged to George, her George, and as the memory of every glorious, wanton thing she'd done with him this night came racing back to her, she let out a long, low sigh of amazement, even as she blushed there in the darkness. Being country-raised, she thought she'd known what to expect from her first time with a man, but the reality of the pleasure that George had drawn from her body was far, far beyond her innocent imaginings.

But what had been the price of that knowledge?

She was naked in the great curtained bed of Captain Lord George Claremont, and everything in her life had changed. She was most definitely no longer a virgin, neither respectable nor decent in the eyes of the world, at least not once the ears of the world heard of it.

She'd become yet one more sorry servant to be tumbled by her master, and she'd never be able to look at that broad cushioned bench near the window the same way again. Ending her family's long if lawless connection with the Winslow Company would pale to nothingness beside her playing the whore to an aristocratic officer, making her a traitor to her own class and blood. The only way she could possibly compound such a disaster would be if she bore a Claremont bastard.

And yet none of that mattered because he loved her.

That was the greatest wonder of it all, and from any other man than George, she wouldn't have believed it. But George—ah, George wasn't like any other man under heaven. She could marvel or wonder at such a declaration, but she'd never, ever doubt the truth of it. She was the one who'd always lived with deception, not him. He loved her, Fan Winslow, without a care for his own position or rank, and she'd returned his pledge with one of her own, giving him her body along with her heart.

Carefully she slid back down against the pillows, curling her body around his. She was fascinated by the differences between them, the roughness of the dark hair on his chest and legs and the stubble on his jaw, the play of his muscles, the warmth of his skin against hers, his musky male scent so unlike her own. Instinctively in his sleep he shifted closer against her, as if there was no other place she could possibly belong than with him. She smiled, nestling against his chest, and as she did her foot brushed against the heavy bedcurtains.

Brilliant morning sunlight burst through the narrow parting that she'd created, slicing across her, across George. With a yelp of horror she flung back the coverlet and scrambled from the bed, snatching up her clothes from where they'd been discarded here and there around the room last night.

"What the devil," muttered George, burying his face in the pillow to avoid the light. "Come back here, Fan, and close those infernal curtains."

"I can't—I can't!" she wailed, fighting her arms through the sleeves of her shift as she pulled it over her head. "Oh, George, it must be half past nine already, and all the others will have been awake and working for *hours!*"

"What if they have?" With a grunt of resignation, he rolled onto his back, linking his hands comfortably behind his head. It also made him as tempting as sin itself, sprawled naked without a lick of self-consciousness against the rumpled sheets. "They'll manage perfectly well without either one of us to interfere, lass."

"I *know,*" she tried to explain as she struggled with a knot in the drawstring at the neckline of her shift. "But it's all my responsibility as Feversham's housekeeper. I have to be certain that everything is properly done for your guests."

"It will be, sweetheart," he said, his lordly conviction unshakable. "You've done nothing else for days. But a good officer must know when to step back and trust his followers to carry out his orders. You can't do everything yourself."

"I know, I know, I *know*," she said, finally dropping on the edge of the bed with a sigh, the neckline of her shift still untied. "But I've never had so much to do, or such a chance to make you proud before the finest folk in the county, and—oh, George, we're both of us usually awake before the roosters, and the whole house knows it. Leggett, Small, Danny, your brother and the others—they all could have guessed by now why we haven't showed ourselves."

"Doubtless they have," agreed George easily. "They're all clever enough. Except perhaps for Danny, though I imagine the others will have enlightened him by now."

"Oh, *bother*." She bowed her head, letting her tangled hair fall on either side of her face. He was right, of course, and she'd no reason to act surprised. Given the proprietary interest George's men had in him and his actions, they'd be bound to uncover such a fascinating revelation about their captain and the housekeeper in no time at all.

George leaned forward, curling her hair behind her ear with a tenderness that made her shiver. "Regrets, Fan?"

"No regrets, no," she said softly, and she meant it. In this single night, he'd taught her the joy to be found in love, a lesson she intended to remember always. "Not at all."

"Well, then," he said, his smile endearingly lopsided. "You must know I still do love you, even here in the full glare of the morning. That hasn't changed.''

"And I love you," she said, her own smile wistful, all too aware of how fleeting that love of his might be if he ever learned of her role with the Company. "But you forget what a humble little country lass I've always been before you came. I'm not like you, George, so noble and grand that people have to gawk, especially when you're bedecked with gold lace and medals.''

He cocked one skeptical eyebrow. "You underestimate yourself, sweetheart," he said. "And overestimate me. You're a proud, beautiful woman, Fan, nothing humble at all, and tonight in that new gown of yours you'll rival every titled lady in the realm. There won't be a single glance spared for me.''

She couldn't help flushing with pleasure at the compliment, nor could she keep from running her fingers lightly along his whiskery jaw. Ah, how much she did love him!

"Not one, excepting one from every last woman in the room," she said wryly. "Recall the way the Blackerby ladies fell upon you, and reckon that by a hundred.''

"How fortunate, then, that I shall have you there to defend me," he said, taking her hand to press her fingers to his lips. "I'm proud of you, Fan, deuced proud. Side by side on the quarterdeck we'll stand, and no prisoners taken, either.''

"More likely those two same fools together," she warned as he kissed her fingers, and wished she could forget everything else except the deliciously teasing sensation. "Mind me, George. Kitchen gossip flies upstairs faster than a cinder on the wind, and your guests will hear of—of *us* before they've had time to leave off their cloaks.''

''They'll know it sooner than that if they see us together, lass,'' he said, nibbling gently on one finger to try to distract her. ''Let them look their fill, I say.''

''They will do that.'' She sighed, wishing she could be so brashly confident about the future. She knew the scandal would race among the well-bred guests tonight, but how long would it take before it reached the hearths of the cottages in Tunford? And how many days after that would she have before the other side of the same scandal, the part involving her role with the Winslow Company, swept from those same cottages back to Feversham? ''I've lived alone here for so long that it's not easy to now have so many others watching me—*us*—like players on a stage for their amusement.''

''I told you before, Fan, that they don't matter,'' he said firmly. ''The only ones we must please are each other. Now forget about those harpies and the wines to be uncorked and every other infernal nuisance that is plaguing you, love, and bring your sweet self back here where you belong.''

He patted the bed beside him, making his desire so abundantly clear that she had to look away before she could speak. She was such a hopeless coward, even in this!

''Do you love me enough that you would ignore whatever scandal you heard whispered about me?'' she said hurriedly, before she lost her nerve. ''Would you trust me and listen to my reasons, no matter how wicked or wrongful the tale might seem? Do you love me enough for that?''

''Tales of an innocent like you, Fan?'' he asked

incredulously, grinning as if she were making a jest. "What in blazes could anyone say of you, sweetheart?"

"I didn't say there were any such tales," she said in a rush, hedging against the truth that she still couldn't bring herself to tell. "I only asked that if there were any, then would you take my side?"

"Ah, so that is it, a test to prove my love." He relaxed visibly, his smile warmly inviting as he drew her back against his chest and into his arms. "Consider my challenge passed, then, sweetheart. No matter how vile the gossip or scandal, I vow to turn away my ears and not listen to a word of it against my own dear Fan."

Troubled, she closed her eyes and listened to the steady beat of his heart. She should confess everything now, and not let him hear of her past from another. If he truly loved her as he claimed, then she could tell him the truth, and he would forgive her. For her sake, just this once, he'd have to put aside all his scruples and allegiances and his life's devotion to doing what was honorable. If she promised that there'd be only one more run and then she'd be done with the Company forever, then he'd understand, wouldn't he?

Wouldn't he?

But if she truly loved him as she said, how could she ever ask him to make such a sacrifice for her worthless sake?

"Oh, George," she whispered unhappily. "I love you so much—so much!—but it's not as simple as that."

"But it is," he said, brushing her hair back to kiss her forehead. "And I'll make it so for you if it isn't.

All you must remember is that I love you, and you love me. That will be enough, Fan. For us, that will always be enough.''

Yet as he tipped her back into the crook of his arm to kiss her, Fan could only pray that he was right.

The vagaries of life had made George leery of declaring anything a certainty, but on this morning he was absolutely sure that his brother would seek him out. The only variable would be how long it would take Brant to find his way to George's rooms after Fan had left.

"Good day, Your Grace," murmured Leggett, bowing with George's razor in his hand.

George twisted in his chair to find Brant, his brother's expression exceedingly grim. Twenty minutes was all it had taken, then, scarce time for George to be shaven. He'd never known Brant to be so prompt.

"Leggett, leave us," he said, wiping the last of the soap from his face with a towel as he rose from his chair. "His Grace and I wish to speak alone."

Pointedly Brant stayed silent, watching the servant bow himself from the room, hardly a fortuitous sign. Brant was seldom silent, and even without a word spoken, the tension between them was thick as a Channel fog.

"So," said Brant at last, every word clipped. "I suppose I must congratulate you on taking another prize, even if swiving your housekeeper is not quite of the same order as seizing Spanish treasure ships. Or perhaps it is. Was she worth the wait, George?"

"No more, Brant," said George, determined to keep his temper because Fan would wish it. "I won't have you speak of Fan as if she were one of your own tawdry harlots."

"Why the devil shouldn't I?" demanded Brant. "Clearly you have. This room smells like a Chelsea whorehouse on a Sunday morning."

"Damnation, Brant, I said no more!" George forced himself to take a deep breath, then another. "I love Fan Winslow, and I won't listen to her slandered like this. I love her, mind?"

"Love." Brant's chuckle was remarkably unsympathetic. "Did you ask her where she goes at night, George? Did you ask her who she sees, what she does, that's such a great bloody secret?"

"I asked," said George, "and I was satisfied with her answer."

That wasn't exactly true, for George had found her answer about where she went in Tunford as cloudy and roundabout as that nonsense about loving her despite her past. But as long as he had her heart, he'd be willing to grant her a secret or two. God knows he'd a few of his own.

"Regardless of Fan's station," he continued, "she is the most honorable woman I have ever met, and while it may be impossible for you to understand, Brant, because I love her, I trust her as well."

But Brant had stopped listening. "You had her first, didn't you?" he asked, his expression full of fascinated disbelief. "That's what all this idiocy really means, George, isn't it? You took her maidenhead, and in return you've made her a saint."

"I respect her, Brant, and if you can't see how—"

"How can you say you respect her when you've done this?" Brant shook his head. "I'll grant you Fan Winslow is a good woman, George, and likely far better than any Claremont male deserves. But consider how thoroughly you have ruined her. Every last person through your door this night will realize that she is your mistress. You couldn't have chosen a more ostentatious way to proclaim her fall to the world. You won't be able to hide it, and neither will she.''

''Why the devil would I want to?'' demanded George. ''I told you I loved Fan. Would you rather I were ashamed of her?''

''Oh, hardly,'' said Brant. ''But what comes next? Shall you set Fan up in keeping here at Feversham, Captain Claremont's infamous harlot? She'll be scorned wherever she goes in Kent, that much is certain. She'll simply have to make do with your short-tempered company. But what will become of her when you sail away again, or worse, sail away and don't return? Do you intend to settle a handsome amount upon her to ease her way? You should provide for a bastard, too. Brats can prove costly, yet a gentleman must always be prepared for the possibility.''

''Blast you, Brant,'' muttered George, turning away from his brother and towards the long window overlooking the sea.

He couldn't face his brother, not now, because his brother was *right,* speaking from experience that George didn't have and didn't want. Brant knew what was expected for gentlemen of their rank regarding women, while George had been so busy basking in the heat of his lovemaking with Fan that he'd completely forgotten this chilly, unromantic side of the same coin.

Yet as sober and realistic as George now tried to

be, he still couldn't picture Fan as an outcast here at Feversham with an ill-founded reputation for sin. He couldn't regard what they'd shared as no more than a financial obligation for the solicitors, or dismiss any child they'd conceived together as a mere costly inconvenience.

Why the devil did it have to be like that? He stared out at the sea over the tops of the windswept trees, thinking of Fan. He'd always scoffed at the mournful, sentimental ballads that the sailors sang between decks, but here he was living one himself, having found the one woman put on this earth for him.

He'd made his name and fortune by seizing what the fates had dangled before him. How, then, could he hesitate now, when the greatest prize of all was within his reach?

"I'll give you the address of my solicitor," Brant was saying. "The man's as clever as they come with contriving arrangements that both please the gentlemen without offending the women."

"Thank you, no, Brant," he said without turning. "I believe I'll see to my own contriving."

"Don't ruin yourself over this," warned Brant. "There's scant pleasure to be found in letting a woman make a fool of you."

But George knew it was far too late for that, and as the smile spread slowly over his face, he knew that he'd never wish it any other way.

"You look most lovely, mistress," said the lady's maid, hired by George to help Fan dress for the evening, as she gave one final pat to Fan's gown. "You'll make Captain Lord Claremont so proud the buttons will burst from his chest, see if they don't."

"I should hope not," murmured Fan with dismay, staring at her reflection in the looking glass with wary disbelief. She couldn't recall the last time she'd worn anything other than black, let alone a peacock-green gown as elegant and fashionable as this one. She did look lovely, as the woman said, but she also didn't look like herself, not with so much bare arm and bosom and her hair piled high into glossy, thick curls.

She didn't feel like herself, either, without the familiar support of her stays, and as she tentatively turned and twirled before the glass, the glistening silk seemed to spill like liquid over the curves of her hips and breasts, accentuating her womanliness in a blatantly seductive way. Madame Duvall had assured her that this was the most modest gown imaginable by London standards, and entirely appropriate to her position as housekeeper, but as the moment neared for Fan to join George and the others downstairs, she felt a rush of panic.

"I can't wear this," she confessed to the maid as she tried to tug her bodice higher over her breasts. "It may be a lovely gown, true, but it doesn't seem proper for—"

"Mistress Winslow!" called a young woman shrilly from the hall as she knocked frantically on the door. "It's Mr. Small, Mistress! Oh, please, please, come!"

At once Fan forgot the gown and hurried to open the door. The young woman was one of the Tunford girls brought in to help in the kitchen, her round face flushed with excitement and her hands twisting in her apron.

"Beg pardon, mistress," she said, "but Mr. Small says he's nigh ready to bust his scuppers if'n you don't come an' show him where the damned—beg pardon, but that be what he said—fish platter's stowed.''

"Oh, he knows exactly where it's stored, the great baby," scoffed Fan, already heading towards the stairs with the girl scurrying after her. "He just wants me to share his confusion."

"Wait, Mistress Winslow, your shawl!" The lady's maid followed, the luxurious cashmere shawl fluttering in her outstretched hands.

With an impatient sigh, Fan flung the shawl around her shoulders and wrapped it modestly over her bodice. That, at least, would solve one problem with Small, for there was no way under heaven she could speak to him with so much of herself on display. He'd likely have expired from apoplexy there in the middle of the kitchen, and so much for George's grand evening.

"Come now, Polly," she said to the girl as they marched down the stairs. "We must find that fish platter directly, before the kitchen's filled with Mr. Small's busted scuppers."

In his full dress uniform with his medals on his chest, George stood on the landing of the front stairs, his hands clasped behind his waist and his face as grim as if preparing for battle. Behind him the last candles were being lit in the ballroom and the musicians were finally bringing their squeaking fiddles into tune, while in the hall below servants ran back and forth with a frenzy that only served to irritate him more. He himself was always prompt, even early, and as the tall clock solemnly began chiming the hour, he expected his guests to being arriving before the last chime was done.

"Where the devil is Fan?" he demanded as Brant sauntered up the steps to join him. "She should be here by now."

"Why?" asked Brant, smoothing the ruffles on his shirt's cuffs. "You know that even here in the benighted country, no one will have the audacity to arrive for at least another half an hour."

"Damnation, I know nothing of the sort." Restlessly George drummed his fingers on the rail. He hadn't seen Fan for hours, and he missed her. "I need her, Brant. I'll be a helpless, babbling nincompoop without her to guide me. She should be here by now, shouldn't she? Fan? *Fan!*"

Below them, one of the startled servants looked up. "Miss Winslow be in the kitchen, Captain My Lord," she said, bobbing a quick curtsey. "She be with Mr. Small."

"A pox on Small and his infernal interference," he grumbled as he raced down the stairs towards the kitchen, leaving bowing and curtseying servants in his wake. "Fan! Where in blazes are you when I—*Fan?*"

The kitchen was chaos, filled with smoke and steam and shouting and clanking and swearing and kettles being lifted up and platters being set down, and in the very center, standing on a small stool to reach into a cupboard, stood Fan, like the green-silk eye of a furious hurricane. At the sound of George's voice, she turned towards the door, a small silver charger still in her hands and an instant smile of purest joy on her face for him. He grinned back, unable to help it, and amazed by the intensity of the happiness that her smile alone could bring to him. How could Brant warn him against the falseness of women if he'd ever experienced such a feeling for himself?

But then she lowered her hands with the charger and the paisley shawl slid from her shoulder, uncovering the front of her gown and considerably more of the front of *her*.

He gulped, too stunned for much else. He'd always known she was a beauty, but nothing could have prepared him for the sight of her this way, in this gown, with her skin glowing against the green silk and her barely covered breasts fair begging for his touch. It was only an instant, a glorious, frustrating instant before she realized and pulled the shawl back into place, but as instants went, he'd remember it forever.

"Fan," he said hoarsely, tongue-tied and bumbling like the greenest midshipman while everyone stopped to gawk at him. "Ah, that is, Miss Winslow."

"Captain Lord Claremont," she answered, her eyes twinkling impishly as she handed the charger to a waiting maidservant. "Forgive me for keeping you waiting."

"Not at all," he mumbled, watching her hop down from the stool, the green silk doing all manner of interesting, shimmering things that accentuated the curves of her hips and legs as she walked towards him. Only when she passed him and left the kitchen did he recall that he was supposed to be walking with her, too, as well as looking at her face like a sensible man instead of staring like an obsessed idiot at the undulation of her silk-draped bottom.

"Fan, wait," he said, catching her arm and drawing her into one of Feversham's window alcoves. The shadows filled the narrow space, with the moonlight fragmented by the old-fashioned diamond-shaped panes in the window.

She smiled up at him from beneath the unfamiliar curls in her hair. ''You're not supposed to be calling me that tonight, at least not before the others.''

''Hang the others.'' They'd only a minute or two at most before someone would come this way, and he wanted to make the most of even that. ''Will I muss you too much if I kiss you?''

''No,'' she whispered, chuckling as she rested her hands on his chest, ''nor would I care if you did.''

He kissed her then, fast and hard, in equal measures of desire and love. Hang the others, and the whole party with them; he'd much rather take her upstairs to bed this moment and not come down again for a week.

She chuckled again, a sound that promised so much that he almost did take her upstairs. ''We can't stay here, George,'' she murmured, ''though I would wish it.''

''No,'' he said. ''Yes. That is, I don't wish to leave, either.''

He took a deep breath, striving to calm himself, especially the part of himself that was inconveniently large in his breeches. He reached into his coat, finding the two little leather-covered boxes he'd tucked inside when he'd dressed: one for now, one for later.

''Here,'' he said as he drew out the first box. ''Rigged out as fine as you are tonight, I should be draping you in pearls and diamonds. These, I fear, will have to do for now, to show that I love you.''

''I love you, too, even without pearls and diamonds.'' She grinned shyly as she took the box. She flipped open the lid, and her grin melted away.

"Oh, George," she whispered, tears in her eyes as she lifted out the first of the garnet earrings, the same ones she'd admired that first day in Tunford, the ones he'd tried to give her and she'd refused. "You remembered."

"I didn't have to remember," he admitted sheepishly. "I saw how much you liked them, and I bought them then, hoping you'd, ah, change your mind about keeping them."

He hadn't expected tears, not over gimcrack jewels like these. What would she do later when she opened the second box and saw the Brazilian emerald ring he'd claimed from the treasure ship, a ring once meant for a Spanish princess, and now destined for his lady wife?

"They are so beautiful," she said, hooking the earrings into her ears and giving her head a quick toss to make them bob against her cheeks. "And you, my dearest George, you are—oh, my, listen, George, the first guests are here! Hurry, hurry, we must go!"

With the same pleasant half smile on her face that she'd employed all evening, Fan stood slightly apart from George while he listened to an ancient local squire describing an equally ancient foxhunt. The half smile came naturally, for the evening was going far, far better than she'd ever dreamed possible. The food, the music, the dancing, the conversation, even the candles had all been declared perfection itself, and the company had been so determined to behave with a duke and his brother in their midst that there'd been not a single indignity, outrage, or shed tear, at least not that Fan had witnessed.

To be sure, she and George together had drawn

their share of curious glances, but no one had dared comment in her hearing, not even when he'd claimed her hand for three of the country dances. The gossip was certain to begin later, in the home-bound carriages and chaises, but by then, she and George would be dropping their own polite facades as well. Fan's smile widened with anticipation, and she lifted her head to feel the swing of the garnet earrings he'd given her earlier.

But perhaps more importantly for Fan, the gentlemen's conversation had seemed completely preoccupied with the Frenchman Buonaparte, with not a single word to squander for local smuggling. Now that the weariest of George's guests were beginning to make their farewells, Fan was daring to hope her earlier worries had been unfounded.

"Remind me of the day again, Fan," teased George, leaning closer so that no one else could overhear. "Tell me I haven't truly been standing in this room for the last month or so, and that it's only some demon trick that makes it seem so."

"Hush," she whispered back. "Though perhaps by now we may have slipped from one day into two. It must be close to midnight, isn't it?"

He slipped his heavy silver watch from his waistcoat pocket just far enough to check the time. "Five minutes to midnight it is." He cleared his throat, and watched the dancers for a moment. "When this tune is done, Fan, I would like a word with you."

She glanced at him sideways, curious. "You are having words with me now."

"More words, then. Different ones." He cleared his throat again, oddly ill at ease for the first time that evening. "Blast it, Fan, don't make this—now what the devil is that ruckus?"

Like everyone else in the ballroom, they turned towards the stairs and the front door, where the clamor of excited voices threatened to drown out the musicians. Finally Sir Simon Blackerby pushed his way through the crowd, half-dragging a young servant with him to the edge of the dance floor.

Uneasily Fan felt for George's hand for comfort. She had a bad feeling about anything involving Sir Simon, and his crowing, red-faced exhilaration sent ripples of dread through her.

Not tonight, not like this, not now. Please, please, please, don't spoil the first love and happiness I've ever known....

"Where's Sir Henry?" Sir Simon shouted as the dancers stopped raggedly in mid-step. "Where the devil is the magistrate when we need him?"

"I'm here, Blackerby," answered an older gentleman, making his way through the others. "What has happened that you must interrupt us this way?"

Blackerby gave the servant a little shove in the back to move him forward. "Tell him, Falk. Tell him the great news!"

The servant flushed, unaccustomed to being the center of so much attention, but still eager to deliver his message.

"It be grand news from Waverly Point, M'Lord, not far from th' town," he said, raising his voice so everyone could hear. "This very night, not an hour past, th' soldiers from the garrison at Lydd killed or captured a whole pack o' them Tunford smugglers!"

Chapter Fourteen

At once George let go of Fan's hand, and stepped forward.

"I'll come with you into Tunford, Sir Henry," he said, his voice ringing out easily over the din of excited conversation. "I offer you my experience in dealing with the French, and besides, there's nothing I'd like better than to see these rogues brought to justice."

Applause rippled through the crowd, along with several hearty "huzzahs" and "hear, hear's", while Sir Henry bowed to George. Of course they would all be thrilled by George's offer, thought Fan unhappily, her dread blossoming into full-fledged fear.

What a noble display of duty and patriotism, courage and confidence he made, there with the candlelight shining on the medals on his chest! What sorrow and pain his offer could bring to them both!

"I shall be honored by your assistance, Captain My Lord," said the magistrate as a footman came hurrying with his coat and hat. "Though I hesitate at taking you from your home and guests on such an errand."

"I can think of no better reason," declared George, motioning to Leggett to fetch his things, too. "My brother His Grace shall play Feversham's host in my stead, won't you, Brant?"

George scarcely waited for his brother's nod of agreement before he was striding off to lead the way, down the stairs and through the front door, with Fan racing to keep pace with him. The night air was clean and chilly after the crowded ballroom, the men's voices louder out-of-doors, more full of bravado as they milled about, waiting for horses and carriages.

Shivering, Fan stood to one side, hugging her shawl around her bare arms and wishing desperately for some way to keep George from this dreadful errand. She knew she must go to Tunford herself as soon as she could, to learn the truth of what had happened and make certain none of her own people had been killed or arrested. She was sure to know the men who had, and the families who'd been stricken, for even among rivals, the smuggling community was a small one, and bound to come together at such a time.

On the rare occasions in the past that the beleaguered customs officers had decided to send for soldiers from Lydd as reinforcements, she and every other smuggling leader had learned of it well in advance through the network of companies up and down the coast. There hadn't been a successful capture like this in years, and it terrified Fan to realize that it could just as easily have happened tomorrow night, when she had been on the beach with the others waiting for Markham.

What would George have done then, if he'd found that she were one of the ones waiting in irons for the magistrate? What if she'd been one of the bodies now

*lying stiff and cold and ignominiously tossed beneath
a tarpaulin in the back of some wagon, to be held
until morning as evidence?*

"Arm yourself, Captain My Lord," advised Sir
Simon Blackerby with relish. "There could be stragglers from the band, lying in wait to ambush you.
These smugglers are dangerous villains, you know,
not to be treated lightly."

"I never underestimate any enemy," said George
gravely, taking the pistols that Leggett had brought
along with his coat. Now Fan saw that the rest of his
old crewmen had joined him as well, making a swift
transition from Feversham's staff back into stern-
faced fighting sailors.

"Please, George," said Fan, too frightened to keep
silent any longer. "Please don't do this, I beg you!"

He turned towards her, his smile bittersweet. "I'm
sorry to leave like this, Fan, but this is something I
must do. I want you to be safe here at Feversham,
and that won't happen until this coast is rid of these
smuggling gangs."

"But why can't you let the soldiers handle this?"
she pleaded. "You are supposed to be on leave,
and—oh, George, I don't wish any harm to come to
you, not now!"

"You worry over me that much, Fan?" Touched,
he took her hands in his, linking their fingers together.
"I do believe that's the first time anyone has ever
said that to me before I went to—that is, before I
left."

"How could I not, when I love you so much?" she
cried. She knew he'd stopped just short of saying he
was going into battle, and she knew, perhaps better
than he did himself, that it wasn't an exaggeration.

That splendid blue and white uniform with the row of medals would make an easy target in the night for any coward with a musket bent on revenge.

"I love you, too," he said softly. "If I didn't, I wouldn't have to do this now. And when I return, Fan, regardless of the hour, we will talk, and I wish you to be ready."

She nodded, not trusting her voice to answer. Of course they would talk when he came back—when did they not talk?—and though she would pray with all her heart for his safe return, she would also have to do her best not to weep when he told her how many Tunford smugglers he'd helped send to the gallows.

"My own dearest Fan." He kissed her quickly, his lips warm upon hers, and held her for a final moment before he left her standing on the steps.

She pulled her shawl more tightly around her arms, a miserable substitute for his embrace as she watched him mount Caesar and pause to speak to Sir Henry as the magistrate climbed into his carriage. He looked back to her and waved, but did not smile, and then he was gone with the rest into the night. She sighed, and shivered, staying on the step until she heard the last of the rumbling wheels of Sir Henry's coach.

A sad night, she thought, a sad night indeed, and as she hurried upstairs to change her clothes, she realized the worst could still lie ahead for them all.

"A sullen lot, Captain My Lord," muttered Sir Henry with disgust as he sat, his black silk evening breeches and waistcoat at odds with the rough slatback chair that was the best the Tunford gaoler's front room could offer. "I've never seen thieves so able to hold their own counsel and say not a word in their own defense. 'Companies', they call themselves, you know, smuggling companies, though a pack of mongrel dogs is closer to the mark. Let them hang together, I say, if they wish to be so damned uncooperative.''

"Perhaps," said George, purposefully noncommittal as he warmed his hands over the tiny fire. He and his men had spent the last hour making a final sweep of the beaches around Waverly Point, hunting for any stragglers or latecomers, and he'd come to the gaol in time to hear only the last few minutes of Sir Henry's interrogation. George agreed that the prisoners were a sorry enough group, but he'd noticed more about them than their silence, especially after he'd been shown the bodies of the three who'd been shot.

Yet still he'd hesitated to share his observation, not only because the customs officer who'd made the capture had been rightly territorial about the prisoners when faced by a Navy captain. But also, and far more importantly, George wondered about the possible larger significance of these seven silent, threadbare prisoners.

"Pity their boat got clean away from us," continued Sir Henry, inhaling a large pinch of snuff to soothe his indignation. "That's where the army always fails, eh? If we'd only had a good Navy man like yourself in some swift little cutter, we'd have more than a single cask of burgundy and a handful of Tunford's worst to show for the trouble.''

"They weren't from Tunford," said George quietly. "At least the ones you tried to question weren't. They weren't even English. They were French, which could explain why they didn't understand you to answer.''

"Eh?" Sir Henry looked at him sharply. "What the devil are you saying?"

"What I'm saying shouldn't go beyond this room," said George firmly, clasping his hands behind his back as he turned to face the magistrate. "At least not yet. But I'll swear to this—what those soldiers interrupted was no ordinary smugglers' run. The seven men captured are French sailors, not English. The way they dress, how they crop their hair, even their gestures when they didn't, or couldn't, answer your inquiries—there's a score of little things that give them away.''

"Upon my word," said Sir Henry, shaking his head. "Frenchmen on our very beaches!"

"They could simply be smugglers, too," said George, wanting to consider every possibility, even though his instincts pointed to a single likelihood. Here he'd been reading the London papers, searching for news of a formal declaration that the peace had ended and the country was once again at war.

But given the anarchy that now ruled France, their lack of respect for rules and traditions, who was to say that the republicans in power would bother with declaring war at all? Why couldn't they simply launch a fresh attack on the unsuspecting English coast like this, a few boats at a time with men trained to infiltrate the countryside? Because smuggling was so openly condoned, the harbor masters were notoriously blind to all kinds of small incoming vessels, and even if the invaders were captured, the local authorities would most likely be as unsuspecting as Sir Henry. It would be the perfect arrangement for France; for all George knew, it had already succeeded in other villages.

He thought of the small box with the emerald ring, a little square lump waiting inside his waistcoat. Had it really been this same night that he'd been laughing and dancing with Fan, with no greater care than to choose the best words to use to ask her to be his wife?

"The French ferry their share of untariffed English goods back to their own shores, too," he continued carefully, unwilling to share all his suspicions. "I could ask them in French myself, though I doubt we'd get even a quarter of the truth in return. But what makes this perplexing is that the dead men are all English, likely your Tunford rascals. Yet all three were killed by French pistols at close range, not the Brown Bess muskets carried by the soldiers who made the capture."

Sir Henry shook his head again, his expression growing more solemn by the moment. "Forgive me, my lord, but how can one judge such a thing?"

"There is a great difference in the wounds, Sir Henry," answered George quietly, remembering all the men, good men, he'd seen die by gunshot, some so close he'd been splattered with their blood. "Unfortunately, I've seen far too many of both kinds in my career."

"To be sure, with your gallant record," said Sir Henry with the heartiness of a man who'd never seen battle. "But what are you to make of this, my lord? Your observations are suggesting a far different version of these events than the testimony given me by the soldiers."

"I do not know what to make of anything as yet," said George with a sigh. "For now, however, I would accept the soldiers' version, and make that the public explanation. That, and with the cask of burgundy as evidence, are sufficient to keep the men in gaol. By your leave, I shall write of this to my superiors, and perhaps in a day or two we shall be able to discover the rest of the answers.''

"Excellent, excellent," said Sir Henry with approval. ''We need to prove that such wickedness will not be tolerated in this county.''

"One other recommendation, then," said George. He didn't want wickedness in this county, near his home and his Fan, but he didn't want war, either. ''Release the bodies of the dead men to their families.''

''*Release* them?'' sputtered Sir Henry indignantly. ''Tonight? You are new to this region, Captain My Lord, else you would never make such a suggestion with these people. They were villains, sir, perhaps even traitors in collusion with these Frenchmen, and now, my lord, they are evidence!''

"They were never convicted of any crime," said George, his voice turning more forceful, ''and they are beyond any punishment now. The only ones you shall hurt are their widows and children. Compassion is not a weakness, Sir Henry, not even in the British courts of law.''

Sir Henry grumbled, shifting unhappily in the chair. ''Niceties are wasted on the lower sort, my lord, especially the stubborn variety here in Tunford. The only way to gain their notice is through direct punishment, and making a hard and fast example of those that are caught.''

"If you do not show these people—*any* people—a measure of respect," George said sharply as his impatience grew, "then you can expect precious little in return, and you'll never learn what really happened on that damned beach this evening."

"Then have your way, my lord," said Sir Henry crossly, throwing up his hands in unwilling surrender. "I shall oblige your request. But mind you, I do not believe for a moment that such coddling will put an end to this sort of mischief."

"Nor do I, Sir Henry," answered George curtly. "Just pray that it isn't only the beginning of something far, far worse."

Wearily Fan untied Pie's reins from the fence where she'd left him, and the pony nickered happily, glad at last to be returning home. Fan wished her own life could be so simply resolved, that once again her greatest challenge would be not giving in to the delicious impulse to kiss George before his guests. But in these last few hours she'd seen and heard things that would remain forever in her conscience, and darken every memory she'd have of George's grand candlelit party.

She'd been at the gaol just as the soldiers had grudgingly been ordered to stand back from the wagon with the three bodies. She'd seen the contempt on their faces as the Tunford women had rushed forward, pulling at the tarp as they held their lanterns high. She'd heard the keening wails of three new widows, the murmurs of those who offered comfort, the curses heaped on the villains who'd done such a thing, and she'd watched as the cold, stiff bodies were carried to their cottages one last time, their faces twisted into final grimaces of pain and surprise and their clothes flapping heavily with dried blood and

sand. The men weren't from her Company, but she'd
known them just the same as Tunford men: sons,
brothers, husbands, fathers, friends, shipmates, with
many in the village to mourn them.

She'd tried to join the other women in the ragged
little processions, to offer her solace and respect as
was proper, especially for her position in the small
community. But to her shock and shame, she was not
welcomed. She was pushed away, shoved aside, her
way barred by strong arms and set faces full of hate.

"Ye don't be wanted here, Fan Winslow," one
man had finally said, voicing what the others hadn't
dared. "Go back t'where ye belong, whoring at Feversham wit' yer murderin' lord."

"Captain Lord Claremont didn't do this!" she
cried defensively, even as the others muttered their
hostility against her. "He was at Feversham, giving
a party for all the fine folk of the county!"

"Couldn't ye keep him in yer bed, then?" jeered
another woman. "Your fancy Navy-man was here not
an hour past, pokin' an' proddin' at these poor fellows
like they was no more than meat at th' market."

"That's—that's not true!" cried Fan, faltering as
her heart raced with fear. The pistol beneath her skirts
would be of no use to her now, even if she could
draw it before the others challenged her. She was
painfully conscious of how alone she was in the narrow street, and conscious, too, of how George's garnet earrings still swung from her ears, and how above
her rough woolen cloak her hair was still elaborately
arranged for the formal evening. These people were
right: she didn't belong here with them. She didn't
belong anywhere.

"That can't be true, none of it!" she said again, trying to make her voice sound steady and sure.

But she was too late for that, far too late. When she felt the first stone strike the ground near her feet, an ominous thud, then the second, she didn't wait for the third. Instead she'd turned and ran, as fast as a terrified coward could, until she'd come here to reach Pie.

Her fingers trembled as she untied the reins, and tried to set her thoughts straight. She had to leave now, before the others decided to follow her, and she had to find George, to learn the truth. She had to decide what she'd do about tomorrow night, whether taking her place with the Company for the last run as she'd planned would mean risking her life, or proving her innocence to the people of Tunford. And most of all, she had to determine her place in George's life, and whether the joy of loving him would be worth having stones tossed at her.

How had everything gone so wrong so fast?

"Mistress Winslow, here, here!"

She looked down as Matthew Carr darted around the pony, his knitted cap pulled down low over his eyes.

"Matty, don't stay," she whispered urgently. "You'll only bring sorrow to yourself and your mother if you're seen talking to me now."

But the boy only shook his head. "I know what they be sayin' about you and the lord, an' I don't believe it, mistress, not a word."

"Thank you, Matty," said Fan, unexpected tears stinging her eyes. "But you really shouldn't—"

"I saw what happened at Waverly Point, mistress," he interrupted, his voice shrill with urgency. "I was comin' back from my auntie's house when I saw th' boat comin' in off the Point. I went down to th' beach then, on account of maybe makin' a shilling or two if they needed a watcher, same as I do for you and th' Company.''

Fan nodded, encouraging the boy to continue. Matty wasn't the only one in Tunford who would greet boats at night like this. There were a good many men, even those in regular smuggling companies, who'd earn extra money by simply appearing on the beach at night. An extra pair of hands and a promise to secrecy were almost always welcome.

''But it didn't go right, mistress, not at all.'' Matty swallowed hard, worrying the hem of his cap. ''Them three men that be dead now, mistress, they was there to help out, same as me. But them others in that boat, when they rowed up in th' shallows, jabberin' Frenchie-talk, they just pulled out their pistols and fired coldhearted at th' Tunford men, shootin' them dead for no reason at all. Then the soldiers came, and I ran away, and they took up them murderin' men in th' boat, and likewise took all th' credit, th' lyin' windbags.''

''Oh, Matty,'' said Fan softly, shocked by his story. ''You could have been killed, too!''

''I know that.'' His voice quavered perilously before he swallowed back the tears. ''It be a good thing I weren't, else Mam would've been left without anyone. But it all be queer, mistress, queer as anything, and wrongful, too, t'blame such a thing on us smugglers. Even those three caskets o' wine were false, tossed into th' sea by th' sailors in the boat, t'look on purpose like smugglers. Them soldiers don't have one part of it right, exceptin' puttin' them Frenchies in th' gaol.''

"You have to tell the magistrate what you saw, Matty," said Fan, realizing that this was exactly what Sir Henry needed to hear. "You're the only one who knows the truth. Come, I'll take you myself."

"Nay, mistress, I'll not do that!" exclaimed the scandalized boy, ducking beneath the pony's neck to put more distance between them. "That old magistrate'll put me in th' gaol, too, just for spite, and then who'll look after Mam?"

"Matty, if you don't tell them, then it could happen again," coaxed Fan. She never thought she'd hear herself advise turning to a magistrate for anything, but then she'd never heard such an ominous story as this one, with Frenchmen shooting good Tunford men dead on their own beach. "You have to tell him, at least for the sake of the trade and the rest of the companies on this coast."

Unconvinced, the boy only scuttled farther out of her reach. "Nay, I told *you,* mistress, so's you could tell your captain, and set things to rights like that, without poor Matty Carr in th' middle."

Her captain: she still didn't think of George like that, even if the rest of the world did. "Wait, Matty, please!"

But Matty was already gone, lost in the shadows and the darkness that were like another home to him. The boy had trusted her with this story, and trusted her, too, to know what needed to be done next. Fan wouldn't fail him, not now when so much was at stake. Quickly she swung herself up onto Pie's back and turned the pony's head towards Feversham, and George.

* * *

For several reasons, George chose to return through the house from the stable by way of the kitchen instead of the grand front door. He was still too preoccupied by what he'd seen and heard in Tunford to wish to leap back into the festivities that still lit his house like a lantern. Most of the guests had long since left—it was, after all, nearly dawn—but the few that did remain would likely be well into their cups by now, and full of garrulous questions that George was in no humor to answer.

But he'd also wanted to walk through the kitchens to reassure himself that everything in his house was still as it should be, from the lingering scents of cooking food to Small swearing and crashing about with his pots, to the gossiping scullery maids elbow-deep in sudsy wash water. No invading Frenchmen had disturbed this place that to him seemed peculiarly English, and he was determined to risk his life to keep it that way.

Yet the last reason was the most immediate: he was far more likely to find Fan down here in her usual domain, and he wanted to find her as soon as he could.

"Polly, isn't it?" he said to the first maidservant he met, a young Tunford girl who dipped a curtsey of respectful acknowledgement with a wet teacup in one hand and a cloth for drying in the other. "Would you please tell Mistress Winslow I wish to see her directly?"

"Can't, Cap'n My Lord," she said, her broad cheeks flushing red as a cherry. "Mistress don't be here."

"Not here?" repeated George, frowning. "Do you mean she's upstairs with the guests?"

"Nay, Cap'n My Lord," said Polly. "She be gone in to Tunford on her pony, oh, hours ago, and she don't be back yet, least not that I've seen. Gone to see to them that be grievin', she said."

"Did she take one of the men with her?" he demanded, though he already could guess the answer.

"Oh, nay, Cap'n My Lord," answered the girl. "Mistress wouldn't hear of it, saying all the men were needed here to help with serving the guests. Not even Mr. Small could change her mind."

Of course Fan would go to Tunford, and from habit, of course she would go alone. With her kind heart for the people in the village, she'd be unable to keep away from sharing the grief and the losses that had struck the village tonight. He was surprised he hadn't seen her as he'd stood at the gaoler's window and watched the families claim the victims' bodies. He could hardly fault Fan for being there at such a time; to expect her here now waiting at Feversham would be unconscionably selfish on his part.

Yet he hated to think of Fan out there on the roads or in the marshes alone, with only that infernal pistol of hers for protection. What if she stumbled across another band of these Frenchmen? He'd wring Small's neck for not insisting she take one of the footmen with her. For that matter, he was a damned idiot himself for not predicting what she'd do, and leaving Leggett or Danny or one of the others to ride with her.

He considered taking Caesar and going back out after her, but he wouldn't know where to begin. Fan was like every other native of the county who knew a score of different routes to the same place, and

blithely prided herself on never travelling exactly the
same path twice.

But such knowledge wouldn't be enough to keep
her safe against a pack of desperate smugglers, English or French, and far too easily George imagined
scores of dreadful dangers waiting for her in the night.
How could he live with himself if any of them happened to her? Likely she'd be furious if he came after
her, but how could he not? She was the one woman
he loved more than any other, the one he'd meant to
ask to be his wife, if only she'd had the good sense,
just this once, to stay put and wait for him to return
and propose.

"Thank you, Polly," he said, swallowing back his
doubts and worries. He wouldn't panic. He'd write
his letter to the Admiralty, a quarter hour at most, and
if by then she hadn't returned, he'd begin searching.
"But as soon as Mistress Winslow returns—the absolute minute, mind—be sure to send her to me."

Unfastening her cloak, Fan hurried up the back
stairs, thankful that she'd met no one else on her way.
Because she'd no wish to be distracted by anyone or
anything else before she saw George, she'd taken Pie
around to the old stable, away from the grooms and
drivers gathered by the main door. She had seen Caesar through the window, so at least she knew that
George had returned as well.

Most likely she'd find him in one of the parlors,
back with his brother and the last of his guests. When
Brant had cheerfully warned her that such parties
could go on until dawn, she thought he'd been ex-
aggerating, but she had seen the lights still blazing
clear from the main road. At least George wouldn't

have already gone to bed himself, she thought as she climbed the last steps, and then froze.

A thin line of light gleamed from beneath the door to her rooms, a light that should not have been there. She distinctly recalled snuffing out the candles when she left earlier—she'd never be so careless as to do otherwise, not in a house as old and dry as Feversham—yet they were most definitely lit now. Yet who would have entered her rooms while she was away, and now be so brazen as to light candles, too? One of the hired servants, a nosy guest from the party, even one of those hate-filled people who'd thrown stones at her in Tunford?

Her heart racing, she drew her pistol from under her petticoat and cautiously pushed open the door. She just glimpsed a figure darting into shadows and hiding behind her bed's curtains.

"Show yourself, you thieving coward!" she ordered sharply. The intruder was wrong to test her like this, when her nerves had already been so sorely tried this evening. "I've aimed my pistol your way, and though I'd hate to tatter those curtains, I've no scruples at all about shooting you!"

She saw the curtains shiver, and with the vilest of oaths, the old man stepped into candlelight.

"Fine sort of homecoming this is, daughter," growled her father. "Since when do you greet your old da by pointing a gun at his gut?"

Chapter Fifteen

"*Father!*" With a happy cry Fan raced across the room and threw her arms around her father. "Oh, Father, I cannot believe you're really here, that you're alive after so long!"

"What else would I be but alive, lass? Dead?" Clumsily he patted her back. "There's already enough mischief in hell without the devil coming to claim me just yet. There now, Fanny, don't cry, don't cry. No woman that's got the nerve to aim a pistol like you do has any business at all blubbering like this."

"I cannot help it," she said, wiping the tears from her eyes with her fingers as she stepped back to look at him. Though her father's spirit—and tongue—remained as unchecked as ever, he seemed shorter and older than she remembered, and that first hug was enough to prove that, in the time he'd been away, he'd grown so thin as to be almost frail, every rib a bony ridge beneath his patched coat. His hair had turned completely white above his weather-worn face, and his snowy brows bristled emphatically over his dark eyes.

"Wherever you've been, Father," she said with concern, "you've not had enough to eat, have you?"

"France," he said succinctly, patting what used to be his belly. "That's where I've been, and that's where I've nigh starved, too."

"France?" repeated Fan incredulously. "But why didn't you come back sooner, or send me word?"

He puckered up his face almost as if to whistle, an expression that Fan knew seldom brought the complete truth with it, and her heart sank. This was hardly the warm, wonderful homecoming for her father that she'd longed for, but rather instead the one she should have expected.

"Oh, sweet Fanny, it's a long, sad tale," said her father dismissively, clearly disinclined to tell the details. "On that last night I was here, Tom Hawkins and I had a mite to drink, enough to make us take a boat and row ourselves to France, just like Will Hood's always bragging about doing. We were doing well, too, until one of those damned French cruisers gathered us up, almost like they was told to expect us."

"Who would do that?" she scoffed uneasily, wishing she couldn't think of so many in Tunford who'd do exactly that to her father, given the chance.

"Who would, I ask you, two old sots like us of no use to anyone!" marveled her Father. "Plunked us down in some sort of half-prison in Marseilles, picking oakum and feeding fleas, until another new set of king-killers in Paris decided we wasn't worth the gruel and tossed us into the street, with nary a shilling in our pockets. Still an' all, Tom decided to stay. He'd become a great favorite of this red-haired brothel-keeper, you see."

"But how did you come back here?" asked Fan, her initial delight at this reunion now dampened by an ominously growing suspicion. "And why tonight?"

"Why tonight, and why not?" he answered easily, without giving any real answer. "Seems there's changes a-plenty here at Feversham, though I'll warrant not so great that you can't find a morsel or two of good English beef for your poor old father, there's a good lass."

But Fan wasn't going to be a good lass, not about something as important as this. "Father, I have to know the truth," she insisted. "Did you take passage here on a French boat?"

"Aye, aye, how else would I come?" he asked with an exasperated sweep of his hands. "In return for my crossing, I acted as pilot, steering the way to Waverly Point for a crew of Frenchmen. A fool's sort of voyage, to my mind, for they'd brought more guns than goods to trade, with but three paltry casks of burgundy. But they set me ashore a bit to the south, as I asked, wanting to keep myself clear of another company's trading."

"Oh, Father," said Fan softly, dropping onto the edge of her bed as if the weight of what she'd seen, and what she now knew, were too much to bear. She'd no choice now but to tell everything to George, including her father's part in it. "What trouble you've made for yourself!"

"I could ask the same of you, daughter." He gathered up the peacock silk gown from where she'd left it on the bed and shook it in her face. "What's this, eh? Since when do you wear such harlot's finery? Look at you now, with sugar-curls and scarlet earbobs! High time you stop asking me questions, Fan, and start giving me answers of your own.''

"There's a new master here now, Father," she explained carefully. She didn't know which was going to be worse: George meeting her father, or her father meeting George. "He's a good man, and he's done much to improve Feversham. He wishes me to dress in London fashions when he entertains guests, and as his housekeeper, I oblige him. Did anyone see you come up the back stairs, Father?"

"Shamed of me, are you?" he said, raising his voice. He balled up the gown in disgust and threw it across the room. "Maybe I should be the one who's shamed, having a daughter like you keeping such close company with the master!"

"Hush, Father, please, and listen to me." Her father was exactly the same as he'd always been, all bravado and bullying. The difference was that she was the one who'd had to change while he'd been gone, and now she couldn't afford to change back. "Those Frenchmen that brought you here tonight didn't come for smuggling. Before they'd even landed, they killed three Tunford men who'd come to help. You're lucky they didn't shoot you, too, and God only knows what they would have done if the customs men hadn't blundered along to take them up.''

Her father looked at her sharply. "What manner of talk is this, daughter? Salvation from customs men? Every man and woman in our trade knows the dangers and the risks, and takes them along with the gold. I don't care if those three poor dead bastards were from Tunford, and them being dim-witted enough to get killed isn't going to make us in the Winslow Company turn tail and tremble, is it?''

She had to tell him *now,* and slowly she rose, standing before him with her shoulders squared and her hands clasped before her.

"You're too late," she said, the words sounding far more wistful than she intended. "Our family's done with the Company. The men are choosing another leader, and most likely another name as well."

"A new leader?" Shocked, her father shook his head in disbelief. "Not a Winslow? Who? *Who?*"

"Most likely Will Hood," she said, trying to sound as if this were absolutely for the best. "You've always liked Will, and he'll make as good a leader as any."

"Did Will do this to you, then?" he fumed, so furious his face grew mottled. "Or was it some other bastard traitor that forced your hand? You tell me the name of the black devil, and I'll—"

"No one forced me," she said firmly, "though there's plenty in the Company who thought I'd held on too long for your sake. For your sake, because you'd wish it, I carried on as leader, to make decisions that were for the best. This is what I decided, Father, and now it's done."

"The hell it is!" he sputtered, so filled with rage he was shaking, and when he raised his fist to strike her, Fan realized to her sorrow she'd almost been expecting it. Yet even so she held her ground and didn't flinch, her gaze never falling away from his.

For nearly a minute they stayed like that, neither willing to take the next step, until, with another oath, her father swung away and struck his fist hard against the mantelpiece.

"You can't know how this hurts me, Fan," he said, staring into the hearth. "You can't know at all. I never thought you'd be the one to betray me. The whole time I was wasting away in that damned frog prison, I kept thinking and dreaming on coming back here and having everything same as it used to be."

"But that's just it, Father," she said urgently, coming to rest her hand on his arm. Her father had already unwittingly blundered tonight with disastrous results, and she would do her best to keep him and his temper away from the beach tomorrow night when Markham's boat landed. "Nothing can be the same as it was, even from last summer. Times are different now. Markham demands a hundred crowns for each delivery, and—"

"A hundred crowns!" Her father jerked around to face her. "Why, Markham is worse than a highwayman, to charge that! I'll make him see what's right, I will, else he'll see the wrong end of my pistol for his troubles."

"It is the same with the other companies, Father," she said, taking his corded, callused hand the way she had as a little girl. "All the captains who cross the Channel are charging more, and squeezing our customers' poor pockets until it's scarcely worth it. And now these Frenchmen—"

"Since when have you been a coward, Fan Winslow, afraid to stand up for yourself?"

"Since I realized I *was* a coward, Father," she said, linking her fingers more tightly into his. She was struck by how different it was to hold George's hand, how just the touch of his fingers reassured her and made her feel safe and protected and loved, while holding her father's seemed more as if she were holding him back, restraining him from yet another rash act.

"I want to live my life like everyone else," she continued softly, "sleeping when it's night and rising when it's dawn. I don't want to worry over keeping secrets, or watching my back, or who I can trust or not. I don't want to die on the gallows or alone on a dark beach, and I don't want you dying like that, either."

"I told you, Fanny, the devil's not ready to claim me just yet," said her father bitterly. "It's the new master, isn't it? He's made you see things different, hasn't he, all honorable and right-and-wrong?"

She flushed. "Is that so very bad?"

"What, that your master's stolen your maidenhead, and given you a missy-miss conscience that turns you against me?" He muttered another halfhearted oath, and pointedly freed his hand from hers. "You wish me to be happy over that?"

"Captain Lord Claremont is a good, honorable man," she insisted, "and I won't hear you say otherwise."

"A captain?" asked her father suspiciously. "A shipmaster, then? But what's this lordly nonsense?"

"Yes, he is a ship's captain," she said, carefully omitting that it was Navy ships he captained. "And he is the youngest son of the Duke of Strachen. But none of that matters as much as that he loves me, Father. He loves me."

"Oh, aye, he loves you, he loves you not, but I see no wedding ring upon your finger to prove it, or give your bastards his name." Unimpressed, he fumbled a grubby handkerchief from his pocket and loudly blew his nose. "Now go fetch me supper, daughter, before I perish from all your bad news."

"It's the truth, Father, not bad news," said Fan. A year ago, she would have meekly obeyed and let herself be dismissed, but not now, not even when her heart was crumbling along with her dream of what she'd hoped this reunion would be. "I'll bring you your supper. You'll find I've kept your rooms down the hall exactly as you left them."

"I know," he said with a final belligerent sniff. "I looked. Though you took away the bottle of rum I'd kept beside the bed."

"I'll bring you a new one," she bargained, "but only if you'll promise you'll stay up here, and won't go causing mischief with the others here in the house."

He scowled, his white brows bristling fiercely. "Why shouldn't I, considering all the mischief and sorrow you've caused me? I've been gone for months, daughter. I've matters to attend to in Tunford."

"Father, please," she said. "Please. Only for a day or two, until I can learn exactly what happened with the Frenchmen on the beach. The last thing I'd wish is to lose you again to the magistrate so soon after you'd returned. Here I know you'll be safe."

"They'd have to catch me first, wouldn't they?" He grunted, the weariness finally catching up to him, and making him look old and tired and, to Fan's worry, eminently catchable. "But maybe you're right, daughter. Maybe I should squirrel myself away here for a bit, to build up my old strength."

"That would be the wisest course, Father," she said, hoping he meant to keep such a sensible resolution. "You can rest all you want, and I can look after you the way I used to."

Cautiously she opened the door, checking to make sure there was no one else in the hall before she beckoned for him to join her.

"Aye," he said, following her to his old room. "Besides, I've a deal of planning to do before I settle with the bastards that forced your hand. Oh, I know you did your best, Fanny, and I'm grateful for it, but now that I'm back, things will be different."

Yet Fan knew that a great many things already were, and not likely to change back. She kissed her father good-night on his stubbled cheek, and with both heart and conscience heavy as lead, she hurried down the stairs to find George.

"My uncle'll be here any moment with his dogs, Cap'n M'Lord," promised the footman as he bowed to George. "If anything can find Mistress Winslow, they can."

George nodded curtly. His horse was saddled and waiting, the other men already mounted, and, at his orders, also armed. After what had happened earlier this night, it was best to be prepared for the worst as they searched the countryside for Fan. He squinted out over their heads, to where the horizon was just beginning to pale with dawn. Daylight would make their hunt easier, but hell, how he wished—

"What is all this, George?" asked Fan with concern, suddenly beside him on the step. "Has something else dreadful happened? Must you ride out again?"

Startled, he swept her up in his arms, not giving a

damn who saw him do it. "Ah, Fan, thank God you're safe."

She hugged him quickly, then pushed away from his chest. "Of course I am safe. George, listen to me. I have so much to tell you, and it cannot wait!"

He frowned. "I have much to say, too, Fan, the first being that you shouldn't have gone off alone to Tunford like that. How in blazes was I to know what had become of you, especially tonight? What else was I to do when there was no sign of either you or Pie?"

"What were you to do?" she repeated, perplexed. "Why, is that what all this is? Because I tied my pony in the old stable, away from the crowds? Because of that, you thought me lost, and were taking all these others to go hunt for *me?*"

"That's the gist of it, yes," he admitted gruffly. He was now acutely aware of the unnecessary search party listening openmouthed to every word he and Fan said, as if standing here on these steps was the stage at Drury Lane. "I do love you, you know. Why, I'd even sent for hunting dogs to track you, and if that isn't love, I don't know what the hell is. Though discovering you were already here makes me feel like a damned ass."

"Oh, but you shouldn't," she said softly, her gray eyes becoming misty in a way that could turn his own insides to a most unmanly mush. He thought again of the little box in his waistcoat; perhaps this would be the time after all. "No one else would do such a thing, not for me. That you would care so much for me that you would want to rescue me from the Frenchmen—"

Instantly the mush vanished. He grabbed her arm and hustled her inside the house before she could say

more before the others. The nearest room was one of
the few at Feversham that he had yet to refurbish, the
small parlor where Mr. Trelawney had displayed his
collection of stuffed gamebirds. Their dusty glass
eyes peered down from the shelves as soon as George
lit a candle, mute, molting witnesses to their conversation.

"What do you know of Frenchmen, Fan?" he
asked, latching the door for more privacy. "What did
you hear in Tunford?"

"Nothing," she answered quickly, pacing back and
forth with her hands clasped before her. "That is, no
one in the village was saying anything about any
Frenchmen. They blamed what happened on—on the
customs men."

He didn't miss the little hiccup of apprehension.
Clearly more had happened in Tunford than she was
saying; he only prayed she'd confide in him.

"But you heard of them somewhere," he coaxed.
"Tell me, love. I need to know."

"That's why I've come to you." She stopped her
pacing for a moment, and raised her chin with determination, and by the candle's light he could see how
her gray eyes were ringed with shadows of exhaustion
and strain.

"You must trust me that what I say is true, for I
can't tell you who told me," she began, her voice
taut with urgency as she began her restless pacing
again. "The men in the boat tonight weren't smugglers, but Frenchmen bent on mischief, who hired an
English pilot to bring them exactly to Waverly Point.
The Tunford men they killed had only come offering
to help, and the Frenchmen shot them dead, without

a thought, and who knows what they would have done next if the soldiers hadn't bumbled upon them."

She paused, searching his face anxiously for his reaction. "It's bad, George, isn't it? Those Frenchmen, and guns, and all?"

"Yes," he said heavily, thinking of the courier he'd already sent racing to London with his letters to the Lord of the Admiralty, and how, after this, he'd soon be sending a second rider with more. "It's very bad indeed. You are certain all of this is the truth?"

She nodded. "Neither had spoken to the other, yet both had nearly the same tales."

And every word of both, thought George grimly, gave credence to his own suspicions. "Is there any chance I could speak to these men myself?"

She shook her head. "I swore to keep their secret, George. But I could take you to Waverly Point myself, and show you exactly where the boat came ashore."

"Perhaps later," he said, gently drawing her into his arms. "After you've rested. You're so weary now you can scarce stand upright."

"We'll go now," she declared, the red garnets in her earrings swinging against her cheeks as she looked up at him. "I have had the exact same hours of sleep as you, George. If we can do anything to help, then we should. If you had seen the poor men who'd been killed—"

"I did," he said quietly. "Because of my experience, there was certain...certain evidence that I needed to observe for Sir Henry before the bodies were given over to the families. Not that Sir Henry was happy about that, but it was the proper thing to do."

"It's not always easy to do what is right," she said with a wistfulness he couldn't miss. "If we go to the Point now—"

"Fan, to be honest, there would be precious little to be gained by doing so," he said, smoothing her hair back from her forehead. "Not after the soldiers and the tide and likely half the town as well have crossed it by now."

"Too late," she said, thumping her hand against his chest with frustration. "Oh, George, if only I'd come to you sooner!"

"It would have made no difference," he said firmly. "No, what would serve us best would be to know when the next smuggling run will come in from France. To be able to ask such men what they'd seen and heard across the Channel, if they'd been approached as your pilot was, to learn if the French were, in fact, considering some sort of invasion as a prelude to war—now that would be invaluable, Fan, without price."

"And a French war would take you from me and Feversham," she said, almost a whisper. "But what you ask, George, what you want! You're a Navy officer, sworn to serve the king. What smuggling folk would put their heads through the noose to confide their trade to you?"

"I've sworn to serve the king, true enough," he admitted carefully, "but I've also sworn to protect Britain and her people. In such grave circumstances as these, I would have to consider even the most blatant rascal first as an Englishman to be protected, and cast a blind eye towards the untariffed goods. Any other time, I'd call them the worst sort of thieves. But now—no."

She bowed her head, the misery of her conflict as stark as the pale parting in her dark hair.

"More Tunford men could be killed if we don't learn what we can from them," she said, clearly striving to convince herself. "Times have been bad enough without another war. Surely they—the smugglers—must understand that."

"They would be safe, Fan," he said gently. "I'd make sure they were not taken or charged. You have my word."

He'd long suspected she'd ties to Tunford's smuggling brotherhood. He'd only to recall the mysterious boy who'd come to the house last evening, the way she'd raced off tonight, even the rumors he'd heard about her wicked old father. Now he was hoping she'd choose to convince these same people to trust him instead; a large order indeed.

True, he'd stopped short of asking her outright, but he also knew her well enough to realize it wouldn't be necessary. With so much at stake, she wouldn't hesitate. She was, quite simply, too honorable a woman not to.

"My own brave lass," he said gently, turning her face up towards his. "Is there any wonder I love you so much?"

Yet instead of the smile he'd expected, she looked away from him, towards the window and the sky pink with dawn, enough to light the tears tangled in the lashes.

"And because I love you, George, I cannot refuse to join you in this," she whispered miserably. "Because I could not bear to lose you to another war, because you are wise and noble and honest in ways I never can be, because others need me to be strong when all I want is to be weak. But this time—*this time*—I will do what is right."

"Don't say such harsh things of yourself, Fan," he said gruffly. He hated to see her cry, especially over something like this. "Not another word, mind? I love you as you are, and I always will. Nothing is decided about what we'll do next with these damned French, nor will it be, at least until I've had my chocolate and breakfast."

"But it is decided," she insisted sadly, not bothering to wipe away the tears that now trickled down her cheeks. "Didn't I tell you I've made up my mind? I *will* do what is right."

"You are certain of this, Fan?" he asked, his uneasiness growing. "You are telling me everything?"

"Of course I am certain," she said, slipping apart from him to stand by the door, hugging her arms around her sides. "Come with me tonight, and I'll take you to the beach to meet all the smuggling-folk you could wish."

"That could be dangerous, sweetheart," he said, acknowledging the fear he saw in her eyes. How could he blame her for being otherwise? Unlike his own life, hers as Feversham's housekeeper could hardly have prepared her for this kind of risk. "I'll bring my men with us, to help keep things honest."

"No!" she exclaimed, then paused with a gulp, visibly struggling to compose herself. "That is, you are right, George. It will be dangerous, not just for me, but you as well. I won't pretend differently. But bringing the others will only unsettle my people, and make them trust you even less."

"No more than I'll likely mistrust them." He held his handkerchief out to her, and to his relief she took it, accepting at least that small comfort from him. "Am I at least permitted to arm myself?"

"Oh, yes," she said, dabbing at her nose and eyes. "You'd be rather a fool not to. But mind you dress yourself plain, in dark clothes."

"Aye, aye, captain," he said softly, holding his hand out to her and hoping she'd return. "Sackcloth and ashes it shall be."

She looked at his hand, but didn't come, instead crumpling the handkerchief into a tight ball in her palm. "It's important, George. There's nothing to be gained by reminding them how you answer to the king and Admiralty."

He let his hand drop back to his side. "I haven't exactly hidden which side I favor, sweetheart."

"Oh, love," she cried sadly, and to his surprise she now rushed back to him, wrapping her arms tightly around his waist. "Can't it just be us together, with no talk of sides, or who is right or wrong? For today, tonight, can't that be enough?"

He held her tight, the way he knew she wanted, and the way he wanted, too. "It's enough for me for always. Or is this another of your tests for me, Fan?"

"No test," she said. "Only—only you've said you would love me forever, and now that we will be together for always, and—and I hope that that is true."

"Damnation, Fan, so there *is* more you're not telling me, isn't there?" Gently he turned her face up towards his, searching for the truth. After all they'd shared together, he suddenly felt as if he were losing her, letting her drift away as surely as if she were being carried off by waves beyond his reach. "No tests, but no riddles, either. Tell me how I can help you, sweetheart. Tell me what I must do."

But all she did was shake her head, lowering her eyes to escape his scrutiny. "Tonight you'll have your answers, George. And whatever you learn, remember that I'll—I'll always love you."

"Then I've one last question for you, Fan." He dug his fingers into his pocket for the little leather box, urgency making him clumsy as he unfastened the tiny brass hook on the lid. He'd played the words out a thousand times in his head and before the looking-glass, but now that he had to say them aloud to her, he was infinitely more nervous than he'd ever been facing an enemy broadside in battle.

"Fan, Fan, my dearest lass," he said, clearing his throat as he held the box out to her. "You've become the one certainty in my life, the one I cannot do without. Will you honor me, Fan Winslow, and be my wife?"

With more of a fumble than a flourish, he opened the box to offer her the ring. The large oval emerald sparkled as green as the grass in the spray-fed lawn, the smaller diamonds around it as bright as the morning dew on those same blades.

But though this betrothal ring was the kind that would take most women's breath clean away, Fan didn't spare so much as a glance at it, her eyes enormous and intent only on George.

"You would marry me?" she whispered. "Me?"

"Yes, you," he said, his confidence growing. "I love you, Fan, and can't fathom loving any other woman more. Say yes, lass. Please say yes."

"You would marry me," she repeated, too overwhelmed for more.

"I would," he said. "I will, as soon as the banns are read."

She stared at him for what seemed like years to him, before she gently closed the box with the ring.

"I cannot, George," she said softly. "Not the answer you wish or deserve. Not yet, not now."

He felt the certainty of his hopes lurch beneath him. "Why the devil not? What must I do to change your—"

"Oh, George, you must never change one blessed hair for me!" she cried unhappily. "It's me, all me, for one more time, I must do what is *right* rather than what I wish!"

He shook his head, refusing to understand. "But what you wish—what we both wish—*is* right, Fan!"

"Then ask me again tomorrow," she said, reaching up to kiss him, more pledge than passion as she threaded her fingers into his hair. "Ask me tomorrow, if you can, when the dawn is as new as it is now. Then you shall have all your answers, George, and I pray for both our sakes that they're the ones you wish to hear."

Chapter Sixteen

"Why didn't you tell me, daughter, that your new master-lover was a king's man?" Her father glowered as he took another swig from the bottle, then spat contemptuously into the grate. "Don't try saying he's not, for I saw him from the window last night with my own eyes, the two of you standing cozy-close outside in the yard. All that gold braid and epaulets surely would make for an easy spot of shooting, wouldn't it?"

"Father, don't," ordered Fan, setting the plate with his supper down before him. "Don't even begin saying such things."

"I'll say them if I mean them," he answered, suspiciously studying the roast chicken. "I'd only be defending what's left of your good name, which must be wicked little. I'll wager he doesn't even know I'm here in his house, does he? Hidden away up here like a hermit?"

"A good thing he doesn't, too, if he learned you'd been ferrying Frenchmen to his doorstep," she said, wiping her hands in her apron.

She was already on edge enough tonight without a conversation like this with her father. How could she not be? In less than an hour, she would be meeting George in the stable, and though she knew what she must tell him about her role in the Company, she hadn't begun to find the words to say it. Then, together, they'd have to face Will Hood and Bob Forbert and the others she'd summoned, and after what had happened to her last night in Tunford, she knew she must be prepared for the worst. Before the night was done, she could not only lose her joyful, love-filled future as George's wife, but her own mortal life as well.

And she could not honestly say which would be the greater loss.

"Go on, Father," she said, trying not to think of the warm rush of pure love she'd felt when George had asked her to marry him. "Eat your supper. I'm not about to poison you."

"I don't know what you're about to do, Fanny," he grumbled, taking a chicken leg daintily between his thumb and forefinger as he sliced away with his own long-bladed knife instead of the one she'd brought. "What does your fancy lord captain make of you and the Company, eh? Or is that the trade you've made, that if you warm his bed, he'll keep you from the magistrates?"

"Maybe I *should* poison you for talking like that," she said defensively. How dreadfully wrong her father's guess was; she couldn't imagine George making such an agreement, any more than she would accept it. "I thought you'd be happy to be home in your own snug room again, but I'm sure the Tunford gaoler can find a place for you there with all your fine new French friends.''

Her father looked at her sharply. "So are you keeping company with the town gaoler, too, daughter? Friendly-like with all of them that can save your skin, and the Winslow Company be damned?''

"You've had too much to drink." She snatched up the empty bottle, determined to leave before either one of them said more that they'd later regret, and gave him a quick, guilty kiss on the forehead. "I must return to the kitchen now, Father, but I'll come back in a bit for the tray.''

But to her surprise he dropped the chicken and seized her wrist, holding her so she couldn't escape.

"You know you'd be breaking your poor mother's heart, Fan, taking to sinning so natural with such a man," he said, his expression too serious to blame entirely on the rum. "She wanted more for you than this sort of harlotty rubbish.''

"Please don't, Father," she said helplessly as she looked down at her hand in his, her emotions too raw to venture more. As much as she wished to, she couldn't tell him of George's offer, not yet, not when he might still take it back when he learned the truth. "Please.''

"Oh, aye, you can stand up to me, Fan, all full of fire and sparks," he said, his eyes flinty. "But do you speak the same to this man? Or is he the one giving all the orders, bidding you lift your petticoats for him?''

"I told you, Father," she said as firmly as she

could, which was now not very firm at all. "He doesn't care that I am his housekeeper. He loves me as I am."

"He loves part of you, you mean," growled her father, "and I can guess which obliging part it is. I don't care how proper and honest you're pretending to be with your pretty lordling. High-bred men like him don't stay with women like you. If he don't care to know about where you've come from or your place in the Company or even that you can aim and fire a gun straighter than most men, why, then he'll never bother with loving you true."

He was right, and to her sorrow Fan knew it. Why else was she taking George with her to the run tonight? True, she did wish to do what she could to stop more Frenchmen from coming ashore at Tunford. But she'd other, more personal reasons as well. Before George could make her his wife and give her his name, he did need to know about her role with the Company. But he also needed to see for himself that, no matter what gossip he might hear, this was to be Fan's last run. She'd finally, definitively, break with her past to make her future with him—if he still wished to share it with her.

Not that she was about to confide any of this to her father.

"George knows about my gun," she said, purposefully avoiding the rest of what he'd said. "I had to shoot at him once, just to get his attention."

"Then you should've finished the job while you had the chance, and saved me the trouble." He jerked her lower towards him, so close she could smell the rum sweet on his breath, and pressed the flat blade of his knife against the inside of her wrist. "Mark what I say, daughter. I won't be kept in this room forever. You've made a wicked mare's nest of my affairs and my life while I've been away, and I mean to untangle it as soon as I can."

"But it's my life, too, Father," cried Fan as she wrenched free, rubbing her arm where the knife had pressed a red brand into her skin. "It's not just yours! I always tried to do what was right, for you *and* the Company's people *and* for me and for George as well, and I'm still trying, no matter what it costs me!"

"Then instead of all that trying, daughter, remember who you are, or you never will do what's right," ordered her father, his gaze as sharp and relentless as the knife in his hand. "Remember you're a Winslow first, else you'll answer to me. To *me,* mind? You remember, and don't you ever forget."

"Keep to the path," cautioned Fan, turning back towards George over Pie's back as the horses walked single file, "and away from those rushes, there. The marsh sand's so soft it'll swallow you and Caesar like breakfast, and all I'll be able to do is watch."

"Then I must thank you for the warning, lass," said George, drawing his larger horse to the very center of the twisting path. "I'd hate to be anyone's breakfast."

She nodded over her shoulder, her face barely visible in the dark before she turned back to watch the path ahead. He could hardly complain; without Fan to lead the way, he and Caesar might very well become a marshy breakfast, and the sobering thought made him pull the collar of his cloak a bit higher against the wispy damp of the fog. The night was chilly and moonless, even without the fog that had fallen almost as soon as the sun had set, and he already felt the saltwater dampness of the nearby sea settled familiarly into his bones.

Yet the chill was no match for the excitement racing through his blood. It wasn't just the weight of the long-barreled pistols he carried, or the scabbard of the cutlass swinging against his thigh, or the realization that behind every nodding leaf or branch could wait a Frenchman or smuggler eager to blow his head from his shoulders. It wasn't even the challenge of knowing that, no matter what he'd promised, he'd have to be very clever and very quick to garner the information he sought. That was simply doing his duty to his king and country.

No: what made this night so special was having Fan with him. She was his partner, her bravery equal to his, but she was also his woman, the one in all the world that he loved most. If this was to be his final test to prove it to her before she'd accept him, then he was determined to pass with flying colors, leaving no possible doubt in her mind when he asked her again to be his wife.

The path widened, more sand than soil now as they drew closer to the water, and he guided Caesar alongside Pie.

"We must be nearly there," he said, taking care to keep his voice low. "I can hear the waves."

She nodded. "I planned it so we'd be first to arrive,'' she said without taking her gaze from the path. ''There's less chance for surprises that way.''

He agreed, though her foresight in turn had surprised him. ''Are you certain there's a landing here tonight?''

''Oh, yes,'' she answered. ''This company is quite steady, you see. They trade in tea, not wines, brandies, or rum. The returns are not so great with tea, but more constant, and the risk of piracy from other companies is less.''

He glanced at her, impressed by how much she must have prepared for this night. ''I should have had you write to the Admiralty about these smugglers instead of me.''

''Ah, I doubt those fine gentlemen would care for what I'd have to say.'' She shrugged, fussing with Pie's reins. ''Here we are now.''

The horses' hooves sank into the soft beach, laboring until they came closer to the water where the sand was packed hard. Without waiting for George's help, Fan slipped easily from Pie's back, and began unbuckling the bulky pack behind her saddle.

''If you wish to help, you can light this for me,'' she said as she handed George a bulky tin lantern with a tallow candle inside. ''The sloop that brings the tea from France will wait off shore until they see the proper lantern signals.''

''And that sloop's captain will be the one who can answer my questions.'' He took the lantern and lit the candle with his flint and striker, the yellow light spilling out across the sand. ''Do you know him by name?''

"Ned Markham," she said. The candlelight washed across her throat and cheeks, pale and golden inside the dark hood of her cloak. "He's the least trustworthy man to sail this coast, which also makes him the one captain most likely to have dealings with the French."

"Then you take the horses back into the rushes," he ordered, acutely aware himself of the danger they were in. "There's no need to put yourself at risk with a villain like that."

"Of course there is," she said briskly, tucking loose strands of her hair back beneath her hood before she bent to close the door on the lantern. "Markham won't have the faintest idea who you are without me to tell him, and he'll think nothing of shooting you dead for your trouble."

"And you, too, Fan, if he's as bad as you say," he said, thinking of how impossibly dear she'd become to him. "I'm not about to lose you over something like this."

"You won't." She pulled her pistol out from inside her skirts, all business, turning her back to the spray blowing from the water to check her powder. "We are partners for tonight, mind? You need me, just as I need you, and I won't be shuffled off into the bushes so you can play the great hero."

"I don't give a tinker's dam over whether I'm a hero or a coward. What matters to me, Fan, is that you're safe." As often as he'd seen her handle the gun with this assurance and skill, he still didn't like the uncertainty in her life that it represented, or the fresh uneasiness that was curling through him now.

"This won't be like shooting at mice from the kitchen door."

"That's right," she said with maddening evenness. "It won't, not at all. Now listen, because we don't have much more time. As soon as Markham accepts the signal, he'll come in close enough to send his boats into the stream, down there on the far side of those hills."

"You are that sure?" he asked warily, again surprised by the detail of her knowledge.

She nodded, letting her hood blow back from her face as she scanned the horizon. "The company men will meet the boats, and shift the tea from the boats to the ponies, until the bags can be broken down and distributed to the customers around the county. That will be the best time for you to speak to Markham, when the tea is being unloaded but before he's been paid. Ah, there's the *Sally's* light!"

He followed her gaze to see the shadow of a boat not far from land, dark except for the signaling flash of a lantern at the bow. Quickly she tucked the gun into her belt and turned her lantern towards the water. With a practiced ease, she flashed the door open and shut, two times slowly, then one fast, in a pattern that mirrored the one from the boat. Finally she left the door open, letting the light serve as a beacon to the incoming sloop.

Beside her George watched, the dull, angry ache of certainty growing somewhere near his heart.

Why hadn't she loved him enough to trust him with the truth?

"There," she said, her chin high and the spray

blowing tendrils of her hair back from her face. "With this tide in their favor, Markham will be here with his hand out soon enough, the greedy bastard."

But George didn't want to hear any more. "Fan, look at me," he demanded. "Tell me the truth. How long have you been a part of this? Was it your father who made you do it? Damnation, Fan, look at me, and—"

"Mistress Winslow, here!"

Fan was already looking past him as George turned towards the man's voice. A wobbling row of lanterns was coming over the low hill towards them, and in the beams of their candlelight he could see at least a dozen men trudging across the sand. Though their faces were purposefully too shaded by their hats and caps to be recognized, the pistols and muskets in their hands were unmistakable.

"What mischief be this, mistress?" called the same tall, thick-chested man, the angry one in the front who George guessed must be the leader. "We've played fair with you, and now you turn traitor by bringing your king's man to spy on us!"

"I didn't bring him here to spy, Will Hood!" Fan shouted back, purposefully staying close to George. "Captain Lord Claremont's here to help us all, if you'd stop raving like a madman long enough to listen!"

"Best you stand aside, mistress," warned Hood, raising his musket, "and I'll show him how we help ourselves."

At once George stepped in front of Fan, shielding her behind his body. He didn't know how good a shot the man was with his musket, especially at night, but he wasn't going to wait to find out.

"Damnation, man, listen to her! Would I be standing here so openly before you if I meant to spy? Would I come here alone, without any reinforcements, if I intended somehow to bring you harm?"

But Hood didn't lower the musket. "Maybe you're here because sailing for his bloody majesty has made you daft as well as righteous."

"Oh, aye, it's made me daft enough to worry what becomes first of you people and your town, and then the entire country, too," he said, his voice growing louder with well-earned authority. "Those men that died last night were killed by French guns, not British ones. The sailors that were captured were Frenchmen pretending to be English."

"Frenchmen?" repeated Hood uneasily. "On our own Waverly Point?"

"Frenchmen," said George firmly. "They weren't smuggling, as they wished the world to believe, but determined to plot an invasion, infiltrating your Tunford—your families, your homes—from within, and making the way easier for General Buonaparte to come with his troops."

A rumble of oaths and outraged disbelief circled through the men, the lanterns in their hands swinging back and forth as they glanced uneasily at their neighbor.

Hood lowered the musket from his eye, the better to glare suspiciously at George. "How are we to know you're telling the truth? And what's it to us if'n you are?"

"Why would he lie, Will Hood?" demanded Fan, slipping around George to stand in front of him, her arms crossed bravely over her chest. Instantly he rested his hand on her shoulder, wanting the others to know he was with her: still partners, no matter what else she'd done, still his proud, clever Fan.

"Captain Lord Claremont wants to talk to Markham," she continued, "to learn what he's heard from other captains crossing the Channel. He will use that information to keep other Frenchmen from landing on our shore, and other Tunford men—men like you, Will—from getting themselves killed."

"I heard them prisoners was Frenchies, too," said a man in the back. "I heard it from my wife's brother, what heard them talkin' their lingo together at th' gaol."

Hood's musket dipped lower as he considered. "But Ned Markham won't go with them republican frog-eaters, mistress," he said doggedly. "He's a good stout Englishman, and he's served us and the Winslow Company for years and years."

"Markham'd sell us all and his granny besides without a thought," scoffed Fan. "You should know that, Hood, if you ever hope to take my place as this company's leader."

Her place as leader of the Winslow Company: so this, thought George, was the real test of his loyalty and love. All the little puzzles about Fan—the pistol she always carried, the long solitary rides at night on Pie, her intimacy with the lowest sort among Tunford's sailors, even the detailed knowledge of smuggling that he'd admired earlier that same evening—

were finally clicking together into painfully sharp relief. He shifted his hand from her shoulder to his side, ready to reach for his own gun if needed. God knows even that half second could make a difference. He'd known this situation would be full of risk when he'd come with her, but he'd no idea it would mushroom into *this*.

The woman he loved above all others, the one he'd asked to be his wife, was not simply a member of a smuggling gang: she was the outlaw queen of a company that bore her family's name.

"Too late for that, mistress," Hood was saying. "I've told the rest o' the men you wished to be done with the trade, on account o' your father being gone, and they've made me their leader. After tonight we'll be the Hood Company, right and proper."

"Right and proper," repeated Fan, striving to keep the sadness from her voice. "That's how I've always tried to do things, you know."

There were no secrets left between her and George now. These last minutes had put an end to those secrets, exactly the way she'd intended, and she'd never made a bigger gamble. But what her father had said was true: before she and George could consider any future together, he'd needed to know exactly what kind of woman she was, and whether he could still love her that way.

Now, without a doubt, he did. Didn't the way he'd just pulled his hand away from her shoulder prove it?

Yet as much as she longed to turn around and tell him again, here before this crowd of witnesses, exactly how much she loved him, she didn't, and she didn't tell him she was leaving the Company for his sake as much as her own, either. Instead she stood with her back as straight and unyielding as a poker, pretending to be brave and stoic when in truth she was simply too great a coward to search George's face for her fate.

"You have brought Markham's gold?" asked Hood. "He won't give us the tea without it."

"Have I ever once forgotten it?" Fan turned back to her saddlebag for the leather bag of coins, for the increase that Markham had demanded now made the bag too heavy and bulky to carry beneath her petticoats. The extra gold also made her more vulnerable, more liable to robbery, and even now she could sense the greedy interest of her own men as she cradled the bag of coins in the crook of her arm. "Markham will have his gold, but not until I have judged the tea, and not until he speaks with Captain Lord Claremont—"

"The boats be here, Mistress!" called one of the lookout boys, and in a single movement the men turned and began hurrying back over the hill towards the stream.

"I'm coming with you, Fan," said George, taking her arm as they climbed the low hill. "I'm not about to let you go into this alone."

"Thank you." Her smile was tight with nervousness. She paused at the crest of the hill, drawing him up short, and with her head high, she finally met his gaze. "I do not believe I could do this alone, not tonight."

"That's why I'm here, Fan," he said, as if this were the most obvious explanation imaginable. She had always loved that gravity in him, and the sense that she could trust him—especially now. "For you."

"You had to know," she said, her words now tumbling over one another in her haste to tell him. "About the Company, about me. But oh, George, I decided I wanted more from life, that I had to do what was right, not only for you, but more myself. I want you to know that, too."

"Because I love you," he said, still grave even as he slid his hand from her arm to her waist. "Because, miracle of miracles, you love me."

"Yes, George, yes!" she said breathlessly. "And because I love you, I swear by all that's holy that this part of my life is almost done."

"Not quite, sweetheart," he said softly, looking past her. "Not quite."

She turned, and understood at once. Markham himself had jumped from the first boat and waded ashore, roaring furiously both at his own men to keep back and at the Company men, led by Hood, to keep their distance.

"An explanation, Mistress Winslow!" demanded Markham as he charged up the hill towards her, and Fan couldn't recall having ever seen him so angry or full of bluster. "An explanation for why you have doubled your men this night, mistress, and it had better damned well make sense if you wish me to give the word to unload your tea!"

"You asked for more money, Captain," she countered, aware of how the hill had been turned into a stage with the rapt audience of men below watching and listening to every word. Markham's outburst had made certain of that. "And I've brought more of my people to guard it. You have the tea, haven't you?"

Despite the chill, he was sweating visibly, his pale face slick in the lantern light as he wiped his sleeve across his forehead. "I keep my word, mistress."

"And I keep mine, too, but cautiously." She raised her voice so the others could hear her as well as she glanced down at the boats. It was odd for Markham to keep his crew waiting like that. Usually he preferred to land his cargo and be gone as quickly as possible. "Listen to me, Captain. Three Tunford men were killed last night by Frenchmen pretending to our trade."

"The—the devil you say!" stammered Markham, and swore violently. "But what the hell does that to do with me, eh? Why would you tell me that?"

"Mind yourself before the lady," ordered George curtly, "or you'll answer to me."

Pointedly Markham spat in the sand to the left of George's feet. "And who are you, you black-haired bastard, defending a shrewish whore like this one?"

"I am Captain Lord George Claremont of His Majesty's Navy," thundered George, "and if this lady is willing, soon to be her husband. If you do not treat her with the civility and respect she deserves, then I shall thrash you myself from here to Brighton and back again."

Fan gasped, as stunned by how he'd defended her as by how he'd declared his love for half of Tunford to hear in openmouthed astonishment. But before she could accept George's offer, or throw her arms about him and kiss him as he deserved, or even blush or smile, she realized that she was the only one of them still facing the water, and worse, the only one who'd noticed Markham's three boats creeping closer to shore. Nor did the boats themselves look quite the same as they had on the other runs. They sat lower in the water, forcing the men at the oars to pull harder from the extra weight, and the tarpaulins protecting the rounded sacks of tea from being splashed seemed different, too, lumpier somehow, more irregular.

And then, in an instant, she knew why, just as she knew what she must do next.

"If you have nothing to do with the French, Captain Markham, why then, that is that," she said nervously, striving to ease the tension vibrating between George and Markham. She knew both men carried pistols hidden beneath their coats, and she hated knowing they might be driven to fire at one another, especially at such close range. "You are a man of your word."

"Yes, mistress," said Markham, not daring to look away from George. "My word's my honor."

"Then I'd say it's high time, Captain Markham, that we inspected the tea," she said, her voice rising with excitement as she raced away with the bag of gold still clutched tight in her arms, slipping and sliding in the sand in her haste to reach the water. She was determined to undo what Markham had done, to steal everyone's attention from him and George and return it to the water, and as she ran she saw a blur of startled faces and lanterns, every man watching her exactly as she'd hoped. She ran hard, not caring how her petticoats flew above her ankles, for that would make the men look more. If they looked at her, then they'd look next at the boats, and see what she had before it was too late: that instead of smuggling sacks of tea tonight, Ned Markham was importing Frenchmen.

She ran, she ran, and heard Markham's grunted oath just before he grabbed her arm and jerked her to a stop and shoved her forward into the sand, sending the bag of gold flying from her hands and into the sand. She fell hard, the wind knocked hard from her lungs, forcing her to struggle to breathe even as she needed to escape. But Markham was a large man made stronger by desperation, and despite her flailing he'd soon pinned her close against his chest, his arm like an iron band across her chest as he dragged her to her feet.

"Quit your fighting, girl," ordered Markham, tightening his grip around her. "Be still, I say, or pay the price!"

"Why should I take orders from you?" she gasped, twisting against him to break free. "You're—you're a traitor and a coward, and—and a low, lying thief, too! You've—you've brought no tea, have you? You—you meant to let those Frenchmen kill—kill us dead, then steal my gold!"

"Shut your mouth, I say," ordered Markham, and suddenly she felt the cold steel barrel of a pistol pressing into her cheek.

At once she went still, so still she could hear the raggedness of Markham's breathing and the thump of his heart and the rush of the waves over the sand. Everything else came into sharp focus as well, the ring of Company men unsure of what to do, the boys waiting with the ponies, the flickering light from the lanterns glinting off the coins that had spilled from the split bag in the sand. Behind them the Frenchmen hiding under their tarpaulins must be waiting, too, wondering what had gone wrong in their plan.

And in the center of it all—of the men, of her world—stood George. He, too, had drawn his pistol, but his was now aimed harmlessly into the sand.

"Let her go, Markham," he called sharply. "She's no use to you. Take the gold, but let her go."

Markham laughed bitterly, a low rasp in his chest against Fan's ear. "You can keep the gold, my lord, and I'll keep your little bride. She's my safe passage back to France, unless you'd rather risk her life to try otherwise. You raise that gun—if any of you do—and she dies."

"Do not hurt her," said George, the pistol in his hand useless and his expression full of pain and fury and frustration and sorrow. "Damnation, Markham, let her go!"

"Don't," warned Markham, inching backwards towards the water and dragging Fan with him. "Or she dies."

She dies: oh, dear God, she did not want to end her life like this. Silently she pleaded with George to understand, to know she loved him no matter how this ended. All she'd ever wanted was to marry him. She wanted to be with him forever at Feversham, his love and his wife and the mother of his children, and she did not want to go to France and *she did not want to die.*

"You always were a stinking coward, Ned Markham!" shouted the man from the top of the hill: a voice that was rough with years and rum, but still could call the attention of every man within hearing, and Fan, too. Her father stood with the musket raised to his eye and pointed at her and Markham, and behind him were more men: Leggett, Danny, all the rest of George's crewmen from the house.

"I didn't believe Fanny when she said things had turned so sour, she was giving up the trade," he continued. "But seeing this sorry show makes me realize what a wise, steady child she is. I wonder you want to take my place at all, Will. I say better to sit in the chimney corner with my pottage now than deal with lying, cheating bastards like you."

"The same warning holds for you, Joss Winslow!" called Markham, moving faster towards the boat. "You're an old fool, and unless you want to see your daughter dead, you'll drop that musket."

"The hell I will," answered her father so cheerfully that Fan's despair grew. As far away as he was, and as shaky as his hands had become, he would as likely shoot her as Markham.

But maybe her father didn't mean to shoot anyone. Her father was old, true, but he was no fool. Perhaps all he wished was to break Markham's concentration, and with a flash of hope she glanced at George. He'd been waiting for her to look, and in return he nodded: all the encouragement she'd need.

"You should've stayed in France, Winslow," called Markham again, unable to resist taunting her father. "Then you wouldn't have had to see me take your whore of a daughter."

Her father laughed, and Fan felt Markham's arm slacken—not much, but enough.

"There's where you're wrong again, Markham," said her father. "My Fanny's no whore. She never was. She's going to wed this lord here, and be a true lady, while you—you'll always be—"

But Fan never heard her father's prediction. Instead she whispered a tiny prayer for bravery and luck, and threw all her weight to one side, breaking Markham's grip. She heard the crack of the gunshot as soon as she stumbled free and pitched forward into the sand, the impact making her cry out. Gunsmoke stung her eyes, and there was something wet and warm splattered across her bare arm.

"Fan! Fan, love, look at me!" said George, dropping the smoking pistol so he could gather her gently into his arms. "Are you hurt, lass?"

She shook her head and smiled through her tears. She hadn't died. She still lived, and George was with her, his handsome, dear face so full of concern and love—*love!*—that no wonder she was weeping with pure happiness. Carefully he was wiping his handkerchief across her arm: Markham's blood, not her own.

"Don't look," ordered George, turning her away from the body, and she didn't. All around them men were running and shouting, the Englishmen, whether Navy men or smugglers, working efficiently together to make prisoners of the French still waiting in the boats. "Markham's gone straight to the devil now, where he won't trouble you or anyone else again."

She shuddered, but not even Markham's death was going to keep her silent. "Ask me, George," she said, slipping her arms around his shoulders. "Ask me now. *Now!*"

He frowned, still worried. "You're certain you're unhurt, Fan?"

"Don't be daft, Claremont," said her father as he joined them. "I heard you declaring yourself earlier, and so did Fanny. Then recall I never did have my chance to fire this old musket, and think a bit harder about the question you should be asking my daughter."

"Ah." He cleared his throat and ducked his chin, and as he fumbled for the ring in his waistcoat, Fan knew she'd never love any man more. "Ah, Fan Winslow. Will you marry me, Fan?"

"Yes," she whispered, her joy too boundless for any other words than the one that mattered most. "Yes, yes, yes."

Epilogue

They were married on the first perfect day of summer, when the roses had just begun to bloom against the old stone walls, but the golden lilies in the marshes had not yet faded, and even the sun seemed to smile down upon them. Though Brant had offered them the splendid grandeur of the duke's private chapel at Claremont Hall for their wedding, Fan and George had chosen the humble stone church in Tunford instead, preferring to have their joy pealed over the countryside by the single bell in the church's squat, square tower.

The wedding feast at Feversham spilled from one night into three days, all to the music of the blind fiddler from the Tarry Man. Among the guests were three admirals and a score of peers, the crewmen from the *Nimble* in their best white trousers and gold-buckled shoes and members of the old Winslow Company with sprigs of green boxwood for luck tucked into the buttonholes of their Sunday coats.

To no one's surprise, the customs officers from Lydd and Hythe were not invited.

And on the day after St. Valentine's Day, the happy product of so much celebration was born. He was christened with a long string of names worthy of being a Claremont, but to George and Fan he was simply, perfectly Baby Jack, and Jack to them he would always be.

"Oh, George, he must be the most beautiful little boy ever born," whispered Fan in awe as she stroked the velvety skin on her son's sleeping forehead. "Have you ever seen such an angel?"

"I've not only seen him," said George wryly, "I've heard him, too, crying out to the rest of the cherubim while you and I were trying to sleep."

"Hush," she scolded, but her smile had only love in it. "And who's the first to rush to his crib, day or night, whenever he cries?"

"Guilty, guilty," admitted George softly, linking his fingers into hers. "Our Jack was rightly born to be an admiral, I think, already giving orders."

"I always did wish to do things right, George," she said, letting him pull her into his arms. "Just as I love you, Captain My Lord, and that is the rightest thing I've ever done."

"Right and proper, my love," he said, kissing her. "Right and proper for always."

MIRANDA JARRETT

considers herself sublimely fortunate to have a career that
combines history and happy endings, even if it's one that's also
made her family far-too-regular patrons of the local pizzeria.
With over three million copies in print, Miranda is the author of
over thirty historical romances, and her bestselling books are
enjoyed by readers around the world. She has won numerous
awards for her writing, including two Golden Leaf Awards and
two *Romantic Times* Reviewer's Choice Awards, and three times
has been a Romance Writers of America RITA® Award finalist
for best short historical romance.

Miranda is a graduate of Brown University with a degree in art
history. She loves to hear from readers at P.O. Box 1102, Paoli,
PA 19301-1145, or MJarrett21@aol.com. For the latest news,
please visit her Web site at www.Mirandajarrett.com.

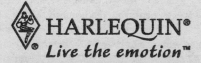

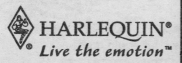

COMING NEXT MONTH FROM

HARLEQUIN HISTORICALS®

- **LADY ALLERTON'S WAGER**
  by **Nicola Cornick,** author of THE BLANCHLAND SECRET
  Lady Beth Allerton's wager with the Earl of Trevithick was the most
  dangerous thing she'd ever done. If she won, her prize would be an
  estate. If she lost, the penalty was to become his mistress!

  HH #651 ISBN# 29251-1 $5.25 U.S./$6.25 CAN.

- **McKINNON'S BRIDE**
  by **Sharon Harlow,** author of FOR LOVE OF ANNA
  When Jessie Monroe's husband was killed in the arms of another
  woman, she vowed never to experience that kind of pain again and
  set off for her brother's ranch. There she met Cade McKinnon, who
  fell in love with her at first sight, determined to win her hand and
  her heart. But when Jessie learned he'd been lying to her, would she
  ever be able to forgive him?

  HH #652 ISBN# 29252-X $5.25 U.S./$6.25 CAN.

- **ADAM'S PROMISE**
  by **Julianne MacLean,** author of
  THE MARSHAL AND MRS. O'MALLEY
  Madeline Oxley eagerly traveled to Canada to marry
  Adam Coates, the man she'd adored since childhood. Upon her
  arrival, however, she discovered that he really wanted to marry her
  older sister. Unable to return to England, Madeline hoped Adam
  would learn to love her. But when her sister arrived, which one of
  them would Adam choose?

  HH #653 ISBN# 29253-8 $5.25 U.S./$6.25 CAN.

- **HIGHLAND SWORD**
  by **Ruth Langan,** book one in the *Mystical Highlands* series
  A fierce warrior traveled to the Mystical Kingdom, a hidden land in
  the Highlands where ancient magic has not been forgotten, to find a
  woman to heal his dying son. But little did he expect this woman
  would heal his broken heart, as well!

  HH #654 ISBN# 29254-6 $5.25 U.S./$6.25 CAN.

KEEP AN EYE OUT FOR ALL FOUR
OF THESE TERRIFIC NEW TITLES

HHCNM0303